Savannah had just dropped off to sleep when the telephone rang, exploding in her right ear and sending her pulse racing.

"What?" she shouted, ready to kill whoever was calling her at—she squinted at the red, glowing numbers on the bedside clock—1:22 A.M.

"Van . . ."

Savannah sat straight up and flipped on the bedside lamp. "Dirk, what's going on?"

"It's Polly. She's dead."

"A car accident?"

"Murdered."

She could hear him, feel him shaking through the phone. His teeth were chattering, and he was having trouble breathing.

"Calm down," she said as she jumped out of bed and reached for the jeans and sweatshirt she had tossed into the hamper upon retiring. "Where are you?"

"At home . . . in my trailer."

"And where is the bod—I mean, where is she?"

"In my trailer. Shot with my gun."

"Don't do anything," Savannah ordered. "Don't touch anything. Don't say anything to anybody." There was silence on the other end of the line, except for his shaky breathing. "Do you hear me?"

"I hear you. Hurry."

"Hang tight, buddy. I'm halfway there."

Books by G.A. McKevett

JUST DESSERTS

BITTER SWEETS

KILLER CALORIES

COOKED GOOSE

SUGAR AND SPITE

SOUR GRAPES

Published by Kensington Publishing Corporation

• G. A. McKEVETT •

SUGAR
AND
SPITE

A Savannah Reid Mystery

KENSINGTON BOOKS
Kensington Publishing Corp.
http://www.kensingtonbooks.com

KENSINGTON BOOKS are published by

Kensington Publishing Corp.
850 Third Avenue
New York, NY 10022

All Kensington titles, imprints and distributed lines are available at special quantity discounts for bulk purchases for sales promotion, premiums, fund raising, educational or institutional use.

Special book excerpts or customized printings can also be created to fit specific needs. For details, write or phone the office of the Kensington Special Sales Manager: Kensington Publishing Corp., 850 Third Avenue, New York, NY 10022, Attn. Special Sales Department. Phone: 1-800-221-2647.

First Kensington Hardcover Printing: January, 2000
First Kensington Paperback Printing: January, 2001
10 9 8 7 6 5 4 3 2 1

Printed in the United States of America

This book is lovingly dedicated to Linda Hynson, a dear friend who knew me "way back then." Thanks for everything, sweetcakes!

CHAPTER ONE

Not for the first time, it occurred to Savannah Reid that she led a less than conventional existence. Not every Southern Californian spent their morning lying on a park bench, dressed in bag-lady garb, staring up at the rustling palm fronds overhead, waiting to be attacked. And, also not for the first time, it occurred to her that if it weren't for the guy lying on a bench a hundred feet away from her—similarly outfitted, equally bored—she might have a real life.

Naw.

As much as she would have liked to blame her eccentricities on Detective Sergeant Dirk Coulter, Savannah had to admit she loved lying there, hoping the s.o.b. who was going around spraying homeless people with red paint swastikas would mark her as his next target. He would be in for a little surprise. His previous victims hadn't been armed with a 9mm

Beretta, a black belt in karate, and a wicked temper made worse by PMS.

Then there was Savannah's vigilante mentality, a hold-over from a childhood spent in rural Georgia among feisty nonconformists. A stint in law enforcement hadn't mellowed her much. Although she was reluctant to admit it, her rebel attitudes were largely the reason why Savannah was no longer a member of the San Carmelita Police Force.

She might not be a cop anymore—like the guy stretched out on the bench opposite her—but as a private detective Savannah loved to get the bad guy and make him pay, pay, pay for his wicked ways. Nothing relieved the symptoms of PMS quite so effectively . . . except maybe a bag of nacho-flavored Doritos, chased by a two-pound box of See's candies.

"I'm bored," growled the bum. She could hear him through the tiny earpiece hidden under the gray thrift-store wig she wore under her red thrift-store stocking cap. "It ain't gonna happen today. I can just tell."

"We've only been here twenty minutes," she whispered into the microphone tucked into the collar of her lumberjack's plaid shirt. Also a thrift-store acquisition. "Have a little patience."

"Screw patience. I gotta take a leak."

That was what she liked about Dirk: his delicacy, his genteel manner, his laid-back, "go with the flow" outlook on life, and, of course, the way he always addressed her as a lady.

He was hauling his body off the bench as though he were a ninety-five-year-old with lead-plated underwear. "Gonna go tap a kidney . . ." he grumbled. "Dangle the snake . . . hang a rat."

Oh, yes, and she adored his colorful vocabulary.

She watched him stumble across the park lawn to a small, cement-block building that served as a public rest room. Ladies to the right; gents to the left.

Dirk made a good drunk. He had the stagger down pat, and he looked the part—even when he wasn't deliberately dressing for the role—in a baggy sweatshirt, faded jeans with ripped knees, and battered sneakers. To go "undercover" he just raided the laundry pile on the floor of his house-trailer bedroom for something dirty and rumpled, but the basic wardrobe remained the same.

Except for a little beer roll around his middle, Dirk had a pretty good body for his forty-plus age. He wasn't a bad-looking guy, in a street-tough sort of way. Dirk just didn't know the words "vanity" or "fashion." "Adequate hygiene" was his only personal standard.

A moment later, the sound of his urinating tinkled in her earpiece.

"You wanna turn down the volume on your mic?" she said into her collar. "I don't exactly need to hear you . . . ah . . . draining your dragon."

"Like you haven't heard it before," she heard him mutter just before the sound went dead in her ear.

Of course she had heard it before. For years, Dirk had been her partner on the San Carmelita Police Force. Many times she had pulled over to the side of the road while he emptied his thimble-sized bladder behind a secluded bush. But that didn't mean she was going to pass up a chance to complain about it now.

This stakeout was a freebie from her to Dirk, a favor for an old friend, because he didn't like to work alone, and the department was too tight with the purse strings to give him a partner for this little detail. And if she was going to do the old boy a favor, he was going to pay in guilt . . . or maybe chocolate. Expensive Valentine chocolate. She hadn't decided which.

When Dirk didn't come out in thirty seconds, she knew it would be another five minutes at least. She had seen the newspaper tucked under his arm when he had disappeared inside the "library."

Yes, she decided. She knew Dirk Coulter and his habits far too well. It was a simple case of familiarity breeding contempt. She made her decision then and there on payment. A big box of candy. A red heart-shaped one. After all, Dirk was the closest thing she had these days to a Valentine.

Now *there* was a scary thought.

Corey McPherson stood at the edge of the city park, checking out his next victim. The excitement was building inside him, and his palms were wet as he clutched the can of spray paint he had hidden inside his camouflage jacket.

He had seen the old lady shuffle over to the bench and lie down about twenty minutes ago. She'd been there, stretched out, staring up into the big palm tree and mumbling to herself ever since. A nutcase if he'd ever seen one.

Corey was nineteen and more than a little pleased with himself. A few weeks ago he had been accepted into the White Warriors, a skinhead, white-supremacist group, which had further inflated his already bloated ego. He and his newfound compatriots met twice a week in the leader's basement, beneath a six-foot swastika scrawled—along with some cool skulls and crossbones—in red chalk on the wall. They would have painted the symbols on, but the kid's mom had complained about having "that ugly crap on my wall," so they had to wipe everything off after every meeting.

At their biweekly gatherings the Warriors discussed what an awesome dude Hitler had been and how the Nazis had been right on, getting rid of the Jews, bums, fags, and retards. The Warriors weren't in any position to actually get rid of anybody ... yet ... but they did their part for society by making life miserable for anyone they decided fit in one of the "undesirable" categories. And that was pretty much everyone outside their small group.

The old gal on the bench was obviously a society reject. The Nazis would have picked her up and shipped her off right away. It irked Corey that he couldn't actually kill her— although he fantasized all the time about that sort of thing— but he could make a statement. That's what the bloodred paint was all about. Making a statement.

Maybe someday it would be more than just paint. At the age of five, Corey had wanted to be a fireman or astronaut. But lately he had narrowed it down to anarchist or maybe serial killer. He figured he'd be good at either one, and neither career required a high-school diploma.

But, for now, he'd just settle for spray-painting bums.

He made his way quietly across the grass toward the old woman on the bench. His heavy combat boots with their white laces, symbolic of his white-supremacist affiliations, made no sound as he crept closer to her. His fatigues were baggy enough to be fashionable in his age group and didn't come close to the standards of army neatness. His auburn hair was cut short and spiked with gel ... also pseudomilitary. The can of spray paint inside his jacket was definitely not GI issue.

As he drew nearer to his intended victim, he could hear

her still muttering something to herself, no doubt holding a conversation with some figment of her tortured imagination. Corey wished he could put her out of her misery, rather than just scare her silly.

Oh, well. If he frightened her badly enough she might pack up her one bag and get the hell out of his town. They certainly didn't need her type stinking up the place.

For half a second, he saw her glance his way, focus on him, then stare up at the palm tree again and mutter to herself again. That was good. Corey didn't like it when they got a good look at him. He wanted to just spray them in the face, squirt a quick swastika on their chest, and then run away before anyone could get a good description of him. He had done this more than a dozen times and not been caught yet. Yep, he was good. And proud of it.

He took a few more steps and waited for the woman to notice him. She didn't seem to. In fact, she looked the other way. Toward the rest rooms. His pulse rate doubled and throbbed in his ears.

Now was the time.

He rushed her, paint can in front of him, pointed at her head. "Hey, you . . . you old bitch!" he shouted at her.

He waited for her to turn around and face him. He tensed, finger on the trigger, ready to depress the button and give it to her full force.

But when she turned to look at him, she raised her own hand. And Corey saw a gun that was roughly the size of a cannon. Or it seemed that large, because it was aimed directly at him.

"You talkin' to me?" she asked as she sat up, pistol still trained on him. Her voice didn't sound shaky or quavery like an old lady's. It was soft and sweet, with a heavy Southern accent. But the cold, hard glitter in her blue eyes wasn't that of a gentle Dixie belle ... or that of a feebleminded street person either.

The red stocking cap slipped to the side of her head, along with the ratty-looking gray hair. Corey saw the black curls sticking out from beneath the disguise and knew he'd been had.

"Take your finger off the button," she told him as she stood to her feet and took a step closer to him.

Corey couldn't move. He was so scared he couldn't even breathe.

"I said ... take your finger off the button ... or I swear I'll shoot you dead." She sounded like she meant it. She looked like she meant it.

Corey removed his finger from the spray button.

She held out her left hand. "Give it to me," she told him. Slowly, carefully, he surrendered the can.

A second later, both her gun and his paint can were aimed at his face. The angry gleam in her eyes seemed to change. She smiled a little, as if she were enjoying herself.

That was worse. Much scarier.

"So, you like to terrorize old people ..." she said. "Poor people, sick people, folks who've got a few screws loose, huh?"

Corey squirmed inside his baggy fatigues. "Ah ... no ... I mean ... I don't terrorize them. I just mess with them ... a little ... you know."

"Yeah, I know. I know all about you, you little Nazi-wanna-be punk. You think you're real bad. Well, you're not. You've got no balls, or you wouldn't be hurting people weaker than you."

Corey felt his face flush, scalding hot with embarrassment and fury. He wanted to hurt her, kill her, show her she was wrong about him. But she had that gun . . . and that scary grin on her face.

"Are you a cop?" he asked in a small, squeaky voice that shamed him even more.

"Nope," she said.

"Then who are you?"

"Just somebody who doesn't like nutless Nazi punks."

She took another step toward him, and for a second Corey thought she was going to shoot him after all. He started shaking, a violent tremble that coursed in waves through his body from his head to his combat boots.

"Look at you, big tough guy," she said, "shaking like a mange-bald hound dog in a snowstorm. How does it feel to be so scared that you don't have any spit in your mouth? To have somebody treat you like you're less than dirt under their feet?"

Corey glanced around quickly, hoping that maybe someone would see what this crazy woman was doing and come to his rescue. But they were the only two in sight. He had picked a solitary place, a solitary victim. And now it looked like *he* was going to be the victim. The game had definitely gone sour for Corey McPherson.

"There's something else you need to experience first-hand," she continued in that cold voice with the deceptively soft, feminine accent. "You need to find out how much fun it is to scrub paint off your bare skin, to get it out of your hair once it's all dried and matted. Oh . . . yeah . . . and then there's the humiliation."

She lowered the barrel of the pistol, and for a moment,

Corey was relieved. Until he saw she was pointing it at his crotch.

"Pull out the waistband of those baggy breeches of yours," she told him. Her nasty grin widened. "Do it now."

Corey couldn't believe what he was hearing. Didn't want to believe it. "What?"

"You heard me. You've got enough room in those pants for you and the jackass you rode in on. Now do what I said and hold the waistband out in front of you."

Corey shook his head. "No. I won't. What are you, some sort of pervert?"

"Maybe I am." She laughed. "Now there's a scary thought, huh? If I'm a real sicko, heaven knows what I'll do to you before I'm finished with you. Pull those pants open, now!"

Corey was afraid to. But he was more afraid not to. He did as he was told.

"Your underwear, too," she said. She took a step closer to him.

"I haven't got any on," he replied, feeling four years old.

"How unsanitary."

She closed the small gap between them. Pressed the barrel of her gun against his neck. Pointed the spray can directly down the front of his opened pants.

"You're not gonna . . . you're not . . . !" he shouted.

"Oh, yes-siree-bob," she replied in that silky Southern voice. "I most certainly am."

"I don't quite understand this," Tammy Hart said as she watched Savannah add three eggs to the skillet and several slices of bread to the toaster. "*You* help *him* nab the bad guy and *he* rewards *you* by letting you fix him breakfast?"

The "him" she was referring to was sitting at Savannah's kitchen table, a satisfied smile under his nose. Dirk was always happy when food was imminent. Especially if that food was free. And in keeping with her Southern heritage of hospitality, Savannah made sure that everyone in her presence was stuffed like her Granny Reid's Christmas turkey. Heaven forbid anyone should feel a pang of hunger. It wasn't to be tolerated.

"So I'm a sap for a pretty face," Savannah said.

"And what does that have to do with Dirk?" Tammy shot a contemptuous look toward the table and its occupant, who was still dressed like a street bum.

Savannah chuckled and took a sip of the hot chocolate she had poured for herself . . . laced with Bailey's . . . topped with whipped cream and chocolate shavings. Savannah suffered few hunger pangs herself, as was evidenced by her ample figure.

Tammy, on the other hand, was svelte, golden tanned, golden blond, the quintessential California surfer beach beauty.

Savannah loved her. Anyway.

So the kid was scrawny and ate mostly mineral water, rice cakes, and celery sticks; everyone had their faults.

Savannah retrieved several jars of homemade jams and preserves from the refrigerator and shoved them into Tammy's hands. "Put these on the table," she told her.

The younger woman took the jars and looked at the labels disapprovingly. "Gran's blackberry jam . . . probably full of sugar."

"I'm fresh out of sea-kelp spread," Savannah muttered under her breath, and swigged the hot chocolate.

Tammy sashayed over to the table and plunked the jars in front of Dirk, who gave her a cocky smirk. "Now I have to cook for him, too?" she complained. "It's bad enough that you're his slave, but now I have to—"

"Oh, stop ... enough already." Savannah snapped her on her teeny-weeny, blue jean-covered rear with a dishtowel. "I'm not Dirk's slave, but you *are* my assistant, so assist. Butter that toast."

"With real butter?"

Savannah sighed. "Yes. Cholesterol-ridden, fat-riddled butter. I'm fresh out of tofu."

"I'll go shopping for you."

"No, thanks."

"Why are you having breakfast at four o'clock in the afternoon, anyway?" Tammy dipped only the tip of the knife into the butter and made a production of spreading the one-eighth of a teaspoon over the slice of bread.

"Because we didn't eat this morning," Dirk replied, watching the meal's progression with the acute attention of a practiced glutton. "We were working, remember?"

"Spraying the genitalia of youthful offenders," Tammy said with a giggle. "That's work?"

"Savannah did that all by herself. Thank God, or I'd be up on charges. You shoulda heard that guy screeching when they were scrubbing him down in the emergency room."

He and Savannah snickered. Tammy shook her head, pretending to be appalled.

"There are advantages to going freelance," Savannah said as she dished the eggs, some link sausages, and thick-sliced bacon onto the plate, then ladled a generous portion of cream gravy beside a scoop of grits. Where she came from, grits might be optional, but gravy was considered a beverage.

Dirk's eyes glistened with the light of hedonism as he

picked up his fork. "Van, you've outdone yourself. This looks great."

"Yeah," Tammy said as she sat down to a bowl of long-grain rice across the table from him. "She's good at CPR, too. And if that doesn't work, I'm pretty good at angioplasty." She hefted her knife and punctuated her statement with a skewering motion.

Savannah was reaching into the cupboard for a box of marzipan Danish rolls for herself, when she heard a buzzing, coming from Dirk's leather coat, which was draped across one of her dining chairs.

"I see you've got it set on VIBRATE again," she said, digging through his pockets and handing him the phone. "Your love life in a slump?"

"Eh . . . bite me." He flipped it open and punched a button. "Coulter here."

"He's sure grumpy when somebody gets between him and his dog dish," Tammy whispered to Savannah. "Reminds me of a pit bull I knew."

Savannah didn't reply. She was watching the play of emotions over Dirk's craggy face: irritation, fading to surprise, softening to . . . she wasn't sure what, but she was fairly certain the party on the other end was female.

"Ah, yeah . . . hi," he was saying. He turned in his chair, his side to her and Tammy. His voice volume dropped a couple of notches. "I'm . . . ah . . . here at Savannah's. No, not like that. We were working together this morning. No, really."

Savannah didn't like the sound of that. Why, she wasn't sure. She and Dirk weren't anything "like that," but she didn't like to hear him saying so . . . so clearly . . . to another woman.

Another woman? *Where did that thought come from?* she

wondered. *To hell with that,* she quickly added to her mental argument. *Who is he talking to?*

"Yeah, I was going back home right after . . ." He looked wistfully down at the plate of goodies on the table in front of him. ". . . actually, I was leaving right now if you want to. . . . Yeah, that's good. Sure. See ya."

He flipped the phone closed and rose from his chair. The look on his face reminded Savannah of a sheep after an embarrassingly bad shearing. "I . . . ah . . . gotta go," he said. "Sorry about the"—he pointed to the food—"ah, breakfast. But I really should—"

"No problem," Savannah said as she snatched the plate out from under him and carried it over to the cabinet. "If you gotta go, you gotta go. Obviously it's an important meeting."

"Ah, yeah, it is . . . kinda." He slipped on his jacket and fished for his keys. "I'll see ya later, okay?"

Savannah nodded curtly.

He grunted a good-bye in Tammy's direction, then headed toward the front of the house.

"Don't let the door slap your backside on your way out," Savannah called after him.

Another grunt. The sound of the door slamming.

"Well," Tammy said, recovering from her shock. "I never thought I'd see the day that Dirk Coulter would walk away from a free meal . . . especially one *you* cooked," she told Savannah.

From the kitchen window, Savannah watched his battered old Buick Skylark as it pulled out of her driveway. He was practically spinning gravel.

"Hmm," she said thoughtfully as she took his heavily

laden plate from the cabinet and carried it back to the table. She sat down, picked up his fork, and dug in.

"That's all you've got to say?" Tammy asked her. "Hmmm. That's it?"

"I'm thinking."

"And eating." Tammy watched disapprovingly as Savannah shoveled in a mouthful of grits, dripping with butter.

"I think best when I eat."

"That explains your mental prowess," Tammy mumbled.

"Shut up. I've almost got it."

"Got what?"

"The plan of action."

"You've gotta know, huh?"

Savannah snorted. "Only if I intend to sleep tonight."

She downed a few more bites, then jumped up from her chair. "Be back later," she said as she snatched her cell phone off its charger base.

"What's the story?"

"He forgot his phone."

"That's *your* phone."

She shrugged. "We bought them at the same time. They look so much alike. It's an honest mistake."

"Going out there is a mistake," Tammy grumbled as she followed her to the front door. "There's nothing honest about it."

"I don't recall asking for your editorial comments. Go on the Internet while I'm gone. See if you can drum up some business for me so that I can continue to pay you that high, minimum-wage salary you've grown accustomed to."

Tammy sputtered, stood between her and the door, then moved aside with a sigh of resignation. "That's it? The phone story? It's a bit thin."

Savannah grinned and tossed her purse strap over her shoulder. "Yeah, well . . . Dirk's a bit thick. It'll work."

CHAPTER TWO

As Savannah pulled her 1965 Camaro into Dirk's trailer park, she grimaced at the cloud of dust that was settling on her new red paint. There was a nice mobile-home park down by the beach, but Dirk was far too tight to spring for that. He had parked his ten-foot-wide in the Shady Vale Trailer Park fifteen years ago, and once Dirk was parked anywhere, he tended to stay until he rusted.

Shady Vale was inappropriately named. Flat as a flitter, without a tree in sight, the property's picturesque description must have been a figment of some developer's imagination.

Dirk's neighbors were mostly transient, and more than once he had been forced to arrest one of his Shady Vale-ites for everything from armed bank robbery to blowing up half the park while cooking up a nice batch of methamphetamines in one of the trailer's kitchens.

The only residents who had been at Shady Vale longer than Dirk were the Biddles. They were a cantankerous, nosy old couple who watched the comings and goings of everyone in the park, as though they owned the dusty, gravel road themselves. From their #1 spot at the entrance, they saw every arrival and had an opinion as to whether that person had legitimate business in Shady Vale.

Their trailer was right next to Dirk's, which was parked in spot #2, and Savannah was hoping she could avoid her usual argument with Mr. Biddle or an interrogation from Mrs. Biddle. If luck were on her side, she might be able to recognize Dirk's mystery visitor's vehicle and find out who his guest was without having to use that ridiculous cell-phone ruse.

But the new silver Lexus parked beside his Buick didn't ring any bells. Since when did Dirk have a girlfriend . . . let alone one that could afford to drive a new Lexus?

Looks plumb out of place in this neck of the woods, Savannah thought as she slowed down to see if the car had vanity plates. But the series of random letters and numbers told her nothing.

She saw Harry Biddle sitting in his broken-down lawn chair, swigging a beer, scratching the roll of hairy belly that was protruding from beneath his gray undershirt. As she drove by he watched her with a lascivious gleam in his eye that made her want to crawl out of the car and slap him goofy. Half a slap would probably do the job.

Feeling like an adolescent whose curiosity was about to land her in trouble, Savannah parked her Camaro behind the Lexus and got out. Harry perked up when he saw her walking in his direction, until she turned toward Dirk's trailer.

"Wouldn't go in there right now," he said, his ugly, snaggled grin widening.

"Yeah, why not?" she asked, knowing she wasn't going to like the answer.

"Let's just say, he's already got hisself some company." He waggled one bushy gray eyebrow suggestively. "I think three'd make a crowd, if you catch my drift."

"Well, catch mine, you old coot. Mind your own business."

"Or then ... maybe you three are into that kinky stuff. ..."

"And maybe you're a dork with a dirty mind and a grubby undershirt."

Leaving Mr. Biddle behind to mutter obscenities into his beer can, Savannah strode to the door of Dirk's trailer and rapped a shave-and-a-hair-cut greeting. Might as well be friendly. Might as well be casual. Might as well pretend she wasn't there to snoop.

Dirk might even believe it.

He didn't. She could tell right away by the irritated look on his face when he opened the door. Considering his less than cordial mood, she pushed past him before he could ask her to enter ... or to leave, which was far more likely.

"Gee, I hate to drop in on you unannounced like this but ..."

Savannah's voice trailed away when she saw who was sitting on Dirk's 1973 vintage, beige-and-gold-plaid sofa. It was the last person she expected to see.

The former Mrs. Dirk.

The hated and often maligned—though not often enough in Savannah's book—ex-wife who had run away with a shaggy-haired, twentysomething rock-and-roll drummer several years ago.

"Polly!" Savannah replaced her look of shock with a carefully constructed facade of nonchalance. The act probably would have been more convincing if she hadn't been choking on her own spit. "What are you doing . . . I mean . . . what a surprise. I didn't expect to ever see you again."

"You mean, you *hoped* you'd never see me again."

"Yeah, that too."

Polly leaned back and propped her arm along the top of the sofa. She looked as casual as Savannah was pretending to be. Her long legs were stretched out before her, every inch of them bared by her short-short shorts. Savannah noted with just a bit of catty satisfaction that her knees were starting to sag a little.

So was her heavily made-up face. Foundation applied with a trowel, spider eyelashes, red lips that had been painted too far outside the natural lipline to fool anyone . . . except some fool like Dirk. He had admitted to Savannah that he had actually thought Polly was a real blonde for the first year of their relationship. Savannah could spot Golden Sun Frost a mile away . . . especially when it was on a swarthy-skinned woman who, undoubtedly, had been born with dark brown hair.

Like most of the men who had crossed Polly's path, Dirk had been taken in . . . in more ways than one . . . by a used-to-be-pretty face and a not-too-bad body, and lots of skillfully worded female flattery. Those had always been Polly's greatest weapons when hunting.

"Hope I'm not interrupting anything," Savannah said smoothly. She was pretty sure by the frustration on Dirk's face and the way he was pacing the ten-foot span of trailer floor that she had. If she hung around long enough, she might just put a stop to this nonsense all together.

Some might call it interference; she called it charity. The guy needed to be saved from himself. On a nearby TV tray lay a single red rose. Probably a pre-Valentine gift from her to him or from him to her. The thought completely irked Savannah . . . either way.

"No problem," Polly said smoothly. "I'm sure you'll be leaving soon. Right? I mean, now that you see Dirk has company . . ."

"And now that you've seen who that company is," Dirk growled as he nodded, not so subtly toward the door.

In her peripheral vision, Savannah could see Dirk's cell phone sitting on top of the television set in the corner. She sauntered across the room in that direction.

"Actually, I had a good reason for dropping by, old pal," she told Dirk. "I brought you something. It's in my car."

She craned her neck to look out the window at her Camaro. As she had hoped, they did the same and she took the opportunity to sweep the cell phone into her jacket pocket.

"What is it?" Dirk said. She could hear the suspicion in his voice. She didn't really expect him to buy this pitch. The best she could hope for was that he would be a gentleman and not call her "liar, liar, pants on fire" to her face.

"Your cell phone," she replied. "You left it at my house. I figured you'd need it."

Dirk shot her a "yeah, right" look and glanced around the room. He didn't see his phone. But that wasn't unusual for Dirk. The guy would lose his rear end if it weren't stapled to his tailbone.

"So where is it?"

"In my car."

"Why didn't you bring it in with you, Savannah?" Polly asked, flipping her lush golden mane of split ends back behind one shoulder.

"Forgot." Savannah held out her car keys to Dirk. "Why don't you go get it. I think I left it on the passenger's seat."

He grumbled under his breath and headed for the door. "Aren't you coming with me?" he said, not bothering to hide his anger.

"In a minute, darlin'," she said, much too sweetly. "You go ahead. I'll be along shortly."

He looked from her to Polly and back, then shook his head. "I don't think it's a good idea to leave you two broads alone."

"Go on, Dirk," Polly said, stroking one of her legs as though checking for razor stubble. "I'm not afraid of Savannah. We're old friends, right?"

"You may be old," Savannah replied. "I'm barely middle-aged. And just for the record, you and I have never been friends." She tossed the keys to Dirk. "Go get your phone. I'll be right out."

Reluctantly, he exited the trailer, leaving the door ajar. Savannah waited until he was out of earshot. Then she took a few steps closer to Polly.

In spite of what Polly had said, she did look a bit worried, just enough to satisfy Savannah's perverse streak.

"I don't know what you're doing here," Savannah said. "After the number you did on Dirk, I can't imagine why you would come back into his life, or why he would allow you to. But if you use him and hurt him again, like you did before, I swear I'll beat the tar outta you. And if you think I mean that figuratively, you're wrong."

A flicker of fear crossed Polly's eyes; then she reached for the pack of cigarettes on a nearby TV tray and lit up. She blew a long puff of smoke in Savannah's direction before answering. "Now what is this I hear? Do I detect a note of jealousy? Was I right all those years ago . . . you really do have a thing for Dirk?"

"Yeah, I have a thing for Dirk. It's called friendship. Loyalty. Concern for his well-being . . . all things you wouldn't know about."

"I think you want him all to yourself." Polly released more smoke through her nose.

How perfectly lovely, Savannah thought. *Quintessential femininity. I'd like to snatch her bald.*

Savannah reached over and, before Polly knew what was happening, grabbed the cigarette out of her hand. She crumbled it between her fingers and dropped the remains into a glass of white wine that was sitting next to the ashtray and a bottle of half-drunk beer on the TV tray. Dirk's beer, no doubt. Polly's wine.

"If you hurt Dirk again," Savannah said, using a voice she usually reserved for suspected murderers and child molesters, "I'll hurt you. My interest is not romantic; it's self-preservation. I'm not going to listen to him bellyache for two long, miserable years like he did when you left him before. If I have to pick up the pieces of Dirk, Miss Priss Pot, somebody's going to have to pick up pieces of you. You got that?"

Polly didn't answer. But Savannah could tell by the wide-ness of her spider eyes and the way her too-lipsticked mouth was hanging open that she had heard and believed . . . at least a little.

Savannah left the trailer, slamming the door behind her, and nearly ran, chest first, into Dirk.

"My cell phone isn't in your car," he said, his nose inches from hers, his voice as low and ominous as hers had been a moment before. "But then, neither one of us really expected it to be, right, Van?"

Savannah reached into her left jacket pocket and took out his phone; hers was still in her right. "Oh, silly me," she said. "Here it is. I guess I remembered to bring it in with me after all."

When she handed it to him, he looked puzzled and apologetic enough to make her feel a little guilty. "Oh, you really . . . oh, thanks, Van."

"No problem. Watch yourself, buddy, with that gal." She nodded toward the trailer. "Remember last time?"

"Yeah, I remember. But it ain't like that this time. She just wants me to help her, to take care of somethin' for her."

"That's all she's ever wanted, Dirk, from anyone. She's a leech. That's the problem."

"Naw. I can take care of it. Don't worry."

Don't worry, yeah, sure, she thought as she left him, got in her Camaro, and drove away. Dirk wasn't stupid—not by a long shot. But he had a blind spot where women were concerned . . . especially women he loved.

Why else would he buy a stupid story about a cell phone?

Savannah had no idea what line of bull Polly was going to try to sell him, but she was pretty sure he'd buy it, too.

* * *

Savannah felt a lot older than her forty-plus-a-few years as she walked from her driveway up the walk to her house. The place needed a lot of work. The white stucco could use a coat of paint. Some of the red Spanish tiles were crumbling on the roof. And the bougainvillea—affectionately named Bogey—that had once graced the front porch was a tangled, red-and-green jungle. The mess definitely needed to be hacked back. At one time a pair of ladies' garden shears would have done the job. Now a macho machete would be required.

And she wasn't in the mood for home improvement.

Or catching wanna-be-Nazi adolescents.

Or playing the role of codependent rescuer to a guy whose main problem in relationships was that he was a codependent rescuer.

She was in the mood for a hot bubble bath, a hot chocolate topped with mounds of whipped cream, and a hot, steamy romance novel . . . with a subplot involving mounds covered with whipped cream.

As she walked through the door, her two cats—pampered, four-legged children wearing glossy black fur and rhinestone-studded collars—wrapped themselves affectionately around her ankles. "Cleopatra, Diamante," she cooed to them as she stroked the ebony fur and was rewarded with motorboat purrs.

"Anybody home?" she called as she tossed her purse and keys onto the piecrust table in the foyer and kicked off her loafers. "Tammy, are you still here?"

"In the office," came the reply from what had once been Savannah's sunporch, before she had been kicked off the police force, before she had formed the Moonlight Magnolia Detective Agency . . . back when she had been gainfully employed and could afford cheese with her macaroni and cheese dinners. Ah, those were the days.

Savannah entered the room just in time to see Tammy whip a pair of reading glasses off her face and into the desk drawer. She stifled a giggle as she watched her assistant squirm a bit in her chair, squinting at the computer monitor in front of her.

"Screen fuzzy again?" Savannah asked, unable to resist.

"Yeah . . . kinda." Tammy donned her most officious, computer-expert face and tone. "I think it might be a problem with the connector cord or . . ."

"Or a simple case of premature myopia or astigmatism, combined with a narcissistic personality disorder?"

"What?"

"Nothing." Savannah sat in her favorite floral-chintz chair. The piece of furniture was a tad faded, a bit frayed around the edges, more than a little overstuffed, curvaceous, and comfy. Savannah related, reveling in their similarities.

"Anything new?" Savannah asked. She peered at the computer screen, but as usual, she didn't understand what she was looking at. It was all a bunch of gobbledygook to her. That was why she desperately needed someone like Tammy Hart. A sweet, hardworking airhead who happened to also be a computer whiz kid. A strange combination, but in Tammy, it worked.

And Tammy worked. Hard. And cheap.

At first, Savannah had assumed it was because she had read too many Nancy Drew books as a girl and had some misguided notion that if she hung out with Savannah long enough, she'd become a real, live detective. But now Savannah knew Tammy was there out of love and loyalty. And if she helped nail a bad guy once in a while or find somebody's runaway teen, all the better.

"I was scanning some of the message boards on-line today," Tammy said, clicking away on the keyboard and moving the little white arrow all over the screen with a gadget she called a "mouse."

Savannah nodded, pretending to have some vague notion as to what she was talking about. "I see."

Tammy shot her a doubtful, sideways grin. "You do?"

"Nope, but go on. I'll probably be able to jump in somewhere along the way."

"And I saw that someone had posted a message about you."

"Oh, yeah? On the Internet?"

"Yep. Somebody's looking for you."

Someone hunting for *her*. That didn't sit well with Savannah. She was far more comfortable with doing the hunting.

"Who was it?"

"Here, let me sign on again, and I'll find it for you."

Savannah stood and walked over to stand behind Tammy. She rested her hands on the young woman's shoulders as Tammy worked her magic with the keyboard and mouse. Rude sounds, a series of irritating beeps and hisses, spewed from the computer's speakers as it communicated with the world. Seconds later, Savannah saw a message displayed across the screen.

I am searching for a woman by the name of Savannah Reid, please contact me at the following address. She is Caucasian, in her early forties, approximately 5'8", 135 lbs., and has dark brown hair and blue eyes.

She is from the Atlanta, Georgia, area and was last believed to be on the West Coast, possibly Southern California. If anyone knows the whereabouts of this person would they please contact me at the following e-mail address . . .

"Do you recognize the address?" Tammy asked.

Savannah shook her head. "No. Does it say who posted it?"

"Not really. But there's a city mentioned . . . right down here." She scrolled to the bottom of the page. "There it is. Macon. That's a town in Georgia, right? I wonder why they would give their town but not their name."

Savannah felt her stomach flip into a tight roll like an overwound window blind as she stared at the word. Finally, she found her voice. "Macon is a town, all right. But in this case, it's not a location. It's a name."

"A name? Don't tell me you have another sibling named after a Georgia town! I thought I knew all nine of you."

"He's not my brother," she said.

Tammy looked up at her expectantly, but she didn't fill in the blank. That window blind had rolled all the way up her throat.

"Well, do you want me to respond? If it's an old boyfriend, maybe he wants to wish you a happy Valentine's Day and—"

"No."

The answer was so quick and abrupt that Tammy raised one eyebrow. "Ooo-kaay. Whatever you say."

Savannah turned to walk out of the room. Tammy jumped up from the chair and followed: Nancy Drew on the prowl.

"Do you wanna talk about it?" she asked. "Because if you do, I—"

"No . . . thank you." Savannah stopped in the middle of the floor and was nearly rear-ended. She turned and gave Tammy a kind but don't-push-it look. "Why don't you knock off a little early?" she said gently. "Not much going on around here, right?"

"Ah. Yeah, I guess right."

Savannah watched, feeling a little guilty as her deflated assistant walked into the front hall and retrieved her own purse and keys from the piecrust table. Savannah's grandmother's table. The table where Macon had tossed his keys, a lifetime ago.

"Thanks for everything you do, Tam," she said. "I just want a hot bath and a well-balanced, nutritious, wholesome dinner."

"A pint of Ben & Jerry's Chunky Monkey?"

"You know me too well."

Tammy shook her head. "Junk food is going to be the death of you."

"I'll die a happy woman . . . with chocolate on my breath and a smile on my lips."

"Call me later, if you need me."

Savannah smiled. Yes, Tammy was there for love, not money. "I will, sweetie. I will."

But Tammy wasn't the one Savannah called later that night when the decadent culinary treats and the sweetness of the romance novel wouldn't take the bitter taste away. She called Granny Reid in Georgia. Even though it was late, she knew Gran would still be up, reading her Bible and her *National Enquirer* . . . both the absolute, gospel truth, according to her.

No one could beat Gran when it came to lending an ear and giving advice. In her eighty-five years, Gran had seen it all and lived most of it. Nothing even surprised her, let alone shocked her.

Savannah snuggled under the rose-spangled satin comforter on lace-trimmed sheets as she held the telephone receiver against her cheek and listened to the phone ring once, twice, three times. The sleeves of her white-cotton, Victorian-styled nightgown were also trimmed with lace, the bodice closed with a crisscrossing of tiny pink ribbons.

Around the house and out in the hard, cold world, Savannah was denim and linen, wool and corduroy. But in bed . . . in bed she was all woman.

Southern femininity—her heritage from the lady on the other end of the phone, whose voice was silkier than any satin spread.

"Hi, Gran. It's me."

"What's the matter, sugar?"

Nothing got past Gran. She could smell a whiff of trouble across a phone line three thousand miles away.

"Macon's looking for me."

There was a long silence on the other end. She could tell her grandmother was choosing her words carefully. Southern belles were known for their tact, their diplomacy, their—

"What does that horse's ass want with you?"

Well, maybe not.

"Don't know. I haven't talked to him. He left a message on the Internet."

"On the what?"

"Ah . . . the worldwide computer system."

"Can't imagine he'd be bright enough to operate something like that."

"Maybe he had help."

"Like an accomplice? Naw. That would mean he had a friend. Not likely."

"I see your point."

They both shared a companionable giggle; then Gran got serious. "How do you feel about that, sweetheart . . . him trying to get in touch with you after all these years?"

"Honestly?"

"That goes without saying. I don't ask if I don't want to know."

"I wish he'd just leave me the hell alone. As far as I'm concerned, my business with him is over and done with, and that's the way I like it."

"Then send him a message on that Internet thing and tell him so."

"Or just ignore him, drink lots of liquids, stay warm, and get plenty of rest, and like a bad case of the flu, maybe he'll go away?"

"One can always hope."

Savannah thought she could detect a note of sadness in her grandmother's voice. Gran wasn't the only one who could detect a problem long-distance. "I'm sorry if it hurts you to discuss him," Savannah said. "I probably shouldn't have called you, of all people."

She heard Gran sniff a no-nonsense, but still ladylike, sniff on the other end. "Do you really think I don't know what sort of person Macon is? Of all people, I should know my own son."

Savannah toyed with the ribbon on the front of her gown, allowing it to slip between her fingers. Unshed tears began to burn her eyes. She blinked them away. Why should it still hurt after all this time?

She started to speak, but her throat closed up. As always, Gran filled in the blank. "It's all right, honey. It's okay to cry."

Savannah cleared the knot out of her throat. "I'm not crying." But it wasn't a very convincing denial; even to her own ears, she sounded like a defiant, teary, five-year-old.

"I didn't say you were boo-hooing up a storm," Gran said. "But I could tell you were getting a little weepy on me. And that's all right. I know my son wasn't much of a father to you. And your mama . . . well, she was another story altogether. And things weren't exactly a picnic for you, the oldest in a family with nine young'uns and no full-time parent to take charge."

Savannah flashed back on the mountains of laundry that always needed to be washed, hung on the clothesline, folded, or ironed. The skinned knees, cut fingers, cat scratches, and beestings that had to be cleaned, medicated, and kissed. The endless assembly line of school lunches: stacks of sandwiches, sliced Spam when they could afford it, peanut butter when they couldn't. Babies crying, kids fussing, the verbal quarrels and the knock-down-drag-outs that had to be refereed. A table with not one, but three extra leaves in it, burdened with plates of fried chicken—one piece per kid—and huge bowls piled high with mashed potatoes. If you truly are what you eat, those children's bodies must have been ninety percent mashed potatoes.

But the memories weren't all tiresome.

Granny Reid had always sat at the end of that table,

saying grace at the beginning, and thanking the Good Lord above for every one of them sitting around it. She had cared for her shiftless son's children without one word of complaint, making each of them feel as though they had a special, wonderfully warm spot in her heart.

"I didn't suffer, Gran," Savannah said, wishing she could, like the commercial said, reach out and actually touch the precious person on the other end of the phone. "Not one bit. I have no regrets about my childhood . . . thanks to you."

"Me either, sugar. I wouldn't have missed it for the world. You children kept me young long past my youth. And now the grandbabies are doing the same. As long as there's a youngster in the house, I'm a kid, too."

Savannah took a deep breath and snuggled deeper under the satin comforter. "I wish I could be as young tomorrow as you were yesterday, Gran."

"Well, of course you do, sugar," her eighty-five-year-old grandmother replied with Mae West sauciness. "Or half as good-looking."

Savannah had just dropped off to sleep when the telephone rang, exploding in her right ear and sending her pulse racing like a scared rabbit's. She grabbed the receiver, dropped it on the floor, picked it up, and smacked herself on the teeth with the mouthpiece. She could swear she tasted blood.

"What?" she shouted, ready to kill whoever was calling her at—she squinted at the red, glowing numbers on the bedside clock—1:22 A.M.

"Van . . ."

Savannah didn't need Gran's extrasensitive radar to

detect the distress in that one word. She sat straight up and flipped on the bedside lamp. "Yeah, Dirk, what's going on?"

"It's Polly."

Savannah had a half a second to utter a quick, silent prayer, one that she instinctively knew was pointless. *God, let her be okay. They just had a fight, right? She's alive, but they just argued and—*

"She's dead."

Let it be natural causes, or . . . "A car accident?"

"Murdered."

She could hear him, feel him shaking through the phone. Dirk got excited, but he wasn't a shaker. His teeth were chattering, and he was having trouble breathing.

"Calm down, buddy," she said as she jumped out of bed and reached for the jeans and sweatshirt she had tossed into the hamper upon retiring. "Where are you?"

"At home . . . in my trailer."

She danced around on one foot, trying to get the jeans on with one hand and the nightgown off over her head. "And where is the bo—I mean, where is she?"

"In my trailer. Shot with my gun."

"Oh, shit."

"Yeah."

"Don't do anything. Don't touch anything. Don't say anything to anybody. Just sit down on the floor and put your head between your legs until I get there."

There was silence on the other end, except for his shaky breathing.

"Do you hear me?"

"I hear you. Hurry."

"Hang tight, buddy. I'm halfway there."

CHAPTER THREE

Savannah made the ten-minute trip to Dirk's place in less than six, but that was plenty of time for her to fantasize more than a dozen scenarios of what had happened in his trailer. And she didn't like the way any of them played in her head.

They didn't call it "*hom-i-cide*" for nothing. Most murders were committed in the home and by killers who were either family or friends of the victim.

But Dirk wouldn't kill Polly. He wouldn't. He wouldn't. He just would not do it.

The words gave Savannah comfort, so she kept playing them over and over in her head. But each time she repeated the litany, it had a less convincing ring of truth to it. Savannah had learned several things in law enforcement. And one of them was: Anyone will do anything under the right/wrong circumstances.

Dirk wouldn't kill Polly. All right, he might have if . . .

As she whipped along the narrow, dark, eucalyptus-lined road leading to his trailer park, she tried to fill in the blank. What would it take to put a guy like Dirk over the edge? He had been through a lot with his former wife already, and he had never hit or harmed her in any way. At least, not that Savannah had ever heard. And usually, domestic-related killings were a culmination of abuse that had escalated over a period of time.

If Dirk had shot his ex-wife, Savannah could honestly say she hadn't seen that one coming.

Her headlights shone silver on the leaves of the orange trees that stood in long, straight rows parallel to the road. The groves glimmered in the winter moonlight, and Savannah wished her spirit were even half as peaceful as those orchards looked.

What could have happened in that trailer?

She considered alternative scenarios—the ones where another party had pulled the trigger.

Of Dirk's gun?

Yes, she told the nasty, cynical cop voice inside her head. *It could happen. Well . . . it could.* The killer—not Dirk—could be lurking in the darkness of the groves right then, watching her approach the park.

If somebody else did it, he would have hightailed it out of there right away . . . unless Dirk got him, too. She hadn't taken the time to ask before racing to his aid.

She wondered if he had called the cops yet. Knowing Dirk as she did, she figured he hadn't. But someone must have.

The trailers were pretty close together, and the nosy Biddles wouldn't have missed an opportunity to report trouble and stir up a hornets' nest if possible.

The answer to that question was given the moment she pulled into the spot she had vacated hours before, behind Polly's Lexus. Harry Biddle came bouncing out of his trailer with an energy she hadn't seen him demonstrate before. He was minus the undershirt, but the baggy boxer shorts and surgically attached beer can were still in place.

"I called the cops on your boyfriend, there," he said.

"Yeah, you're a real credit to your community . . . asshole," she muttered as she hurried past him.

"I told them he was shooting off fireworks, and those hills as dry as kindling." He waved a flabby arm toward the foothills, where wild chaparral was waist high and thirsty from lack of rainfall.

"Is that what you told the cops on the phone," she asked. "That somebody was lighting firecrackers?"

"Yeah, but I said it sounded more like cherry bombs to me. And I told them about him running around out here naked."

"Naked?"

"As a jaybird."

Savannah didn't know what to say to that. The mental picture nearly overloaded her brain circuits. She left Harry Biddle, his boxers and beer behind, and hurried up to Dirk's trailer. The door was ajar a couple of inches. A dim gold light came through the opening and cut a line across the dark porch.

Carefully, hand on her Beretta, which was in a shoulder holster beneath her jacket, she climbed the three wooden steps to the door.

"Dirk? It's me, Van. I'm coming in."

No point in charging into a crime scene unannounced. No point in spooking a guy who had sounded pretty shook on the phone less than ten minutes ago.

When she didn't hear an answer, she pulled the Beretta from its holster with her right hand and held it, pointed downward, beside her thigh. She eased the door open a few inches with her left hand.

"Hey, buddy. I'm here. Where are you?"

She didn't see him at first. She saw Polly.

The body was lying sprawled on the floor in front of the sofa. The copious amount of blood puddled on the linoleum and the vacant stare in her glassy eyes told Savannah immediately that Dirk was right. Polly Coulter wasn't hurt; she was very dead.

When Savannah opened the door the rest of the way and stepped inside, she saw Dirk. And the sight made her knees grow weak.

He was sitting on the floor about six feet from Polly's body. As Mr. Biddle had said, Dirk was naked, his knees drawn up and his arms wrapped around them. His head was down, and she couldn't see his face, but his hair was wet and plastered to his scalp in dark strands. He was shivering violently.

As Savannah reholstered her gun and took a few steps toward him, he looked up, as though realizing for the first time she was there. His eyes were red and puffy, and they had a lost, frightened look. Savannah recognized the look. It was the one human beings wore when visited by sudden tragedy.

She hurried across the room and dropped to her knees beside him. When she placed her hands on his shoulders, she was shocked to feel how cold and clammy his skin was. And slick . . . as though he had some kind of soap on him.

"Th-thanks for . . . coming," he said through chattering teeth. "I didn't know who else to . . ."

"Don't be silly. Of course you should call me. Are you all right? Are you hurt?"

He seemed surprised at her question, as though it hadn't occurred to him to check. Unwrapping his arms, he looked down at his bare chest. So did she.

It was covered with blood. His arms and hands were smeared with the dark red gore as well.

"Are you shot?" Savannah said, as she quickly checked his skin for anything resembling an entrance wound. But she found nothing.

"No," he said, "I don't think so." He glanced over at Polly and shuddered. "It's hers. I . . . I was holding her, you know, when she . . ."

"When she was shot?"

"When she died."

"Oh, okay."

With her hands on his shoulders, she could feel his cold, damp gooseflesh, and his shaking seemed to vibrate through her own body. She was afraid he might go into shock if he didn't get warm.

"Wait right there," she said. "I'll be back in a second. Okay?"

He nodded.

She jumped up from the floor and made her way through the tiny kitchen to the equally tiny bedroom in the back of the trailer. As she grabbed his ancient, tattered bathrobe off its hook on the wall beside his bed, she was aware of a sound . . . the spraying of the shower, going full blast.

She stepped into the bathroom and reached for the handle, intending to turn it off. Then she reconsidered and left it running.

Don't disturb anything, a quiet, logical voice told her, even as she mentally registered the explanation for Dirk's wet hair and soap-slick, nude body. *This isn't Dirk's trailer anymore*, the former-cop voice cautioned. *It's a crime scene. Worse, a homicide scene*.

She took the robe into the living room and draped it over his shoulders. "Can you stand up, darlin'?" she said, in the same tone she would have used with an injured, frightened child.

Again, he nodded, and she supported him under the elbow as he rose from the floor and stood on trembling legs. "Here," she said, easing his arms into the robe. "Let's get you wrapped up, kiddo. You're colder than a mackerel." She pulled the terry cloth tight around him and tied the belt in front. "There ya go. Now, come over here and set yourself down.

Next to a fold-down table was a molded plastic lawn chair . . . Dirk's idea of practical dining equipment. She pushed him into it and dragged its mate next to his and sat down. "Tell me what happened," she said, "but make it snappy. Your favorite neighbor has already ratted you out to 911. The cops are on their way, and you've gotta get a call in before they arrive."

"Harry called it in?"

"He told them you were shooting off cherry bombs, so they probably aren't exactly burning the wind to get here. We've got a minute or two. How did that happen?" She nodded toward Polly's still figure without looking in her direction. Long ago, she had discovered that corpses you know are always harder to view than those of total strangers. Even after years of seeing things that made her old for her age, Savannah had never gotten over the shocking difference between a live body and a dead one. In moments . . . such an astonishing transformation. It always made her feel her own mortality.

"Was it an accident?" she asked, giving him the benefit of the doubt, afraid of what she was about to hear.

"No, I don't think so. Somebody broke in while I was in the shower."

"Broke in?" Savannah glanced around. No open windows and the door didn't appear to have been forced or the lock jimmied. Maybe from the outside.

"Yeah, or she let them in. I don't know." His teeth had stopped chattering, and his eyes were losing their glazed look. She looked down at his feet and hands; they were turning from grayish blue to a normal flesh color.

"You were in the shower."

"Yeah. We'd had an argument, and I told her I was going to hose down and go to bed . . . that she'd better be gone by the time I got outta the shower."

"What did you fight about?"

He shrugged and shook his head. "What did we always fight about. Stupid shit. Her bummin' money off me all the time, giving me some sob story about how broke she is."

"So, you went into the shower and . . . ?"

"I was in there a couple of minutes, soaping up, washing my hair, when I heard a bang."

"The gun?"

"Yeah, but I wasn't sure that was what it was, with the

shower running on my head, you know. Anyway, I ran out here to see what was goin' on, and I ran right into the guy."

"What guy?"

"Some dude standing about right there . . ." He pointed to a spot on the floor about four feet from where Polly's body lay. "He had my weapon in his hand and was pointing it at Polly. She was . . . she was down there, where she's at now."

Savannah nodded. "Did you recognize him? Anybody you know?"

"I don't think so. I didn't get that good a look at him, before I jumped him."

"You tackled him?"

"Yeah. He smacked me on the head with the gun, but I got it away from him."

"But you couldn't hold him with it?"

Dirk shook his head. "Naw, my hand was wet and soapy and I dropped the damned thing. He bolted out the door. By the time I picked it up again and chased him, he was gone."

"You chased him outside?"

"Yeah, but he was gone. I didn't even see which way he went."

She nodded thoughtfully. "Your old geezer neighbor said you were running around in the altogether. Come to think of it, he told the cops that, too. You'd better call this in, buddy, before they get here."

Dirk glanced over at Polly, at the pool of blood around her, and he shuddered. "It looks bad, huh, Van?"

His eyes looked directly into hers. She saw and felt his fear. She wanted to say something to allay his concerns. But she and Dirk had always shot straight with each other in times of trouble. This wasn't the time to start lying to him, no matter how altruistic her reasons.

"It looks bad, buddy. She's shot with your gun, in your trailer. You've got her blood all over you. You say you were arguing right before, and you've got nosy neighbors only a few feet away who probably heard you. You're in deep, pal. Right up to your gills." She reached for the cell phone, sitting on top of the television, and handed it to him. "You'd better make that call."

CHAPTER FOUR

Dirk and Savannah sat across from each other at the no-frills table in the no-frills interrogation room in the San Carmelita Police Station. The cubicle-sized enclosure had been designed to give the invited "guests" of the SCPD that claustrophobic, we-got-you-now-sucker feeling. And it was most effective. With nothing to look at but the gray paint on the walls, nothing to sit on but the gray aluminum folding chairs, and the temperature raised to at least eighty-five degrees, the occupants had that snug, cozy feeling usually associated with being inside a pressure cooker.

Dirk was looking a bit better, Savannah noted with a sense of relief. At least he had some color in his face, his hair was dry, and he was dressed in his usual past-its-prime polo shirt, jeans, and sneakers. He seemed less vulnerable . . .

though, from the haunted look in his eyes, she suspected that wasn't altogether true.

"I can't believe they put you in the sweat tank," she said, drumming her fingertips on the gouged surface of the table. "I mean, I'm persona non grata around this place, but you . . . you're still family, for cryin' out loud."

Dirk reached beneath the table and yanked the wire off the tiny microphone installed there. "Yeah, you'd think we could talk this over at Joe's Bar. At least I could get bombed there. Boy, do I feel like it."

"We'll . . . ah . . . raise your spirits later, buddy. Just give them what they want and we'll get outta here. Be careful though. Don't let 'em hang you out to dry."

Dirk cleared his throat and stood, trying to see out the tiny window in the door. "What do you suppose they're doing out there?"

"Fighting, like a pack of jackals, over who gets to pick your bones."

He turned back to her, one eyebrow quirked. "Thanks. I knew there was some reason why I made them let you in here."

"I meant to ask—how did you do that?"

"I told them I wanted either you or a lawyer."

"I'm flattered . . . I guess."

"Don't be. I like lawyers even less than I like doctors."

He sighed and dropped back onto his chair, which complained with a rusty, grinding sound.

"If that chair breaks and dumps you on your rear, you could sue the city for a wrenched heinie," Savannah said brightly. Too brightly.

Again he gave her a rueful not-quite grin. "Stop trying to cheer me up, okay? It ain't cuttin' it."

She nodded. "Gotcha." Instantly, she turned serious. "What are you going to tell them when they ask you what—"

The door swung open and Lieutenant Quince Jeffries marched into the "tank." Jeffries was a company man all the way. Three-piece charcoal suit, thick, prematurely silver hair slicked back in a GQ do, and ramrod posture that would make a Marine look like a slouch.

Savannah had always suspected that a three-feet-long steel ramrod had been surgically implanted in his colon, forever stiffening his posture and detrimentally affecting his personality. Spending time with Lieutenant Jeffries was no afternoon in the park playing Frisbee and barbecuing ribs.

"Well, we see who came out on top of the pack," Savannah muttered under her breath. "The beta male jackal himself."

Dirk shot her a look that told her he understood the reference. Everyone knew that although Lieutenant Jeffries spent half his time exploiting his limited authority and making life unpleasant for his underlings, he spent the other half applying his puckered kisser to the seat of Chief Norman Hillquist's trousers. Jeffries wanted to be chief of police of San Carmelita when he grew up someday; Hillquist wanted to be mayor. Watching them interact with each other, the city council members, and everyone else with money or influence was nauseating for less ambitious people like Savannah, Dirk, and the other cops who were just trying to stay alive and do a decent job.

Jeffries gave Savannah a curt nod and pulled a chair up to the head of the table. He sat down and rested his elbows on the table, folding his fingers in a judicious pose.

"So, I get top-notch service," Dirk said, not bothering to

hide his sarcastic tone. "You're going to squeeze me personally, huh?"

Savannah winced inwardly. Dirk seemed to have a gift for making a bad situation worse. "Diplomacy" wasn't a commonly used word in his personal lexicon.

Jeffries fixed him with cold gray eyes that would have cut through a man with less chutzpah than Dirk Coulter. "We take officer-involved shootings very seriously in this department, Sergeant. I don't have to tell you that."

"Especially in an election year when the chief's trying to bump up to mayor and you're trying to fill his spot, huh? Don't want any bad PR for the department right now." Dirk leaned back in his chair and folded his arms across his barrel chest— the picture of defiance. Savannah longed to reach over and slap some sense into him. This wasn't the time to be cute.

Jeffries's eyes narrowed and his mouth pulled into a tight line. "Election or no, there's never a good time for a cop to blow away his ex-wife," he said smoothly, with a deadly lack of inflection. "It's almost always frowned upon by the local citizenry. Especially the female population."

"And that's more than half the voters."

Savannah couldn't stand it. She kicked him under the table and landed a solid one on his shin. He winced, but dropped a bit of the tough-guy facade. "I didn't kill her, Lieutenant," he said with a convincing degree of sincerity. "I know it looks bad, my trailer, my gun . . . her being my ex, but it was an intruder."

"The intruder you wrestled with and disarmed . . . as in, you had your gun in your hand, but he still got away?"

"My hands were wet, and I dropped my weapon. And I hesitated a couple of seconds to check on Pol—the victim . . .

and he ran out the door. I chased him, but it was dark and . . . well . . ." He shrugged. "I'm not happy about it, but that's the way it went down."

"Uh-huh." Jeffries stood and began to pace the floor behind Dirk. It was a move designed to make the interviewee feel intimidated, having questions fired from behind by an unseen interrogator. Savannah had seen Dirk use it many times. She was surprised that Jeffries would use it on a veteran.

Jeffries stroked his chin thoughtfully. She didn't like the arrogant, assured look on his face. The expression was a common one for him, but all the more disturbing, considering her friend's rear end was in the wringer. And it appeared Jeffries was the one turning the crank. "And nobody saw this mysterious intruder running around outside," he continued. "They didn't see anyone outside except you, that is. Naked."

Dirk's face flushed angrily. "I was in the shower when I heard the shot. I came out of the bathroom and found my ex-wife bleeding all over the floor. What I was—or wasn't—wearing at the time wasn't a big concern of mine."

"What was your ex-wife doing there in the first place?"

Dirk turned in his chair to face Jeffries. "What are you talking about? There's something wrong with my former old lady dropping by to shoot the breeze?"

"But you weren't shooting the breeze. You were arguing . . . loudly. Your neighbors heard you. What was the fight about?"

Dirk released a long, weary sigh and shook his head. Savannah could tell that he was exhausted, and it worried her; Dirk wasn't at his best when he was tired. And under the circumstances, he needed to be top-notch.

"I thought she had come by to . . . you know . . . touch base, to hang out for old times' sake," he said. "She gave me a flower, because of Valentine's Day comin' up. But then she admitted that she was in trouble . . . again . . . and wanted me to bail her out. I got pissed off and told her, 'No way.' I was sick of her using me."

Jeffries walked back to his chair and sat down again. "What kind of trouble did she say she was in?"

"She didn't say. I didn't ask. I just told her I wasn't going to be her patsy this time. Money, or whatever it was she wanted, I wasn't interested. I told her to take a hike; then I took a shower."

"And she got shot. With your gun."

"Well, maybe you take your weapon into the shower with you. I don't. It specifically says not to in the manufacturer's manual."

Jeffries said nothing, but made a five-second attempt to stare Dirk down. It didn't work. The lieutenant was the first to look away.

"I'm tired," Dirk said. "I've had the day from hell, and I want to leave now." He stood and shoved the chair against the table. "I told Jake McMurtry everything I could think of at the scene, and I'll write you a two-hundred-page report before the end of the day. But right now, I've gotta lie down somewhere, or I'm going to fall down."

Savannah stood with him. "He's going to my place. He'll be there if you need him; just call."

It isn't going to work, she thought. No way would Jeffries cut him loose after only half a dozen questions.

"All right. Go get some sleep," Jeffries said. Savannah braced her jaw to keep it from dropping. "Have your report on my desk by five."

Savannah hurried to Dirk, grabbed his elbow, and hustled

him toward the door before the lieutenant could change his mind.

"One more thing," Jeffries said before they could make their exit. *Uh-oh*, Savannah thought. *There's always a catch*. "Don't talk to the press. Not one word, or I'll haul your ass back in here so fast it'll make your dick spin."

"Don't worry, Lieutenant. I'm not talking to nobody 'bout nothin'," Dirk said.

Savannah shoved him through the door and closed it behind them. In less than thirty seconds she had him out of the station and was leading him, like an obedient cocker spaniel, across the parking lot, toward her Camaro.

"So, after all these years," he said, "you're inviting me to spend the night with you."

"Only because your place is a crime scene," she told him, slipping her arm through his. "And don't get frisky on me. You're sleeping in the spare room."

He leaned down and placed a quick kiss on her forehead. "Don't worry, kiddo. I just want to drink a fifth of Jack Daniel's and quietly pass out. Any horizontal surface will do. Believe me: Frisky's the last thing on my mind."

"I know that you never liked Polly," Dirk said as he poured himself the fourth shot of the evening. And the evening—at least the drinking part—was only thirty minutes old.

Savannah watched, a little concerned as his unsteady hand replaced the bottle on her coffee table. He didn't spill it, but he definitely set it down with more force than necessary. Dirk's depth perception was always the first sense to go when he became inebriated. Which wasn't all that often. He liked an evening beer with his Whopper or Big Mac, but she had seldom seen him show his liquor.

But there was a first time for everything, and Savannah figured the night a guy watched his ex-wife die was as good a night as any to get stinking drunk. Excuses didn't get much better than that.

Besides, there were only a couple more hours of the night left. The green digital readout on her VCR said it was 4:25 A.M. She figured she would get him soused, then drag him upstairs and throw him into her guest bed. He could sleep all day . . . as long as he woke up in time to generate a report for Lieutenant Jeffries.

"Okay," she said, "I'll admit it. Polly wasn't one of my favorite people. But then, I didn't know her as well as you did. Apparently you saw something in her that wasn't obvious to me."

Heaven knows what, she added silently as she settled back in her easy chair and petted the ebony, green-eyed purring machine that was curled in her lap.

Dirk tossed back the shot and grimaced as it went down the hatch. Then he leaned back on the sofa and propped his feet on the coffee table. Savannah had told him a thousand times to keep his shoes off her furniture. A thousand and one times, he had forgotten.

"Polly could be sweet, when she wanted to be," he said. "At least, she was in the beginning. She'd say, 'Pretty please,' and butter me up when she wanted something. And when I gave it to her, she acted all grateful, like I was some fantastic sort of hero who'd rescued her."

Savannah listened quietly, stroking Diamante, remembering something that her grandmother had told her once. Granny

Reid had said, "It's not so much the person we fall in love with ... as much as it's the way they make us feel about ourselves."

Perhaps that wasn't such a grand and glorious commentary on the human heart, but the older Savannah got, the more she realized how true Gran's words were.

So, Polly had made Dirk feel like a knight in shining armor, rescuing a fair damsel who was perpetually in distress. Sometimes her dragons were real, other times imaginary, but they were always of her own making. A fact that seemed to elude Dirk.

But the maid-in-trouble routine had worked all too well for Polly. She had never been without male company. Usually she had dangled several on a chain at once.

Savannah tried to recall the last time she had felt a tug on her own chain. Ages. But then, she wasn't in the habit of asking knights to wield their swords on her behalf. Maybe she should take some lessons from Polly on carefully cultivated helplessness.

But then, defenseless Polly was lying in the morgue, next in line to be autopsied. So much for surrendering your personal power to avoid personal responsibility. If she hadn't come over to Dirk's to try to finagle him into bailing her out of some sort of problem, she would probably still be alive and irritating people.

"Do you have any idea what she wanted from you?" Savannah asked, sipping her own hot chocolate, which, for once, wasn't laced with Bailey's or anything else alcoholic. One of them had to stay sober to negotiate the stairs later. And there was another reason for someone to keep a clear head ... a reason she didn't want to think too much about right then.

"Well, she certainly wasn't there to cozy up to me—that's for sure," Dirk said with a sigh as he poured another shot. "Whatever she wanted, it wasn't to kiss and make up."

For the first time, Savannah realized that Dirk had actually hoped, at least briefly, that Polly's appearance, Valentine rose in hand, might have indicated a desire to reconcile on her part. She also realized that he might have welcomed that. The revelation didn't sit well with her.

"If we could find out what sort of problem she had, we might know why somebody wanted to kill her," Savannah said. It wasn't the time to talk shop, but she couldn't help herself. Her mental cogs were already whirring. If things went as badly as she was afraid they would for Dirk, he was going to need some help . . . a lot of help to clear himself of Polly's murder.

He tossed back the shot and shuddered. "Right now . . . frankly, my dear . . . I don't give a rat's ass." As he wiped his hand across his eyes, Savannah thought how tired, how gray he looked. She needed to get him into bed soon. "I guess I should care," he added, slurring his words a bit, "but I don't. I figure I'll care later. Tomorrow or maybe the next day."

Savannah scooped Diamante out of her lap and placed the cat gently on the footstool. The miniature leopard didn't even open an eye. "I think I'd better get you upstairs and into your bunk, cowboy," she told Dirk, "before you pass out on me and I have to haul your mangy hide up those steps with brute strength."

He stood on wobbly legs and took a careful step toward her. "Yeah, I think I've enjoyed about as much of this day as I can stand. Let's put an end to it."

With his arm slung over her shoulders and hers wrapped

SUGAR AND SPITE

around his waist, she helped him up the stairs and down the hallway to her small, but adequate, guest bedroom. She knew he must be exhausted when he didn't even complain about the room's feminine, tulip-spangled quilt and lace curtains.

She barely had time to pull back the spread and sheets before he collapsed across the bed. "Come on," she said, tugging his sneakers off and tossing them on the floor, "we might as well make you comfy. Get out of those clothes."

In much the same way as she would have undressed one of her nieces or nephews, she removed his socks, shirt, and jeans. Although he didn't help her much, he didn't resist. She decided to leave on his boxers. Seeing him naked once in a twenty-four-hour period was enough.

"Bathroom's down the hall on the right if you need it," she told him. "The door on the left is a closet, and if you 'drain your dragon' or 'hang your rat' on my linens there, you're dead meat."

She waited for a reply but got only a cursory grunt as he snuggled into the covers and bunched the pillow under his head.

"Sleep tight, buddy," she said as she leaned over and gave him a peck on the forehead. "If you need anything, give a holler."

When he offered no response, she figured he was already a goner. But after she had turned out the light, as she was softly closing the door behind her, she heard him say, "Thanks, Van . . . for everything."

"You're welcome, sugar," she whispered. "You'd do it for me."

"I would," he said. She could hear the drowsiness in his voice as sleep overtook him. "You know, Van . . . if you needed

me, I'd rescue you, too. And I wouldn't resent it, like I did
with Polly. I'd be glad to help you out."

Savannah felt a little catch in her throat that seemed to
squeeze some unexpected moisture into her eyes. "I know you
would, darlin'," she whispered. "Hush now and get yourself to
sleep."

Dirk began to snore.

When dawn broke, pink, gold, and turquoise, through
her living room curtains, Savannah was still wide-awake, lying
on her sofa, her grandmother's crocheted afghan thrown over
her . . . her loaded 9mm Beretta and an extra clip filled with
bullets lying on the coffee table beside her.

Someone had to stay awake and sober. And, because of
the hellish nature of his past twenty-four hours, Dirk had been
given the honor of *Designated Drunk*.

Because, even though the thought hadn't seemed to have
occurred to Dirk—at least, he hadn't voiced any concerns in
that area—Savannah was worried for their personal safety.

Somebody had murdered Dirk's ex-wife. That same somebody had tried to shoot him, too. Polly might be the one lying
in the city morgue in a special white body bag with a locked
zipper, reserved for homicide victims and those who had died
under suspicious circumstances. But the intruder had entered
Dirk's trailer. And for all anyone knew, Dirk might have been
his intended victim, not Polly. She might have just been at
the wrong place at the wrong time.

Savannah felt a shiver that not even Granny Reid's lovingly crocheted coverlet could chase away. This feeling was
in her bones.

Without knowing who had been in that trailer, why he

had been there, and who he had really intended to kill, there was no way to know if Dirk's life was still in danger. If the killer had made the attempt once and failed, who was to say he wouldn't try again?

So, Savannah had stayed awake the rest of the night, standing guard, so to speak, while lying on her sofa and listening to her brass ship's clock tick. Tammy would be in at nine, and by then it would be bright daylight.

Then she would go to bed and get some badly needed sleep. But for now, the princess had to keep watch over the castle, just in case some homicidal dragon tried to cross the moat. Sir Dirk was passed out cold up in the tower. Even a knight in dusty armor needed some time off.

CHAPTER FIVE

Even before Tammy arrived the phone started to ring; reporters from local papers and television stations wanted to know if Dirk had a statement. Savannah told them, not too tactfully, that if she were to wake him, he would, without a doubt, have several statements, none of which they would want to hear.

Savannah wondered who had tipped them off that he was at her house. But then, journalists were fairly resourceful, and Savannah's name had been linked to Dirk's in print more than once, thanks to some high-profile cases they had worked together.

When the doorbell rang at 8:34 A.M., Savannah threw the afghan onto the end of the sofa and gave up on getting any quick winks. She took her Beretta from the coffee table, shoved it in the back of her jeans waistband, and went to the door.

Looking through the peephole, she saw Rosemary Hulse, one of her least disliked newspaper reporters. Rosemary was tenacious, but not obnoxious, when it came to getting her story. So, in a moment of humanitarian love and consideration, Savannah decided not to shoot her dead on the front porch.

"Rosemary . . ." she said as she opened the door, "you decided to pay me a little visit. How sweet. If I'd known you were comin', I'd have baked a cake." Her far-less-than-enthusiastic tone belied the expressed Southern hospitality.

Rosemary didn't buy it. She gave her a rueful smile, and said, "Sorry, it's not social."

"Didn't really figure it was." Savannah noted that the usually perfectly groomed reporter looked a bit disheveled herself. Her customary pageboy flip didn't flip, and she was wearing wire-rimmed glasses instead of her contacts. "Did they drag you out of bed so that you could drag me out of bed?"

"Something like that. I've been up since three, when they called me about the shooting." Rosemary glanced up and down Savannah's rumpled shirt and slacks. "Did I drag you out of bed?"

"More like off the couch. It's been a long night."

"Is he here?"

"Yeah, upstairs, hopefully sawing logs. I'm not going to disturb him, so don't even ask."

Rosemary reached into her purse and produced a mini-recorder. "Mind if I ask you a couple of ques—"

"Of course, I mind. I haven't had my coffee yet, and my blood sugar level is zero, which means my brainwave level is the same."

Rosemary shot her a winsome smile. "Invite me in for coffee and a Danish, maybe?"

But it wasn't that winsome. "Nope. Sorry. Nothing personal."

"After coffee and doughnuts, when you're feeling better"—Rosemary fished in her pocket for a business card and handed it to Savannah—"if you or Sergeant Coulter do decide to talk to the media, will you give me first crack?"

"Don't hold your breath. I don't know much yet, and Dirk's not exactly the chatty type."

The reporter wrinkled her nose. "I remember. I think he told me to . . . well . . . he suggested some unnatural act that—"

"Don't feel bad. Coulter has offered similar suggestions to almost everyone he knows at one time or the other. Actually, he likes you."

Rosemary looked doubtful. "Really? How can you tell?"

"He actually spoke words to you. If he didn't like you, he'd growl, maybe snap."

"And he's your friend?"

Savannah laughed. "My best one in the world. Doesn't say much for my taste, huh?" Behind her, Savannah could hear the phone ringing again. "Gotta go."

"Give me a call."

"If I talk, it'll be to you."

She shut the door in Rosemary's face, nearly closing it on Cleopatra in the process. "One of you cats is always underfoot," she told Cleo, nudging her with the toe of her sock. "Let me guess. You've got no Kitty Gourmet in your bowl, right?" The cat purred loudly and twined herself around Savannah's ankles as she hurried to the cordless phone she had left on the coffee table. "Hello . . . oh, shit," she said as she tripped over the cat and caught herself just before she hit the rug. "Get your hairy face outta here. I'll feed you in a minute."

"So, Dirk is there. I thought he might be," said a sexy male voice on the phone. Savannah's heart skipped a staccato pitterpat, as it always did when she heard from Ryan Stone . . . or saw his handsome face . . . or even thought of him. He was gorgeous, suave, kind, intelligent, funny, gay. Savannah hadn't been able to reorient his sexual preferences, no matter how she had applied her feminine wiles, which, her being a Southern belle, were considerable.

She had to be content to worship him from afar . . . him and his partner, an older, but equally handsome and charming British fellow named John Gibson.

"We heard it on the local television news this morning," Ryan was saying as she sat down on the sofa and pulled Gran's afghan around her again. "John guessed Dirk would be with you, making a serious dent in your kitchen staples."

"No, so far he's only raided my liquor cabinet."

Ryan chuckled, then got serious. "So, how is he? Holding up all right?"

Savannah was touched at Ryan's concern; she knew that Dirk wasn't his favorite person on the planet. Less than tactful Dirk had dropped enough derogatory comments about alternative lifestyles to alienate both Ryan and John. More than once Savannah had gouged him in the ribs or kicked him under the table for insulting her friends. Ryan and John tolerated Dirk because he was Savannah's, and Dirk avoided bruises and tongue-lashings by at least pretending to tolerate them in return.

"He was pretty shook up last night, when it first happened," Savannah said, plucking at the fringe on the afghan, remembering Dirk, naked, cold, and shivering there on his trailer floor. "But later he composed himself sufficiently to piss off Lieutenant Jeffries when he questioned him."

"That sounds like the Dirk we know and love. Any idea who the killer was?"

Once again, Savannah was pleasantly surprised. Ryan had automatically assumed it wasn't Dirk. Maybe they hated each other less than she thought.

"I'm pretty sure Jeffries thinks Dirk did it. We don't know. He saw the guy, but barely. White, brown hair, medium height and weight, pretty generic-looking. Dirk didn't get that good a look; he was wrestling him for the gun. Polly was bleeding to death on his floor. He had other things on his mind."

"Do you want us to come over, see what we can do?"

Savannah wasn't about to turn down the offer. Ryan Stone's and John Gibson's investigative skills had been invaluable to the Moonlight Magnolia Detective Agency in the past. They were both former FBI agents and still had a lot of connections at the Bureau. John Gibson seemed to know everyone who was anyone in Southern California and beyond. Ryan could find absolutely anybody . . . especially someone who didn't want to be found. They were definitely prize players to have on one's team.

"I'll take a rain check for the moment," she said, "until we see what Jeffries is going to do. Obviously, if they try to pin this on Dirk, I'll have my work cut out for me."

"We all will."

Savannah smiled. "Consider yourself kissed, my friend."

"By you . . . what a nice way to start the day."

She stifled a frustrated moan, just thinking of what it

might be like to start the day by kissing a hunk like Ryan Stone. A nice fantasy. But reality was Dirk snoring in her guest room.

She thanked Ryan again, assured him she would call if she needed them, and said good-bye.

No sooner had she turned off the phone than it rang again. She was prepared to give a reporter an earful of colorful Southern phraseology when she heard a familiar voice, sounding oh so official.

"Lieutenant Jeffries here. I need Dirk Coulter."

"Dirk is in bed," Savannah said, as gently as possible. "He was up all night. Could I possibly have him call you in a few hours?"

"Wake him up. Tell him to come down to the station."

"Now?"

Stony silence on the other end.

"Okay, Lieutenant. I'll get him there right away. Is there . . . some particular problem?"

"Just have him here in twenty minutes and tell him under no circumstances is he to speak to the press. No one!"

"Oh, I see," Savannah mused aloud. "A bit of a public-relations debacle?"

But Jeffries hadn't heard her. He had already slammed the phone down in her ear.

Slowly, Savannah dragged her tired body up the stairs and down the hall to the guest room. Dirk looked pretty much exactly as he had a few hours ago, when she had undressed him and tucked him in. He was sprawled across the covers, looking as though someone had shot him. But he was snoring too loudly for a corpse.

"Rise and shine, Sleeping Beauty," she said, shaking him gently.

He grumbled and pulled the covers over his head.

"Get up," she said. "The lieutenant called. He wants you on the carpet in twenty minutes, and you smell like a saloon."

More rumblings, but no movement.

"Take a hot shower, kiddo, and I'll whip you up some coffee and pancakes."

The head emerged, one eye opened.

Savannah smiled, satisfied. She knew Dirk, his habits, his preferences, the way to motivate him.

Free food did it every time.

As she made her way to the kitchen to stir up some hotcakes, she decided to give him real maple syrup and melted butter. It might be his last meal on the "outside" for a long time.

CHAPTER SIX

Savannah wasn't sure exactly what was wrong with Dirk, but she was sure he was—as her Granny Reid would say— a far piece from being all right. He sat in the passenger's seat of her Camaro, staring straight ahead, like a prisoner being led down the hall toward the electric chair. As she drove, she watched him with her peripheral vision, the way he was shaking all over, especially his knees, which were practically knocking together, like a cartoon character's. But he wasn't funny. Savannah was more than a little concerned by the way he was breathing—fast, hard, and progressively more erratically.

She wasn't sure if he was having some sort of old-fashioned panic attack, or worse, a heart attack. Thinking back on all the cheap pizza, buckets of happy-hour buffalo wings, two-for-the-price-of-one burgers and hot dogs she had seen him happily consume over the years, she wondered if the king of cheap was going to have to fork over big bucks for an angioplasty to clear all that bargain crud out of his arteries.

"You okay, buddy?" she asked, reaching over and jostling his forearm. His muscles were knotted and tight with tension. He flinched at her touch.

"No," he replied with a degree of candor that told her he certainly wasn't his usual cantankerous, closed-off self.

"What can I do to help?" she asked.

"Turn this buggy around and head south until we hit Tijuana."

She shot him a sideways look. "You *are* kidding. Right?"

"Not really. I'm more than half-serious."

"Well, forget it."

"Bad idea?"

"Very bad. You know that tacos and burritos give you killer gas. And the top of your head sunburns the closer you get to the equator, because you're too vain to admit you need sunscreen on it."

"I do not."

"Do, too. You're in denial about your hair loss."

"Yeah, and you still pretend to wear a size ten. Who's livin' in loo-loo land?"

"I haven't been a size ten since I *was* ten, and I've never claimed to be anything other than a voluptuous, full-figured woman. You're just cranky because you think you're going to get sent up the river on a first-degree murder charge and have to spend the rest of your life with roommates that you put behind bars. Huh?"

His face flushed red, all the way up to the receding hairline he claimed he didn't have. "Well, that's a damned good reason to be cranky, don't you think?"

"About as good a reason as I can think of."

They drove along in silence for a while, heading for the downtown, old-town section of San Carmelita ... and the police station. To their left, on the distant horizon bits of blue ocean glimmered between palm trees and stucco houses with red-tile roofs. To their right stretched uniform rows of dark green citrus trees, limbs heavy with fruit. The warm air was scented with the rich fragrance of oranges and lemons. A perfect February day in Southern California.

Except that her best friend in the world was probably on his way to the slammer.

"Maybe it won't happen," she said. She could hear the lack of conviction in her own voice. Dirk was no dummy, and he knew her well. She knew he heard it, too.

"If you were the detective working this case, " he said, crossing his arms across his chest, "would you arrest me?"

Savannah couldn't bring herself to say it. "Would you ... if you were in charge of the case?"

He sighed. "An ex-wife dead in a guy's trailer. Shot with his gun. Neighbors heard them arguing right before. They saw him run outside with the gun in his hand right after. He's got her blood on him and gunpowder residue on his hands. He's blamin' it on some unknown intruder that nobody saw but him. I'd lock his ass up. And you would, too. Huh?"

She couldn't lie to him. There was no point. "Yeah. I would."

Searching for something more uplifting to add, she said, "Of course, I'd also check out his story, just in case he wasn't lying through his teeth. And that might lead somewhere."

Absentmindedly, he reached into his shirt pocket, pulled out a pack of cigarettes, then shoved them back in. Savannah knew he was dying for a smoke, but she had forbidden him, upon threat of a painful death involving kinky torture if he lit up in her Camaro.

Considering the circumstances, she decided to take pity on him. "Go ahead."

He perked up at the very thought of the much-needed nicotine fix. "Really? Don't kid about a thing like that."

"I'm not kidding. You can smoke. This once. But open the window, hang your head out, and pant like a golden retriever."

In four heartbeats, he had lit the cigarette and was taking a long, luxurious draw, which he later released out the window, as instructed.

"Do you think they'll actually check out my story . . . at all?" he said.

"Jake McMurtry's a good man. He likes you. If you hadn't put in a good word for him and taught him the ropes, he wouldn't be a detective now. He'd still be walking the downtown beat with his buddy, Mike Farnon."

Savannah couldn't help grinning when Dirk actually stuck his head out the window to exhale. Despite his occasional cussedness, he could be a sweetheart when he took the notion to be. Damn, she would miss him, she realized with a tightness in her throat and around her heart.

"But," he said, "we don't know for sure that Jake's gonna be in charge. He sorta started there at the scene, then Jeffries seemed to take over back at the station. Somehow, I don't see Jeffries cutting me a lot of slack."

"He wants to be police chief when Hillquist moves up to mayor," Savannah reminded him. "I don't see how it would improve his image if the department was smeared by having a wife-killing cop on the payroll. It would be better PR if the killer were a third party."

Dirk shook his head, and his knees started banging together again. "I have a bad feeling about this, Van. Real bad."

"You don't know yet if—"

"Yes, I do. It's gonna go bad. I know." He reached over and put his hand on her thigh. His hand was shaking, too. "Stop the car," he said. "Stop right up there."

He pointed to a small dirt driveway that led into one of the lemon groves.

"Why?" She didn't like his tone. She didn't know what he had in mind, but she didn't think he was intending to just empty his bladder.

"Just pull over. Do it!"

She did as he said, and before the car had even stopped rolling, he had the door open.

"Dirk, what are you doing?"

"I have to get out of here," he said. "This car is closing in on me. I have to get out. I . . ." He bolted from the car and headed into the grove.

"Wait!" she yelled as she killed the engine, grabbed her keys, and took off after him. "Dirk, damn it . . . hold on! If I have to run after you, I'm gonna make you pay, boy!"

He darted between the rows of trees, and for a moment he disappeared. Then she saw him farther down the row.

"Coulter! Where the hell do you think you're going? You can't run all the way to Tijuana, you moron."

But he looked like that was exactly what he intended to do. With a sinking feeling, she realized that if she didn't give chase, he was going to be long gone.

"Get your mangy ass back here!" she hollered as she ran. "You're just going to make it worse."

Just when she thought she was going to lose him, she saw him step into a gopher hole and stumble. He fell against a thick lemon tree and got his shirt tangled in the thorny branches. By the time he had disengaged himself, she had caught up with him.

"Now that was a crazy fool thing to do," she said, panting as she grabbed his arm and gave it an irritated yank.

He leaned over from the waist, sucking in deep chestfuls of air as he struggled to catch his breath.

She shook her head, disgusted with him. "You aren't in nearly good enough shape to become a fleeing felon," she said, doing some panting of her own. "And I'm far too lazy to hunt you down."

"I was coming back," he said.

"Yeah, sure you were."

"I would have . . . in a few minutes . . . once my head cleared a little."

She stood for a long moment, giving him a searching look. Dirk couldn't lie worth a fig to someone he cared about. On the streets, to the perps, all night and all day . . . but not in his personal relationships.

He was telling her the truth.

And she had to trust him.

She let go of his arm and gave his shoulder a little, affectionate hit-and-rub. "Okay, pal. You need some space. No problem. I'll wait for you in the car."

He looked surprised. Dirk might be trustworthy, but he wasn't a trusting soul. Far from it. Throughout life he had expected the worst from people, and, as a result, was seldom disappointed.

"Thanks, Van," he said, obviously touched.

"No sweat."

She glanced at her watch. When Jeffries had called, she had agreed to have Dirk in the station within twenty minutes. So what if it was more like an hour and twenty?

Dirk was right.

She could feel it, too. Things weren't going to go well for him . . . no matter *when* they arrived.

As they rounded the final curve and passed in front of the city hall complex of buildings, Savannah and Dirk were surprised to see a bevy of reporters, some they recognized and others they didn't, standing on the marble steps leading to the front door. Some carried cameras, others tape recorders with microphones. Rosemary Hulse was there in the center of the pack, her perpetual yellow legal pad in hand. Hulse was an old-fashioned sort of reporter.

"Why do you figure they're out here?" Dirk asked as Savannah headed the Camaro around the far side of the building and toward the rear parking lot. "Bunch of damned vultures, always around when there's a corpse to be picked."

Savannah didn't want to raise his already high anxiety level, so she didn't mention her theory that *he* might be the gasping, prostrate prospector whose body the buzzards were circling. But she had quickly decided that they would enter by a seldom-used back door, rather than the front, just in case.

Unfortunately, a couple of hungry-looking vultures were hovering at that entrance, too. And the moment they spotted her bright red car, they came running over.

"I'm it?" Dirk had opened the door halfway, but he slammed it closed. "I'm the news? Oh, shit. I don't believe it."

The two reporters had posted their positions, one by Savannah's door, one by Dirk's. Apparently the gang in front had noticed her vehicle, too, because they were making hot tracks around the side of the complex and heading in their direction.

"I'm not going in," Dirk said. "I'm not going to talk to them, and I'm not going to wade through them either."

Savannah looked at her watch. They were late, so late, for their very important date with Jeffries. "You have to," she told him. "We've got to get in the building, and that's it."

He looked from one eager face to another, peering in the car at them, and shook his head. "No way. If any one of them says something smart, I'll clobber them, and it'll all be right there on tape." He nodded toward the guy with the video camera. "I can see it now . . . Cop beats reporter to death with his bare hands, still bloody from murdering his ex-wife last night. Film at eleven."

"You aren't fixin' to clobber anybody," she told him. "Because if you do, I'll clobber you. You're going to step out of this car, head high, and walk into that building with all the solemn dignity worthy of a peace officer. And you aren't going to say a word to them. Do you hear me?"

He mulled it over for a few seconds. "Oh . . . all right . . . I guess that's the thing to do."

"That's my brave boy." She gave him an elbow nudge. "On my count . . . one . . . two . . . three. . . . Let's go."

She swung her door open, he did the same, and they were

immediately accosted with microphones and a deafening din of questions.

"Did you kill your wife last night, Sergeant Coulter?"

"Exactly where was she shot and how many times, sir?"

"Are you here to turn yourself in?"

"Why did you shoot her, Detective? Did the two of you have an argument?"

Dirk opened his mouth to speak, but Savannah caught his eye and gave him a don't-you-dare-speak-or-I-swear-I'll-brain-you look.

The look worked. He lifted his chin a couple of notches, and with far more grace than she had ever seen him exhibit, he began the long walk to the back door. They scurried after him, jostling for the position closest to their quarry. But he didn't alter a step.

Savannah flew at them like a mother hen whose nest was being robbed. "Get away from him, you mangy-assed hyenas. He's got nothin' to say to any of you."

"Who are you, his lawyer?" asked the guy with the video cam. He shoved the lens in her face and missed hitting her, hard, by less than an inch.

"I'm Detective Sergeant Coulter's friend," she said with deadly softness. "And if you don't get that blamed thing outta my face, I'm going to whop you upside the head with it, and your ears will be ringing from here to Tuesday."

"Are you threatening me, Miss . . . ?"

". . . Savannah Reid. Of course I'm threatening you, nitwit." She shook her head and brushed him aside. "Not exactly the sharpest knife in the drawer, are you?"

Once they were inside and had the door closed and locked behind them, Dirk turned to Savannah. "You did say you were going to 'whop' him 'upside the head.' That is what you said, isn't it?"

"Yep. That's what I said."

"And you called them mangy-assed hyenas. That's several words."

"And what's your point?"

"You said we were going to walk in here, head high, dignified, and not saying a word."

"I did not. I said *you* had to do that. I didn't say a word about me."

They walked in silence down the hall, past family court, municipal court, and traffic court, heading for the police department hotshots' offices.

As they approached the main door, Dirk said, "I guess you realize . . . it's going to be *you*, mouthing off on the eleven o'clock news."

She shrugged. "Oh, well, it won't be the first time."

"Or, knowing you, the last."

She smiled up at him and nudged him toward the door. "Stop your carryin' on and get in there. The principal's waiting."

Dirk gulped and stared at the closed door several seconds, took a deep breath, and said, "Are you coming with me?"

"All the way, buddy. All the way."

But Savannah didn't go with Dirk all the way . . . or, for that matter, even part of the way. The moment they walked through the door into the reception room—which didn't make visitors feel all that welcome with its cold gray walls and even colder metal folding chairs—they were met by a less than jovial party of department brass. An impatient, cheerless Lieutenant

Jeffries was there to greet him, along with the newly promoted Detective Jake McMurtry and Police Chief Norman Hillquist, one of Savannah's least favorite people on God's green earth.

In a more honest, less emotionally charged moment, Savannah might have admitted, at least to herself, that Norman Hillquist was one of those classic, tall, dark, and handsome types. But, hating him as she did, for kicking her off the force some years back, she preferred to think of him as the creep in the black designer suit and unimaginative white shirt with the generic maroon tie.

Oh, yes . . . and she liked to picture him and his mundane clothing tumbling head over heels down a long flight of concrete steps . . . with a pit full of hungry Mississippi gators at the bottom. Somehow, she found the image comforting.

She shot Hillquist a dark look and received one in return. Mentally, she sent him the silent message, "Up yours, sideways, with a poison ivy bush." She saw the curse register behind his eyes. But old Norman was cool. He looked away as though she no longer existed . . . too inconsequential to warrant any further attention.

Jeffries, on the other hand, wasn't about to ignore her. "What are *you* here for?" he demanded of her. "Coulter doesn't need a baby-sitter."

She took a step toward him, and she could see that he had to fight the urge to step back. She grinned. "You were the one who ordered me to bring him over here, if I recollect our telephone conversation. And you asked so nicely, with the pretty please and all, that I just couldn't resist your charms."

Jeffries glanced at his expensive scuba watch and scowled. "You're more than an hour late."

"Really?" She looked genuinely surprised, batting her blue

eyes and giving him a coquettish grin. "I thought we were twenty-three hours early. You did say tomorrow, didn't you?"

"Don't get on her case about nothin'," Dirk interjected. "It was me that held up the works."

"What matters is that you're here now," Hillquist said in the flat monotone that gave Savannah the creeps. The last time she had heard him use that tone, she had lost her job and one of the most vital parts of her life.

The chief walked over to Dirk, and Savannah saw the glint of a pair of cuffs in his hand. No, he wasn't going to . . .

"I'm placing you under arrest for the murder of Polly Coulter," he continued in that lifeless voice as he pulled Dirk's hands behind him and snapped the cuffs in place around his wrists. "You have the right to remain silent . . ."

"You're cuffing him?" Savannah said, shaking her head in disbelief. "You're arresting him and adding insult to injury by putting cuffs on him? He's a cop, for heaven's sake. He's one of the good guys. What are you doing?"

Even as she spoke the words, a quiet, less emotional, voice inside her head told her that if she'd had the unpleasant duty of arresting Dirk Coulter for murder, she would have cuffed him, too. The guy was known for having a temper and getting a bit physical when he felt he was being treated badly.

But for some reason, Dirk wasn't reacting much at all. He simply stood there, stoic, accepting his fate. Strange behavior for the fellow who roared with rage if McDonald's gave him a hamburger instead of his double cheeseburger, skimped on his super fries or put too much ice in his Coke.

Dirk had never had a problem defending himself before. Usually, his demeanor was that of a cranky bulldog. This wasn't the time to lie down, roll over, and play dead like an obedient cocker spaniel.

Savannah waited for Hillquist to finish his Miranda litany; then she jumped in, feet first. "Lawyer up, buddy. Don't say a word until you've talked to Larry Bostwick. Call him right now."

She turned to Hillquist and Jeffries. "He gets his phone call now! Right this minute! He's calling his attorney, and he doesn't have anything to say until then."

"I think you'd better get out of here, Reid," Hillquist said, his previously lifeless shark eyes lit with a strange light. Savannah recognized unadulterated hate when she saw it. "You drove him here. Your job's done. Now get lost."

Savannah gave him a sickly sweet smile. "And you, my beloved former chief, may go to hell in a handbasket. You're arresting Dirk prematurely, and you know it. The only reason is because the press has already decided he's guilty and with your mayoral election coming up, you want to look good in print. The best thing for you and the department was to prove that your fellow cop was innocent. But since you couldn't do that in five minutes, the next best thing is to prove how tough you are, willing to take down one of your own if necessary. That plays pretty good, too, huh?"

Jeffries walked over to her and placed his hand around her upper arm. He squeezed her biceps and she was mildly satisfied to see the slight look of surprise cross his face. She had inherited Granny Reid's stout physique. Her biceps were better than those of most guys she knew.

"You heard the chief," he said. "Time for you to go."

"Take your hand off me, and I'll leave," she said, imitating Hillquist's deadly quiet voice.

He did, quickly, and she turned to walk to the door. She paused, hand on the knob, and looked back at Dirk. More than anything else he looked tired . . . absolutely exhausted, empty, defeated. "Call Larry Bostwick," she told him. Then she gave the chief and the lieutenant one of her snottiest, nanny-nanny-boo-boo looks. "Never mind. I'll call him for you. From my cell phone in the car. He'll be here in ten minutes." To Dirk she added, "Don't say anything. Not a word, you hear me?"

Dirk nodded. It wasn't much, but she had a feeling he had heard her and, even in his compromised mental/emotional state, she believed he understood.

"It's been lovely, gentlemen," she said as she passed out the door. "But I have a few calls to make . . . and I should have a word or two with the press before I leave."

"You watch what you say, Reid," Hillquist called after her, all pretense of nonchalance gone. "You'd better not—"

"Yeah, yeah, yeah, and your mother looks like she fell outta the ugly tree and hit every limb on the way down."

Savannah decided not to say anything to the reporters after all, figuring a simple "no comment" was best under the circumstances. But the moment she got into her Camaro, she whipped the cell phone out of the glove box and dialed Larry Bostwick, attorney-at-law. The caped crusader, a defender of the underdog, a criminal's last hope and an innocent man's best friend.

In other words, Larry was a crooked defense lawyer who smelled of stale cigarette smoke and wore a bad toupee and rumpled polyester suits. But he was a damned good liar . . . just the sort of guy to have on your side of the courtroom.

"Larry, Savannah Reid here. Have you heard about Dirk Coulter's problems?"

"Heard about it on the radio this morning when I was driving to the office. Does he need me?"

"You have no idea how badly."

"Have they arrested him?"

"Cuffed and rights read," she said with a sigh. "Get down here to city hall lickety-split, would you? He's in a weird frame of mind, and I don't know what he'll say or do that would make his problems worse. And they're bad enough already."

"How bad? How does it look for him, Savannah?"

"It's bad. He's in up to his eyeballs. Hurry."

CHAPTER SEVEN

Summer meetings of the "staff" of the Moonlight Magnolia Detective agency were conducted beneath Savannah's rose arbor in her backyard, with pitchers of fresh lemonade and iced tea, or beer and wine coolers if everyone was officially off duty. The attendees usually wore shorts, T-shirts, and sandals . . . except for Ryan Stone and John Gibson, who came a bit more presentably attired in fresh cotton shirts and linen slacks.

But the winter weather of February called for a seasonal change of menu and wardrobe. Mugs of steaming Earl Grey tea or Irish coffee, hot chocolate with lots of whipped cream, or the occasional whiskey toddy warmed the guests who had changed to long sleeves, as the temperature frequently plummeted to a bitter, bone-chilling seventy-three degrees, rather than the standard seventy-six.

Whether the dead of winter or during a midsummer

dream, the group usually enjoyed these gatherings of minds, ideas, personalities, and resources, pooled to solve a particularly puzzling case.

But this time, the mood wasn't so festive, because one of their members was noticably absent. And even though Dirk could be a sand burr on the back of everyone's britches from time to time, they all liked him . . . whether they would openly admit it or not.

Savannah and Tammy, Ryan and John lounged on comfy chaises beneath the arbor, discussing Dirk's predicament while consuming mug after mug of tea that Savannah had scented with cloves, cinnamon sticks, and slices of lemon and oranges. An array of fresh-from-the-oven, heart-shaped, pink frosted sugar cookies was displayed on a large delft platter—Savannah's token gesture of celebration for the upcoming lovers' holiday. The very fact that the pile of sweets had been sitting there for five long minutes showed a couple of things: One: Her guests were too upset to eat. And two: Dirk Coulter wasn't present to inhale them like a Hoover vacuum cleaner. Savannah missed slapping his hand and telling him to behave.

John took a sip of his tea, closed his eyes for a moment to savor the experience, then fastidiously brushed a drop from his perfectly trimmed mustache. "So, Savannah, we are at your disposal, my dear," he said with his deep, theatrical, British accent. "Please tell us how you would like us to proceed in helping this unfortunate compatriot of yours."

Savannah looked from him, the regal silver fox, to an anxious Tammy and an infinitely attentive Ryan. Dirk's situation was grim, to be sure, but with players like this on his team, maybe he had a chance that was a wee bit bigger than the infamous "no chance in hell."

"It's going to be hard to go after the killer," she said, "with no more than we have on him at this point."

"Dirk didn't get a good look at him?" Tammy asked, as she sat, literally, on the edge of her seat, a pen in her hand, a pad of paper on her lap.

"No. He said he ran into the living room, saw Polly lying on the floor, bleeding, saw the guy for a half a second, and then realized he was holding a gun . . . his gun. From that moment on, Dirk says his attention was on the gun, getting it away from the guy, it going off while they struggled for it . . . him dropping it, then picking it up again and running after the intruder, who, by that time, was long gone."

"But he saw him for that half a second," Ryan said. "What can he tell us?"

"Caucasian. Medium height, medium weight. Brown hair."

"Light or dark brown?" John asked.

"Medium . . . of course. He can't say about the color of his eyes."

Tammy sniffed. "Probably medium brown. What was he wearing?" Savannah grinned. Tammy was always the clothes-conscious one. She was even concerned about what criminals wore to the scenes of their crimes, and frequently she had opinions about the suitability of that attire.

"Dirk said he thought he was wearing a white T-shirt and blue jeans, black sneakers, no coat or hat. But, once again, he was thinking about Polly and the gun. I don't think he was at his all-observant best under the circumstances."

"Did they find any fingerprints?" Tammy asked, scribbling on the pad on her lap.

"I don't know. I'm going to pay Dr. Liu a visit; she's

performing the autopsy this afternoon. And I'll check with the crime-scene tech. But I'm not expecting much in the latent-print department. Dirk is pretty sure the guy was wearing some sort of thin leather gloves."

"Medium brown, I suppose," Ryan said dryly.

"As a matter of fact, that's what he said."

"And he didn't see what sort of motor vehicle the killer drove?" John asked.

"He said he didn't hear a car pulling out. The guy ran off down the trailer-park road and disappeared into a wooded area near the main road."

"Any hope of footprints?" Tammy suggested.

"Nope. The road through the park is gravel. The main one that connects with it is asphalt. Dirk suspects he was parked there on the main road. And before you ask, it's gravel alongside that road, too, so no chance of tire tracks."

"Are they having him look through mug books?" Ryan asked.

"Not to my knowledge," Savannah replied. "But they certainly should let him. I'll ask the next time I talk to Dirk or Jake McMurtry. Maybe we'll get lucky."

"I'll question the residents at the park this afternoon, if you like, " Ryan offered, "and ask if any of them saw anything."

"The old coot in the trailer right next to Dirk's saw and heard quite a bit, and he's blabbering to the cops about it, too," Savannah added. She noticed that her hand, which was holding her mug, was shaking. She realized she hadn't eaten a decent meal for more than twenty-four hours. But with her best friend sitting in a jail cell keeping company with an assortment of grizzly characters who hated cops, she couldn't see herself taking time for a ham and cheese sandwich, a hot fudge sundae, and a snooze.

"That's good," she told Ryan. "You take the trailer park, question the occupants and poke around for anything physical the forensic team might have overlooked."

She stood to replenish John's empty teacup, but he saw how she was trembling and took the pot from her hands. "Let me handle that business for you, love," he said. "I'll also find out the principal players in Dirk's most recent cases and run checks on them. Just, perchance, he was the intended victim and not that poor Polly."

"Good idea, thanks." She turned to Tammy, who for all of her complaining about "dumb ol' Dirk," was eager to jump into the deep end. "And you," Savannah told her, "can start on Polly herself. Go on-line and see what you can find out about her . . . anything and everything."

"Everything?"

"Everything. There's no such thing as a privacy issue here. The woman's dead, and if she were alive, I'm sure she would tell us anything we needed to know to catch her killer. Go for it."

Tammy nodded and scribbled on her pad. "You've got it."

"And I," Savannah said, "am headed over to Dr. Liu's autopsy suite at the hospital. I understand she's due to begin Polly's examination in half an hour. I'd like to be there when she finishes and find out what she knows."

They stood to leave, and Ryan asked the inevitable, inescapable question . . . the one that had to be asked by someone . . . at least once.

"Just for the record," he said, giving Savannah an intense,

calculating look, "do we absolutely know for sure that Dirk didn't kill her himself?"

Savannah thought for what seemed like forever before answering as truthfully and diplomatically as possible. "Dirk Coulter is no more capable of committing murder than any of us."

Ryan just grunted and gave John and Tammy a sad, knowing look. He said, "Mmm . . . That's what I was afraid of."

"Don't kill him," Savannah cautioned herself as she approached the desk where all of the visitors to the county coroner's offices were expected to check in. "If you murder Kenny Bates, you'll wind up in jail yourself and you'll be no good at all to Dirk. Wait until after you get Dirk off, and then you can do it. A machete would be nice. Maybe a wood-chipper."

Morbid imagery flooded her imagination as she stepped up to the desk and the leering idiot who sat behind it. She and Officer Kenneth Bates had a love/hate relationship. He loved—or at least, madly lusted after—her, and she despised him. Her lowly opinion of this blatant lecher was shared by all females on the force. If Kenny had held any real power in the department, his constant come-ons and lewd comments might have been considered sexual harassment. But, since he wasn't anyone's boss and wielded no authority over anyone or anything . . . other than the check-in sheet . . . his annoying behavior was merely a case of odious manners.

"Hey, Savannah . . . my favorite Valentine!" he exclaimed as she strolled up to the desk. "You haven't been around for so long, I was afraid you didn't love me anymore."

"And what were you going to do if you'd found out it was true?"

He shrugged. "Ah . . . I don't know. Probably hang myself. I mean, life wouldn't be worth the hassle. The only thing that keeps me going is the dream that you and me are gonna be doing the Grizzly Bear Hump on my bear rug some Saturday night."

Leaning across the desk toward her, he glanced right and left, then lowered his voice. "You know, I was thinking about you the other day when I was in that adult store on Main Street, The Naughty Lady's Nook, picturing you in some of that red leather bondage stuff that they've got in the window for Valentine's Day."

"Close your mouth, Bates," she told him as she reached for the sheet, which was attached to a clipboard. "Your ignorance is showing."

For half a second, he glanced, concerned, down at his fly; then he laughed. "Yeah, and I bought some of that strawberry-flavored lotion goop. I'll smear it on some secret part of my body and you have to find it with your tongue. How does that sound?"

"I'd rather kiss a freshly bathed rat's ass."

He brightened. She couldn't imagine why. "Well, sure," he said, "I mean, I'd be glad to take a shower first."

Savannah looked Officer Bates up and down, taking in the greasy, slicked-back hair, the lopsided tie, the police uniform that bulged in all the wrong places, having been designed for a body that was far more trim and fit than his.

"Bates," she said with a long-suffering sigh, "there aren't enough showers in the world, and especially in drought-stricken Southern California to transform your body into a delectable morsel. Then, there's that other little problem: I loathe you and always have."

"Naw, you're crazy about me. Don't you ever watch *Oprah* or *Jerry Springer?* What you're feeling is sexual tension."

He reached out to take the clipboard, after she had signed it, and grabbed her hand along with the board. A second later, he had dropped the ledger and was howling in pain as she twisted his little finger almost completely backwards.

"Now *that*," she said, "is sexual tension. That's the pain that's shooting up your arm right now."

With satisfaction she watched his pale, pasty face turn a sickly shade of light green. Finally, just as he looked like he was going to pass out, she released him. "Don't ever grab me again," she told him. "Not any single part of me, ever. Do you understand, Bates?"

He merely nodded as he grasped his hurt finger and rocked back and forth in his chair.

She smiled at him as she replaced his pen on the desk. "I'm so glad we came to an understanding. I'd hate for you to live under the delusion that I'm ever going to have physical contact with you . . . other than the kind that causes you great pain."

He perked up.

"And not kinky contact or feels-good pain either," she added. "So don't even go there with your perverted fantasies."

"But you want me."

"I hate you."

"You're just fighting the urge."

"The urge to wring your neck until your head pops off, like a rooster's who's been invited to Sunday dinner. That's the only urge I'm fighting. And if that camera"—she pointed to the security lens mounted in the corner—"wasn't there, I wouldn't fight it at all."

He flexed his hurt finger. It looked a bit crooked to Savannah, but she chalked it up to wishful thinking.

"See ya later," he called after her as she walked down the hall toward the autopsy suites. "I'll be waiting."

Savannah decided to bring one of Dr. Liu's scalpels back with her and remove some body part from Officer Bates, security camera or no.

From the first time Savannah had met Dr. Jennifer Liu, she couldn't get over the fact that Dr. Liu looked like anything other than what she was, a medical examiner. Slender and graceful with long, shimmering black hair and golden skin, she was the picture of Asian femininity ... with the morbid mind-set of Vincent Price and a wicked laugh to match.

In the law-enforcement world, mostly populated with males, Savannah and Jennifer Liu had bonded, primarily over chocolate bars and barbecued potato chips during coinciding periods of PMS. Even after Savannah was ousted from the force, Jennifer helped her by sharing what she learned during her examinations whenever she could.

It was against the rules for Savannah to be present during an autopsy if homicide was suspected, but, like her Southern soul sister, Dr. Liu wasn't above bending those rules a tad.

So, when Savannah swung one of the stainless-steel doors open and stuck her head inside the autopsy suite, Dr. Liu's pretty face lit up.

"Hey, it's my chocolate connection," she said. "Did you bring me a cherry nut fudge fix?"

"Sorry, didn't know it was that time of the month," Savannah said as she walked inside and winced to see Polly's naked body on the table, chest opened with a huge Y incision, from her shoulders to the center of her chest and on down to the pubic bone.

"What are you talking about?" Jennifer said, holding up bloody gloved hands. "When it comes to cherry nut fudge, it's *always* that time of month."

Savannah walked closer to the table and saw that the doctor had already removed, weighed, and dissected most of Polly's vital organs. The torso was nearly empty. A row of small glass jars sat nearby, holding slices of each organ, preserved for posterity.

"I'll bring you twice as much next time," Savannah told her. "I've got a lot on my mind with Dirk being locked up and all."

"I was really sorry to hear about that. Do you think he killed her?"

"No." Savannah stared at Jennifer across Polly's mutilated body. "But you're the expert. What do you think?"

Jennifer pointed to a tiny lead slug that was lying on a small, steel tray at the body's feet. "That was the bullet that killed her. Ripped into the left ventricle of the heart. Whoever fired the shot was good. Or she was very unlucky."

"Maybe both."

Savannah walked down to the tray and peered at the bullet. "It looks like a .38."

Jennifer nodded, "To me, too. What does Dirk carry?"

"A Smith & Wesson snub-nosed . . . .38."

The knowing look on the doctor's face made Savannah's skin go to gooseflesh. If the people who knew him suspected him, what hope would he have with a jury?

"He told us she was probably shot with his weapon," Savannah said in a far more defensive tone than she had intended to use. "He took it away from the killer, then dropped it."

"Sounds like that gun got passed around like a hot potato," Jennifer said as she lifted the slippery coils of small intestines from the abdominal cavity and examined them carefully.

"What do you mean?" Savannah said, instantly alert.

"Her right wrist was broken. Looks like it was twisted, hard. I'd say someone was wrenching something out of her hand."

"Like the gun?"

"Maybe. Probably."

"Any way to know how long between that and the time she died?"

"Only a moment or two. It didn't have time to swell before she was killed."

Savannah mulled that one over for a while, then asked, "Any other defensive wounds?"

"Two of the artificial nails on her right hand are broken."

"Then the attacker should have had some scratch marks. At least one," she added hopefully. "And Dirk didn't have any."

"That you saw."

"He didn't have *any*. I saw him naked."

Jennifer shot her a quizzical look.

"He was nude when I got to his trailer," she explained, "fresh out of the shower. If he'd had scratches, I would have seen them."

Jennifer's face softened in a sympathetic smile. "I know

how much Dirk means to you, Savannah ... you two being partners for so long and close friends."

Savannah could hear the "but" coming.

She didn't have long to wait. "But," Jennifer continued, "we don't know that she broke them scratching someone. I checked under her nails and found no skin, hair, or blood. I even looked at the broken ones that we found on the floor near the body. Nothing."

Savannah felt her heart sink a couple of notches. "Oh," she said, disheartened.

Jennifer gave her a sympathetic smile. "Savannah, I don't want to tell you anything you don't want to hear, but ..."

"But what? Spit it out."

"But I don't know how objective you're being about this shooting."

"I know how it looks," Savannah said

"It looks like he did it."

"But this is Dirk we're talking about ... and the cold-blooded murder of an unarmed person."

"Even good people make bad choices sometimes in very emotional situations."

"No. That isn't what happened." Savannah shook her head and set her jaw tightly. "What else do you have?"

Jennifer gave her an "okay, whatever you say" look and continued with the examination. She pushed a foot pedal on the floor with the toe of her sneaker, activating the tape recorder on the wall nearby. Savannah knew to be quiet; she wasn't supposed to be present ... let alone on the record.

"Evidence of a recent breast augmentation," the doctor said, "judging from the stages of healing, approximately eight to ten weeks ago. Also, newly applied bondings to the four upper front teeth."

So, Savannah thought, Polly had gone in for a little bodywork and a wheel rotation. Must have been worried about her mounting mileage.

"Intestines seem to be fine," Dr. Liu continued. "No disease of any kind indicated in the abdomen ... except the liver cirrhosis, as previously noted, which was probably due to excessive alcohol consumption."

She pushed the pedal again, turning the recorder off.

"Polly was an alcoholic?" Savannah asked.

"It appears so. I'll know more when I open the skull and check the brain. Sometimes it's visibly smaller than it should be because of alcohol abuse."

"Then we really do lose brain cells when we drink? I thought that was a joke."

Jennifer shook her head as she piled the intestines back into the abdominal cavity. "What excessive alcohol does to the human body is no laughing matter, I assure you. Our friend here may be a woman in her early forties, but she has the liver of a sixtysomething man who spent a lot of time holding down a barstool."

"Any drugs?"

"Nothing overt. But I'll know more once the blood and tissue samples are back from the lab."

Ah, yes, the lab, Savannah reminded herself. Yet another place where she might find more evidence pointing directly to her friend. Why get all the bad news from one source?

"I'll see you later," Savannah said as she walked slowly toward the door. She was weak and tired, and she knew it was due to more than just a lack of food and sleep deprivation. She was losing hope.

"Perk up, babycakes," Jennifer called after her. "That's what you always tell me. You also say, 'It's always the darkest just before dawn.' "

"Yeah, well, remind me not to say that anymore. When you're groping around, without even any moonbeams to light your way, it sounds pretty lame."

CHAPTER EIGHT

Savannah drove across town to the industrial-park section and the county forensic laboratories. Sandwiched between a computer-repair center and a catering-service supply house, the laboratory was low-profile, with only the Great Seal of California and the county emblem above the door.

Fortunately, she had old friends there, too. Her enemies were few and confined to the upper echelons of the police department. She had always been liked and respected among her peers and subordinates. As long as the "suits" weren't around, she was treated as though she were still part of the force.

She parked the Camaro in the spacious parking lot . . . toward the rear to be less conspicuous . . . and walked to the door. As soon as she punched the doorbell button, the intercom crackled to life, and a voice asked who she was and what she wanted. She looked up at the camera mounted above the door and gave it her best raspberry. "It's Reid. Open up, Bradley, or I'll huff and puff and drive my car through your front door."

"And you're just a bad enough driver to do it," the intercom replied. "Hang on. I'm coming."

The door opened and a sixtyish woman with long, curly gray hair stuck her head out. "What do you want?" she asked with pseudoirritation.

"Oh, I think you've got some vague notion of what I'm after," Savannah said, giving her a dimpled smile.

"Dirk?"

"Dirk."

She opened the door. "Come on in."

Savannah didn't wait to be asked twice. She hurried inside and was greeted by a couple of other lab techs, a Hispanic, middle-aged man and a young, freckle-nosed redheaded woman, both of whom had their faces glued to computer screens. All three wore white smocks over T-shirts and blue jeans. Everyone's jacket had the name *Tom* embroidered on the pocket . . . thanks to budget cuts and a previous director named Thomas O'Reilly.

The front of the large room resembled any office area, with cubicles, desks, piles of papers and books, and assorted computerware. Along the back wall was a long counter with microscopes, beakers, and other exotic laboratory equipment which Savannah didn't identify.

In this location law enforcement processed the evidence found at crime scenes . . . other than bodies, which were Dr. Liu's domain. Fingerprints, ballistics, tire marks, scene photos, fiber, and other trace evidence were their tools, used to solve the county's most serious crimes.

And Eileen Bradley and her team of technicians ran the place with the organized regime of a military academy and yet retained their sense of humor—grim though it might be at times.

"So," Eileen said, "Dirk Coulter got tired of paying alimony, huh?"

Savannah wasn't in the mood for Eileen's dark jokes, especially those that were made at her friend's expense. But she fought back her temper. Eileen wasn't being cruel, just insensitive. Savannah knew she liked Dirk, too. They were all hard-bitten characters, and curmudgeons had to stick together in a world of sweeter, kinder souls who didn't appreciate the joy of needling their fellowman.

"Dirk didn't do it," Savannah said quietly. "And I have to find out who did before those bastards Hillquist and Jeffries nail him with it."

Nothing more needed to be said. Both Hillquist and Jeffries were persona non grata in their own departments. Neither would ever be given "Mr. Congeniality" awards by those who served under them. Both had started getting their own coffee from the community pot, after receiving tips about what disgruntled underlings had used to stir their cups.

"How can we help you?" Eileen asked.

"Give me anything you've got."

"That's not much." Eileen sighed, and Savannah noticed she had aged considerably in the past three years, since she had been promoted to head technician. This sort of work could make you old quick. Sometimes Savannah felt older than her octogenarian grandmother, just from all the meanness she had seen in the world.

"Latent prints?" Savannah asked, knowing what the depressing answer would be.

"On the gun, sure," Eileen said. "Dirk's."

"It was his gun."

"Exactly. And a couple of smeared ones. Couldn't read those."

"There were a few on the door and doorknob, and we're identifying those now."

She led Savannah to her own desk, which was slightly larger and centered in the back of the room, near the laboratory equipment. Pulling a chair from a nearby, empty desk, she offered Savannah a seat, then plopped down on her own chair. She propped her white tractor tread nurse shoes on a nearby metal file cabinet and ran her fingers through her gray mop of hair, making it, if possible, more unruly than before.

"Some of the prints on the door may be mine," Savannah told her. "I was there earlier in the day . . . and many times before."

Eileen gave her a smug grin. "Yeah, I know. Yours was the first one we matched. Then there was another that's probably Dirk's. We're working on the last three."

"I doubt that either one belongs to the killer. Dirk says he was wearing gloves."

"Mmmm."

Savannah didn't like the nonresponse or the cynical gleam in Eileen's eye. Why was everyone having a hard time believing the unknown-intruder story? Hadn't they learned anything from poor old Dr. Richard Kimball?

"How about fiber or other trace evidence?" Savannah felt like she was grasping for straws . . . or at least hanging on to threads.

"Dr. Liu hasn't sent the victim's clothing over yet. We didn't see anything outstanding on the body when we looked her over. We haven't processed the rape kit yet, either, but we just talked to the doc and she said she expects it to be negative."

"Raped? Well, of course she wasn't raped. She was with Dirk and . . ."

The distasteful thought occurred to Savannah that Polly and Dirk might have gotten down and dirty sometime that day, before the killing. And if they did, that would mean that his DNA was . . . No, she didn't even want to wander down that mental path. It would just be one more nail hammered into Dirk's coffin lid.

Besides, the thought of Dirk and Polly together made her feel like cold, slippery, slimy eels were slithering up her back. And she didn't want to get into any Freudian analysis about why. It wasn't that she had a thing for Dirk; she just couldn't stand Polly.

Dead Polly.

For half a second she felt guilty.

"Any footprints in the blood?" she asked, changing the subject to another type of bodily fluid.

"Just those made by somebody with bare feet."

"Damn," Savannah muttered under her breath. "And that would be Dirk."

Eileen nodded knowingly. "That's what we figured."

"What else?" Savannah felt a frantic anxiety welling up from her guts. "Don't you have anything to show that someone else was there?"

Savannah noticed that Eileen's two workers were pretending to work, but obviously eavesdropping. Eileen began to doodle on a notepad beside her phone.

"Nope, not at the moment," Eileen said, though Savannah thought she picked up on some sort of hesitation in her voice. She continued to scribble. "I'd like to help you, Savannah," she said, "but that's it for now."

Savannah felt her anxiety level tighten a couple of notches, until she noticed that Eileen was pointing to the notepad where she had just been writing. She was wearing a cocky little grin on her face, like a kid with a secret.

Savannah stood, glanced back at the other two, who resumed their typing and pretending to be busy. Then she looked over at the pad. Eileen had scribbled the words, *Come back after 17:00 hours. Got something to show you.*

Savannah smiled and nodded. "Thanks," she said, "for nothin', I guess."

"Sorry I couldn't be more help," Eileen said as she stood and escorted Savannah back to the door. "But don't hesitate to call or drop by if you think of anything else."

"I may do that," Savannah said as she shook Eileen's hand and gave the other two a dismissing nod.

"Just one favor," Eileen said, as she was going out the door. "Don't let any of the brass know I let you in here."

"Don't worry." She zipped her lips. "Since when am I on speaking terms with those bastards?"

Back at the house, Savannah found a dejected Tammy sitting at the computer. The glass of mineral water, sprigged with celery and laced with a lemon wedge sat, untouched, on the coaster beside her. Apple slices were spread in a decorative pattern on a saucer. The kid was too depressed to eat or drink, Savannah noted. Not a good sign.

"Find anything?" Savannah asked as she took a sip of Tammy's water and grimaced. If a drink didn't have alcohol, chocolate, or at least, some carbonation in it, it wasn't worth drinking . . . except for fresh-squeezed lemonade, of course.

Tammy rubbed her eyes wearily and shook her head. "Not really." She pointed to a pile of pages she had printed on the edge of the desk. "Polly's last seven addresses . . ."

"Last seven?"

Tammy nodded. "In one year. She moved a lot, mostly from one man's place to another's. And she had crummy credit. Big surprise."

Savannah glanced over the list of addresses. "Do you have the guy's names?"

"They're there, too. Most of them are losers. A couple of professionals. One attorney and a dentist."

"Ah, yes . . . I noticed her smile was brighter and straighter than before, and Dr. Liu said she'd had a boob job."

"Trying to stay ahead of the aging game, I guess," Tammy said.

"Hey, I know how she feels. Wait until you look in the mirror and know you've seen better days, and that it's downhill from now on. For a woman who's depended on her looks to get by, that can be a real hard nut to crack."

"Luckily you and I don't have to worry about that for another twenty years or so," Tammy said with a grin that touched Savannah's heart. The kid wasn't always honest, but she was sweet.

"Find out everything you can about these guys," Savannah said, handing her back the list. "See if anybody has a record or has been involved in anything questionable. We'll interview them, one by one, but we want to see who's the most unsavory in the group and start with him. We don't have time to waste. Dirk's in jail with scumbags that he busted. Not a good position for any cop to be in. Have you heard anything from Ryan or John?"

"They haven't checked in yet, but . . ."

Savannah had a bad feeling. She didn't like "buts." "But what?"

"That Macon person did. He left another message. He's got your e-mail address now, and he wrote to you." When Savannah didn't respond, Tammy pushed a little. "I printed it out," she said, offering her a sheet of paper. "If you want to read it, you can—"

"No, thanks, Tammy. I don't think so."

"Okay." Tammy looked a little hurt and a lot confused. "I'll leave it here in the mail-in bin for when you get ready to—"

"Throw it away. I won't want to read it. Now or later."

Tammy hesitated, then placed it carefully in the garbage can. She gave Savannah a concerned look. "How long has it been since you've slept?"

"Last spring, I think," she replied. "Why? Is it autumn? Time to go back into the cave?"

"Maybe you should chow down on some blackberries and apples first. I think that's what bears do before they hibernate."

"Are you implying I'm grouchy?"

Tammy gave her a sympathetic smile. "No more than would be expected under the circumstances. Seriously, can I make you a nice sandwich or something?"

Savannah knew she was sincere, but she shuddered to

think what sort of "healthy" concoction would come out of her kitchen with Chef Tammy in charge. Maybe a tofu and bean sprout omelet with green weed juice chaser to wash it down.

"Thanks anyway," she said. "I think I'll just go make myself a cup of herbal tea or one of your protein drinks."

Tammy raised one eyebrow. "Do you really expect me to believe that you're going to drink something good for you, something with a vitamin or mineral in it?"

"Or maybe just a cup of hot chocolate with a big old scoop of Cool Whip on top."

"Now *that* sounds like you."

Savannah made her way into the kitchen, followed by the cats, who seemed to think that anytime she entered that room, they would receive nibblets of some sort. They had her well-trained. "All right, all right," she said as she opened their special "cookie" jar and took out Kitty Snackaroos, bits of foul-smelling, dry cat food shaped like goldfish that stank like a bait-and-tackle shop. The cats had never even seen a goldfish in their lives. But they had a Pavlovian response to the clanking of the cookie-jar top and wound themselves around her ankles, purring loudly.

It was when she bent over to drop the food into their bowls that black spots began to dance in front of her eyes. She heard the cats purring, but the humming sounded as though it were coming through some sort of filter, and in the far, far distance, she could barely hear Tammy asking her something.

The strength went out of her legs and they buckled. Then the floor came rushing up at her . . . and hit her right in the face. But, fortunately, by that time, she was already completely unconscious, so she didn't feel a thing.

* * *

When Savannah came to, she was lying on her own bed upstairs. Ryan Stone stood on the left side of the bed, a worried look on his handsome face. On the right was John Gibson, who was holding her wrist, staring at his watch, and timing her pulse.

"There we go, lass," he said, "opening those lovely blue eyes of yours. You had us all in quite a dither there for a while. But you're fine now." He shone a tiny penlight in first one of her eyes, then the next. "Ah, yes," he said in a doctory tone. "Pupils equal and responsive. I don't think any great damage was done by her colliding with the kitchen floor."

"The kitchen . . . oh, yeah . . ." She groaned. "I remember now. I was going to make myself something to drink. I leaned over to feed the cats and . . . poof."

"Poof, indeed!" John tenderly brushed a curl back from her forehead, while Ryan grabbed her left hand and softly stroked her palm.

Life could be worse, she decided then and there. If she'd known she would have gotten this much attention, she'd have fainted long ago.

And what was this? Tammy entering the room with a cup of . . . could it be . . . ? Yes! Hot chocolate sporting a big blob of Cool Whip on the top! Miss Health Nut had even added a few chocolate sprinkles to garnish the cream!

No wonder her great-great-grandmothers, pure Southern belles, had swooned at the tip of a hat, if they were treated like invalid princesses.

"Why, Tammy, you shouldn't have," she said as the young woman walked over to the bed and set the steaming mug on the night table.

"I know," Tammy grumbled. "There's enough sugar in that cup to give you diabetes, but I know that's what you wanted. And you probably passed out from lack of sleep and low blood sugar. So, drink up."

"Gladly!"

Ryan lifted her head with one hand and held the cup with the other while she sipped the wonderful combination of soothing heat and cool refreshment.

"When did you fellows arrive?" Savannah asked, when she had licked away her foamy white mustache.

"About five seconds after you did your face plant," Ryan said. "We helped Tammy get you upstairs and onto the bed. We were just deciding whether or not to call an ambulance."

"No! Definitely no ambulances. Heck, I can't even afford my annual Pap smear, let alone a ride to the hospital that would cost more than a limousine."

John looked appalled. "Do you mean to tell me you have no medical insurance?"

"The only medical insurance I can afford these days," she said, "is one or two meals a day and a roof over my head. After that, I'm broke."

"Barbaric," John muttered, "this country's medical industry. Positively savage."

"If you feel you need to go to the doctor, Savannah," Ryan said gently, "we would be glad to take you . . . and cover any expenses."

"Of course we would, my dear," John added. "It would be an honor to—"

"No, no . . . just let me have another big swig of that hot chocolate, and I'll be fit as a fiddle."

They obliged her, and as the life-giving chocolate made

its way into her bloodstream, she did, indeed, begin to feel better.

She sat up. Tammy rushed to fluff the pillows behind her head, then sat on the end of the bed, looking worried.

"Thanks, you guys," Savannah said. "I just got a little swimmy-headed from not eating or sleeping. I've just been so worried about Dirk, and . . ."

She looked from John to Ryan, catching the little glance that had passed between them.

"Oh, no," she said, "what is it? What were you coming over to tell me? Come on, I'm already sitting down. Out with it!"

CHAPTER NINE

"We don't really need to go into all the details now," Ryan said, continuing to stroke her hand. Normally, she would have savored the attention, but she pulled it away from him.

"Don't you hold back on me, Ryan Stone. Spit it out. What did you find at the trailer park?"

He sank onto the chair beside the bed, looking a bit weary himself. "I found three couples who live in three different trailers immediately around Dirk's. They all heard Dirk and Polly shouting at each other, just minutes before the gunshots."

"How many shots did they hear?" Tammy asked.

"One. Then, less than sixty seconds later, another one."

"That would have been when Dirk was wrestling the gun out of the shooter's hand," Savannah said.

The other three gave her dubious looks.

"Now don't tell me," she said, "that you all are having doubts about Dirk, too."

No one replied or would meet her eyes. They each stared down at their hands, or the floor, or the bedspread.

"Well, if that don't beat all," Savannah said. "I swear everybody in this blamed county, except for me, thinks Dirk killed his old lady. Dirk roughs up a bad guy once in a while, when he has to in the line of duty, but he wouldn't squash a bug when he's off duty. You know that!"

Again, no reply.

She sighed. "All right. At least you're all honest about your doubts. What did you find out, John?"

"Dirk's last few cases were: the unpleasant fellow terrorizing seniors in the park, a suspected arson case last month, and a missing person/suspected kidnapping."

"We need to check out that Nazi-wanna-be brat," Savannah said, "just in case some of his misguided friends might have decided to strike a blow for the old swastika. And that arson case. Wasn't that the old lady down near the waterfront whose house went up in flames just before Christmas?"

John nodded. "They ruled it an accident in the end, started by a dry Christmas tree and faulty wiring on the decorative lights."

"And that missing person," Savannah said, trying to recall. "Wasn't that teenager found after all? She hadn't been nabbed, just ran away with her boyfriend?"

"That's correct," John replied. "She's safe and sound at home."

"Tammy, you check out the boyfriend, just in case he's carrying some sort of grudge against the cop who brought her back home."

"Got it," Tammy agreed. "By the way, how did your trip to the lab go?"

"The lab! Oh, shit!" Savannah bolted out of bed so quickly that her head began to spin again. "What time is it?"

Ryan looked at his watch. "A quarter past five."

"Oh, man . . . I almost blew it," she said, "I've got to get back to the lab. Eileen said she had something to show me after five."

"You aren't going anywhere," Ryan said, placing a gentle but insistent hand on her shoulder.

She shook it off. "Oh yes, I am. I have to. She acted like it was something important."

Ryan looked at John. John nodded.

"Then we'll take you there," Ryan told her. "And no arguing, you understand?"

Savannah grinned. "You wouldn't, by any chance, be driving the old Bentley today?"

John laughed, pulled her legs off the bed, and knelt to slip on her loafers. "We are, indeed, madam . . ." he said in his best British chauffeur's voice, "and both we and the automobile in question are at your disposal."

Savannah always felt a bit like Cinderella in the magic carriage when she rode in John Gibson's 1952 silver-and-gray Bentley. He and Ryan further indulged her by allowing her to ride in the backseat, where she usually sipped champagne, took off her shoes, and wriggled her toes into the plush carpet. The dove gray leather seats were deliciously soft . . . softer than any purse she had ever been able to afford. And when Ryan and John were escorting her to dinner, they usually placed a lavender rose in the tiny silver vase attached to the side-window post.

But today the leather beckoned her to lie down, and a second later she was asleep. Her dreams were anything but glamorous. Visions of Polly's bullet-pierced body fought with images of Dirk, cuffed and vulnerable, behind bars with society's worst. In her nightmare, she was holding the key to his cell in her hand, but when she tried to unlock the door, the key crumbled as though it were made of thin glass.

Looking through the bars, she saw a particularly evil-looking inmate with a shiv in his hand, approaching Dirk from the rear. "No!" she screamed. "Look out behind you!"

A gentle hand shook her awake. "Savannah, we're here, sweetheart. Wake up."

Savannah sat up, looked around, and tried to reorient herself to more peaceful surroundings. She realized that they had transported her back to the industrial park and were parked in the lot beside the forensic lab offices. Ryan was sitting in the front passenger's seat, leaning back to lightly jostle her.

"It's five thirty-two," John said. "We've been watching for a few minutes now. A lady and a chap have left, and no one else has entered. Do you suppose your friend Eileen is alone now?"

"A chap and a lady, huh? Well, that's the staff. The coast should be clear. Let's go."

"*Let's?*" Ryan said. "Are you sure she'll talk in front of us? Maybe you should go in alone."

"Naw . . . I'll get more out of her if the two of you are along. Eileen has an eye for a handsome fellow. Times two, I should get good and lucky."

* * *

John was right; Eileen was alone. And Savannah was right; she was instantly, completely smitten by the two men. Savannah had always been amazed to see how women converted into vats of quivering, female gelatin in their presence. The giggling, the tittering, the mincing, the hair fiddling, the eyelash batting . . . it was ridiculous. Savannah didn't want to think about the fact that she had done the same thing for the first year she had known them. Now she was over them. She hardly ever tittered or minced.

"I'm sorry I had to be so secretive earlier," Eileen was saying as she led them back to her personal cubicle at the rear of the large room. "But I didn't want my assistants to know that I had shown you this. I don't want anyone to know. Ever. You have to promise that you'll keep it to yourself. I could lose my job if certain people, who aren't big fans of yours, Savannah, found out that I'd let you see it."

"I double-dog promise," Savannah said, solemnly crossing her heart.

"Okay, then have a seat." Eileen pulled up a few chairs, made goo-goo eyes at Ryan, then took a set of keys from the top drawer of her desk. "Wait right here," she said, before disappearing behind the cubicle's half wall.

They heard keys rattling in locks, metal drawers opening and closing. Savannah had a feeling, a good feeling, the sort of premonition she often experienced just before she got a break in a case.

One look at Ryan and another at John told her they were feeling the same. Ryan even gave her an encouraging little wink.

A few seconds later, Eileen returned, holding several pairs

of rubber surgical gloves and a plastic bag containing . . . something Savannah couldn't quite see. Eileen distributed the gloves, laid the bag on her desk, and donned a pair herself. Then she carefully opened the sealed, signed, dated bag and took out the object.

"What an ominous-looking . . . thing," Ryan said, obviously as stumped for words as Savannah was.

"It looks like some sort of fancy tool, like an ice pick or . . ." Savannah said, staring at the beautiful but deadly instrument.

It did, indeed, look a bit like an ice pick. Only the foot-long steel shaft had squared sides, like those of a screwdriver, and tapered to a deadly point. At the top of the spearlike section was the hilt, a horizontal figure eight, and above that was an ornate handle, fashioned into a rearing cobra's head.

"Is it some kind of dagger?" Savannah asked, inwardly cringing at the damage this sort of weapon could wreak.

"Or maybe a minisword," Ryan added."

"It's a poniard," John said, "and a beauty at that. May I?"

He slipped on the pair of gloves Eileen had given him, then took the weapon carefully from her hand. Turning it this way and that, he examined it closely, the oversize hilt, the ornate handle with its evil-looking snake's head and eyes that were faceted dark red gemstones.

"Are those rubies in the eyes?" Savannah asked, her female interest piqued by any sort of jewels.

John reached into his pocket and retrieved his key chain. Dangling from it was a jeweler's loupe. He used it to study the stones more closely.

"You carry a loupe in your pocket?" Eileen asked. More

than in lust, she was moving toward genuine, lifelong affection for the man with the cultured accent and the silver mane.

Savannah chuckled. "Doesn't everyone? You never know when you'll need to appraise an heirloom or start a fire in the wilderness."

"They're tourmalines," John said, putting his key chain back into his slacks pocket. "Dark pink tourmalines. High-quality. A rather gaudy touch to an otherwise nice piece of workmanship. I'd wager that the added stones were the buyer's idea, not the armorer's."

"Is the handle gold?" Savannah asked, afraid to trust her eyes in the company of such a knowledgeable individual as John Gibson.

"Gold-plated," he said. "Again, a tad risqué for my tastes, but . . ."

"What did you call it again?" Ryan asked. "A pin-yard?"

"A poniard," John replied. "It's a medieval weapon."

"And exactly what would an item like that be used for?" Savannah asked, though she figured she knew the answer.

"A poniard is worthless for fencing or for any display of sportsmanship," John explained. "You can't slice a loaf of bread or dress game with it, because there's no cutting edge to speak of. Historically, poniards were used for only one thing: to kill human beings. And, I might add, although as a tool their repertoire was sadly limited, they were most effective at what they did."

"I'm sure they were," Savannah said with a shudder.

"How do you suppose," Eileen said, handing it off to Savannah, "it got at the scene of the Coulter homicide?"

Savannah nearly dropped it. "This hideous thing was in Dirk's trailer? That's where you found it?"

"It was lying beneath the body, under her hips."

"You're kidding!"

"Not even a little." Eileen smiled, pleased with the effect her words had on Savannah. "When Dr. Liu's people lifted the victim, this was lying under her. It was covered with blood. We're analyzing the blood now, but we expect it will turn out to be all hers. No prints or anything else on that fancy handle. Nothing else was on it ... other than the blood, that is."

"Should we assume," John said, handing the poniard to Savannah, "this doesn't belong to Dirk?"

Savannah took the weapon gingerly and turned it this way, then that, allowing the light to play off the fine scales etched in the cobra's skin. "Of course it isn't Dirk's," she said. "Dirk doesn't even own a paring knife. He just learned how to percolate coffee last year."

"Any chance it belonged to Polly?" Ryan asked.

Savannah shook her head. "I really doubt it. Polly was a prissy girlie type. I don't think she would have packed a Swiss Army knife, let alone something like that."

"Then it probably belonged to the killer," Eileen said. "That's what McMurtry thought."

"Jake McMurtry has seen this?" Savannah asked, somewhat surprised.

"Sure." Eileen gave her a questioning look. "I thought you knew it was his case. He mentioned seeing you at the scene." She grinned. "He also told me that you'd probably come snooping around. He reminded me how much Hillquist despises you and what he'd do if he found out anybody was helping you."

"Don't worry, Eileen," Savannah reassured her. "We won't say a word to anybody who might get back to the bosses.

In fact, we wouldn't say anything even if you let us photocopy this little gem . . ."

"I can do you one better than that." Eileen reached into her desk drawer and pulled out a couple of excellent Polaroid photos of the piece.

Savannah had to restrain herself from clapping her hands and jumping up and down like a kid at a birthday party. But as she took the pictures, she became a bit more somber. "You know, Eileen . . ." she said, ". . . we'd never rat you out to the bosses. But I'm going to have to check this out, ask around, show these pictures to get possible leads."

Eileen shrugged. "You gotta do what you gotta do. We can't let them nail Dirk on something like that, just because . . ." Her voice faded away, and Savannah got the distinct impression she regretted having started the sentence.

"Just because what?" she nudged her.

"Just because . . . he's . . . well, a friend of yours."

Savannah thought that one over for a moment and shivered, as though the temperature in the room had suddenly dropped several degrees. She fingered the deadly, ugly weapon and wondered who the killer had intended to murder with it, Polly, Dirk, or both of them? And was Eileen right? Would Hillquist pin this murder on Dirk, refusing to look down other avenues just because Dirk was closely associated with Savannah?

Did Hillquist really hate her that much?

Years ago, she had exposed some of his own wrongdoings and caused him a great deal of public embarrassment. All this time he had been waiting for the opportunity to get her back. And now the press was clamoring for the bad cop to be hung out to dry.

Of course Hillquist hated her that much. He hated her at least as vehemently as she did him. And even half as much would do the trick.

Ryan's arm stole around Savannah's shoulders, and he gave her a companionable, sideways squeeze. "Savannah isn't the only friend that Dirk has," he said. "Even if he rubs people the wrong way from time to time, he's a good guy. And he's not going to take the rap for a murder that someone else committed. Especially someone who would carry around an ugly weapon like that. Whoever was packing that wicked monstrosity . . . he's definitely one of the bad guys. All we have to do is find him."

Back in the Bentley, Savannah climbed into the rear seat. And as soon as the men were settled in the front, she got right down to business. "Okay, so it's a medieval weapon," she mused. "So, where do we start? Museums, I suppose. Maybe a trip to the university history department."

"Wait a second," John said. "A poniard is a medieval weapon, but I didn't mean to mislead you into thinking that one is a piece of antiquity."

"What do you mean?"

"It's new. A reproduction."

"Mass-produced?" Ryan asked.

"Thankfully, no. It was handcrafted by a talented armorer. I studied it closely for any identification stamp, a hallmark, a signature of some sort. But I didn't see one."

"Maybe the craftsman made it to the customer's specifications and wasn't all that proud of his work," Savannah suggested.

"That's precisely what I think." John nodded thoughtfully.

"The workmanship was actually quite good, much more professional than the gaudy, sensational design. I, too, suspect the artist chose not to claim it as his own."

"So," Savannah said, "where do you suppose we could find this mercenary, medieval armorer who's good at what he does but will sell out for a buck? I doubt he advertises in the Yellow Pages under Poniards-R-Us."

"I know where we could go that we would be waist deep in medieval artisans," Ryan said.

Savannah was all ears. Finally, she had a hot lead, and she was ready to take it and run if she only knew. "Where? Where can we go?"

John smiled broadly and nodded at Ryan. "Grand idea. But I thought they began in April."

"The big one does," Ryan agreed, "but there's another, smaller version going on now."

"Big one? Smaller one?" She leaned over the back of the front seat and poked them in the ribs with her forefinger. "What are you two talking about?"

Ryan glanced back at her and raised one eyebrow suggestively. "Let me put it this way, fair damsel. How lookest thou in a corset?"

When Ryan and John chauffeured Savannah back to her door, she was surprised to see Tammy's hot pink Volkswagen bug still sitting in her driveway.

"Your hired help works long hours," Ryan said as he opened Savannah's car door and handed her out.

Savannah nodded. "She's a jewel. You all are, and I love you to pieces."

His lips brushed her cheek. "And the feeling is mutual."

"Good night, love," John said from the driver's seat. "Remember your promise . . . right to bed. I want you well rested for the Medieval Faire tomorrow morning."

"I will, cross my heart."

"I wish you had accepted our offer to buy you dinner," Ryan said. "I think a nice meal would have done wonders for you."

"I'm too exhausted to eat," Savannah replied with a sigh that seemed to rise from her tired toes. "I never thought I'd say that, but it's true." She blew John a kiss. "I promise: straight to bed."

She dragged herself away from them and into the house. The moment she opened the door, she was greeted with a familiar, heartstring-twanging smell . . . a scent from her childhood.

"Fried chicken?" she said, shaking her head in wonderment. "It can't be, but . . ."

And it wasn't any take-out-in-a-bucket kind either. It smelled exactly like her Gran's chicken . . . and gravy, too!

"Is that you, Savannah?" Tammy called from the kitchen. "I'm in here."

"Well, glory be! Wonders never cease! A beach-bum bimbo in the kitchen! Who woulda thought it?"

Savannah hurried through the living room and nearly collided with Tammy, who was emerging from the kitchen, an actual dishtowel tied around her waist for an apron, a smudge of flour on her nose, and a grin as broad as McGillicuddy's barn door on her face.

"What are you up to?" Savannah asked her. "And what is that heavenly smell?"

"What does it smell like?" Tammy replied coyly.

"It smells like my Granny Reid's fried chicken, but you must be toying with me, tantalizing my taste buds with dreams of what cannot be."

Tammy opened the oven door with a flourish. "*Voilà!* Chicken à la Gran!"

Inside, nestled in a baking pan half-covered with foil was golden brown, crisp, and mouthwatering moist, home-fried chicken. And on the stove, bubbling in a cast-iron skillet was . . . cream gravy.

"When did you . . . ? How did you . . . ?"

Tammy grinned and hurried over to stir the gravy with a wooden spoon. "I called your grandmother. I told her you were having a tough day, and when I mentioned that you weren't even taking time to eat, she knew it was serious."

Savannah sniffed. "Thanks, Tam."

"And I asked her what your favorite homemade dinner was and how to make it."

Savannah opened the oven door and looked inside again, just to make sure it wasn't a starving woman's mirage. The moment she had gotten the first whiff, her appetite had returned with a vengeance.

"And Gran just told you how, and you did it?" she asked, incredulous.

"Well . . . I had to call her back about seven times to ask stuff, but, basically, yeah."

Savannah walked over to Tammy, slipped her arm around her teeny, tiny waist, and gave her a sideways hug. "You know what I'm gonna do, babycakes? I'm gonna give you a great big old honkin' raise."

"A raise? Really?" Tammy did a little in-place, gravy-making jig. "All the way to up to minimum wage?"

"Minimum wage?" Savannah looked at her as though she had lost her mind entirely. "What do you think, girl? I'm made of money?"

Half an hour later, as Savannah licked the last bits of deliciously greasy crust dust from her fingers, a look of sadness crossed her face.

Tammy was sitting across the table from her, too grossed out by the action of actually touching raw animal flesh with her fingers that she was swearing off food of all kinds for a week. She saw the look, and said, "What is it? You're thinking about Dirk, aren't you? You're wondering what he had for dinner tonight."

"That's true. I was." She shrugged and reached for another chicken leg. "Oh, well, whatever they gave him, it was his favorite meal."

"How can you be so sure?"

"Because it was free ... and free food is always Dirk's favorite. It's the only upside to being in jail."

Tammy stayed much longer than she normally would that evening—even missing her Tae Kwon Do workout at the Y— and Savannah knew why. She was being a good friend, lending quiet support, and keeping Savannah's mind off Dirk, at least a little. But, eventually, she had to go. And when she left a little after ten, Savannah was shocked at how empty and lonely her house seemed.

Normally, Savannah liked living alone, just herself and the two furry faces, and Dirk dropping by for a free meal a time or two a week. But tonight, with the thought that Dirk's visits might have become a thing of the past, she was already feeling the loss of his warm, masculine, dearly familiar and comforting presence.

It wasn't going to happen! Not if she had anything to do with it!

They weren't going to string Dirk out to dry just because they hated her and because Hillquist and Jeffries wanted to ascend the success ladder a couple of rungs.

No way!

She wanted to do something more tonight. At least curl up in her comfy chair with a legal pad and make notes, weigh what little evidence they had, brainstorm a bit.

But the dark dots that danced in front of her eyes and made the world spin inside her head warned her that she had to grab a few hours' sleep before she collapsed entirely. Ryan and John said they would drop by at dawn-thirty and, not being a morning person, she knew that hour would roll around quickly. She had a case to solve and a Medieval Faire to go to, whatever the hell that was. And she needed to be at least semiconscious for both.

As she turned out the lights, double-checked the door locks, and headed for the stairs, she passed the desk . . . and its wastepaper can . . . and Macon's printed e-mail, which Tammy had tossed there. Well, she hadn't exactly thrown it in the trash. Delicately placed it there, prominently on top, where Savannah could clearly see it when she walked by was closer to the truth.

Tomorrow was garbage-collection day. She could, should, just leave it there, where it belonged, and in twenty-four hours it would be a part of her past.

Just as Macon Reid was part of her past and not her present.

Just the way she liked it.

If she picked up the piece of paper, he would become her present . . . and, heaven knew, the present had troubles enough of its own and didn't need to borrow sorrows from days gone by.

But her hand picked it up anyway, in spite of her better judgment's warnings to let sleeping, even dead, dogs lie. She held it down to her side as she climbed the steps and walked down the hall to her bedroom. Carefully, without looking at any of the words printed on it, she laid the paper on her night table and walked to the bathroom to perform her nightly grooming rituals.

As she brushed her teeth, she thought about Dirk's predicament and hoped he would pass the night of incarceration in relative safety. While she applied nightly moisturizer, she thought of the poniard with its ugly, snarling, cobra head and wondered how difficult it would be to locate the armorer who had crafted it. When combing her hair, she mentally rehearsed the questions she would ask lawyer Larry Bostwick the next time she had the opportunity to speak to him.

By the time she crawled into bed, she had managed not to think about the paper with Macon's words on it at all. Well, almost not at all.

But there was no point in putting it off any longer. She knew she wouldn't be able to sleep in the same room as that damned paper, unless she had read it. Of course, once she read it, depending upon what he said, she might have problems sleeping anyway. So, she was damned to insomnia either way.

She pulled the comforter and lace-edged sheet up around her throat, as though, somehow, the fabric could shield her from whatever pain the auld acquaintance being renewed might cost her.

For as long as she could remember, she hadn't been able to shield her heart from him. Why was she so foolish as to think she could now?

Allowing herself one quick glance at the words, she saw, *"years have come and gone . . ."*

"Yeah, no kidding," she muttered. Then she took a deep breath and began to read from the beginning. *Might as well get it over with*, she thought. *Just do it quick, like ripping off a bandage. It'll only hurt for a second.*

The letter was short and sweet, at least for Macon, who had never had a way with words.

> Dear Savannah,
>   I don't know if you will ever read this or not, but I'm trying to get in touch with you. I want to see you. It's important. Can I buy you a cup of coffee sometime? Years have come and gone and it's time to make amends.
>
>   Love,
>   Macon

Make amends? What amends could be made? she wondered. There was nothing she wanted from Macon Reid, except to be left alone in peace.

Why was he trying to get in touch after all this time? Did he have cancer or some other terminal illness? Had he experienced some sort of religious conversion and needed forgiveness? Or maybe he had started going to AA meetings after all, the way they had begged him to for years and was trying to fulfill that step about making things right with those you'd wronged.

Whatever his motive, Savannah had learned to live her life without a man's support and protection. She had learned to do without it very early, and she didn't need Macon Reid now. If, at this late date, he had decided he needed something from her . . . well . . . that was his misfortune.

She crumpled up the paper and dropped it in the nearby wicker waste can. Having read it, she decided not to reply, to ignore the fact that she had ever received it. Avoidance, denial . . . yes, those were the best routes to take when dealing with a man like Macon Reid. That had been her mind-set for years; why change it now?

But sleep didn't come as easily or as quickly as Savannah had hoped. She lay there, watching the moonlight filter through the lace curtains and paint delicate designs on the bed's covering. She thought of all the things she had learned from Macon Reid. Lesson Number One: Don't count on men to be there for you. They pretend to be strong, reliable, but when you really need them, they leave . . . laying down skid marks on the pavement.

Then Savannah thought of Ryan and John, their gentle support, their determination to help her with this case. She thought of Dirk, who had put his life on the line for her, literally, a number of times. She recalled how many times he had knocked on her door, just when she needed him most. How he had listened until dawn if she needed a friend to hear her side of an emotional issue.

And she felt ashamed for having applied that lesson to all males.

"No, Macon, it isn't true," she whispered to the father

who had missed so many birthdays, graduations, Christmas plays, and tooth fairy appointments. "It isn't true that men aren't there when you need them. Some are." She sighed and snuggled deeper into her pillow. "Some . . . are."

CHAPTER TEN

"Get off my face, or I swear, I'll make cat soup out of you!" For the third time, Savannah shoved Diamante off her pillow . . . or it might have been Cleopatra, or both cats. Before the break of dawn she didn't have enough brain-cell activity to tell the difference.

The cat returned, purring loudly, rubbing herself in a sweep from nose to tail tip along Savannah's cheek.

"You foul, odious beast, I hope you—" She inhaled a fur ball and choked on the rest of her curse.

Then she heard the doorbell ringing downstairs. "Oh, I see. You're being a good watchcat. Gee . . . thanks," she added without enthusiasm. "If you weren't so conscientious, I could have slept right through it and arisen at the crack of noon."

She had minimal brain function by the time she opened the door and saw Ryan standing there, dressed like Conan the

Barbarian, carrying some other sort of weird outfit slung over his arm.

Running her fingers through her mussed curls, she yawned, and said, "Don't tell me you expect me to put that on."

He grinned his Rock Hudson smile and looked her up and down. "Unless you intend to go to a medieval gathering in your pajamas."

She brightened. "May I? Oh, don't toy with me. Say I can."

He pushed his way inside. "If you think John is going to miss the opportunity to see you in a corset, you've got another think coming."

Taking the odd, burgundy-satin garment with its criss-crossed lacings and the emerald-velvet skirt from him, she gave him a suspicious look. "Are we sure it's John who's eager to see me in this?"

He laughed. "Okay, I'm not exactly dreading the sight myself."

She tucked the garments, along with a white gauzy shirt with long, puffy sleeves under her arm, and marched up the stairs.

"I thought you two were gay and didn't care about such things as damsels in corsets."

"We may be gay, but we aren't blind." He walked to the foot of the stairs and added, "If you need any help with that stuff, just 'give a holler' as you say."

She growled and slammed the bedroom door.

Ten minutes later, she climbed into the backseat of the Bentley, behind an otherworldly wizard in a flowing purple robe, sitting in the front seat. The wiz turned around, and said in a stately British tone, "My dear, how lovely you look this morning in that—"

"John, eat worms and die," she snapped.

She stretched out across the backseat and within seconds was snoring.

"Our lovely princess is a tad snippy today," John whispered as Ryan got into the passenger's seat in front.

Ryan glanced into the back of the car and grinned. "What can I say, Merlin? Our fair Lady Savannah just isn't a morning kind of gal."

"Would you like some sticky buns, m'lady?"

"Would you like a fat lip?"

Ryan grabbed Savannah's elbow before she could clobber the jester in the cinnamon roll booth they were passing on the main street of the faire.

"Sticky buns are considered a delicacy here at the faire," he quickly explained to her. "It's traditional to have one in the morning when you first arrive."

"You mean sticky buns are food?" she asked, still a bit groggy from her long nap on the way there.

"Delicious. That's the cinnamon smell that's floating through the air."

"Oh." She turned to the recently insulted vendor, dressed in tights, a tunic, and a hat with a long sweeping plume. "Sorry," she told him, "I thought you were talkin' dirty. Give me one of those, and some for these guys, too."

"No offense taken, m'lady, " he replied, quickly handing each of them a sticky, perfectly decadent-looking confection. "Though with a lady as well endowed as yourself," he added, with a glance at her abundant cleavage spilling over the top of the tight lacings of her corset, "one might be tempted to suggest a payment not in coin."

"What?"

"I'll take silver from the lords in exchange for my wares," he said, "but would prefer a kiss from the lady."

"Do you have any coffee back there?" she said, nodding toward the back of his canvas-covered tent that served as a booth.

"I can find some," he said, momentarily dropping the thick old English accent.

"And some half-and-half, too," she added.

A few seconds later, he produced a Thermos and poured some of the hot, steaming brew into a mug. When he handed it to her, he puckered up. She waited until the last half-second and turned so that his kiss merely brushed her cheek.

He scowled. "Me hoped for so much more," he said.

"Yeah, well . . . hope springs eternal. Thanks for the java." She turned to Ryan and John, who were already eyeing some daggers displayed in a case in the booth next door. "I've got three of my four basic food groups here: sugar, fat, and caffeine. I'm ready to face the world."

With some calories burning in her system, Savannah felt much better and began to actually enjoy the sights, sounds, and smells of the Medieval Faire. Colorful tents and even larger pavilions lined the thoroughfare, where vendors hawked their period-style goods, everything from wreaths for ladies' hair, to leather codpieces of impossible proportions for overly confident gentlemen.

Games of chance and skill abounded. For a few coins, you could toss balls at a target and dunk the village beauty into a tub of water. The reward was watching her emerge, her thin blouse clinging to her generous bosom.

You could strike a large metal plate with an enormously heavy sledge and ring the bell on a wooden giant's nose.

Colorful banners, sporting family crests, fluttered from tent tops and poles mounted in the ground. And everywhere, festive folks were dressed in costume, enjoying their journey backward in time to a fantasy era, when lords and ladies shared the world with dragons and wizards.

"Do you like it?" John the wizard asked, slipping his arm companionably through hers.

"Love it," she said, drawing in the rich aroma of turkey drumsticks roasting on an open fire with a cute serving wench basting them and eyeing the lads who walked by. "I'd like to come back when we aren't working . . . and bring Dirk."

He squeezed her arm. "We will, dear. I promise."

"Do they have these shindigs all the time?" she asked Ryan, who had just purchased a wreath of daisies for her hair.

"The big one, the official Renaissance Faire, is held in the spring and summer. This is a smaller version, but a lot of the same people attend. Hopefully we'll be able to get a line on our armorer."

Several booths down, they found a burly fellow with a bushy red beard, selling ornately decorated shields.

"This is as good a place to begin as any," Ryan said, as he took Savannah's hand and escorted her over to the armorer, who looked rather bored with the whole affair.

"Good day to ye, m'lord, m'lady," he said, summoning a bit of pseudoenthusiasm. "May I interest you in a fine shield to ward off the enemies' darts and arrows? Maybe one with your family crest thereon?"

"Our interest is more offensive than defensive," Ryan said. "I'm looking for someone to forge a dagger for my lady. Something special, with . . . say . . . a wolf's head on the hilt."

The vendor muttered something about, ". . . turkeys . . ." into his red beard, then said, "I beg your pardon, m'lord, but shields are this craftsman's specialty. You'll have to find another to design your dagger."

"Anyone you would recommend?" Savannah said. "I want a really pretty one, with diamonds in the eyes."

She was pretty sure she saw the vendor shudder ever so slightly. Then he said, "Most of the armorers here prefer to create articles that are true to the period, m'lady. And such a weapon would . . . well . . . would not be historically accurate, and therefore, most of the artisans would . . . decline the honor of designing such a weapon. Even for one so fair as yourself."

John stepped forward, exuding wizardly authority in his purple-and-scarlet robe. "But what if the lady . . . or her escorts . . . were willing to pay handsomely for such a dagger. Very handsomely, indeed."

After glancing in both directions, the fellow leaned toward them and lowered his voice. "Then you could probably get somebody to do it . . . if you promised not to tell where you got it."

"And who might be interested in selling his artistic soul in such a mercenary manner?" Ryan asked, his voice low and equally conspiratorial.

"Oh, almost anybody. Joe Campanella would do it, or Tony Rodriguez, or Patrick McCarthy. Their booths are down there in the gypsy's woods . . . by the tarot-card reader."

"Thanks," Savannah said. "It's comforting to know you can still buy what you want in this world."

As they walked away, she glanced back at the vendor, who had settled down for a nap on a pile of furs among his wares. "Did you guys hear what he was mumbling under his breath . . . something about us being . . . turkeys?"

"That's what I thought he said, too," Ryan replied.

"I'd wager a sixpence that was what he called us," John added.

"Mmm . . . wonder what it means, 'turkeys,' " she mused. "Somehow I'm pretty sure it isn't complimentary."

"I'd wager another sixpence on that," John said. "Maybe even a pound sterling."

The vendor was wrong. Not every craftsman at the faire could be tempted to sell his historically accurate soul for cold hard cash. Both Joe Campanella and Tony Rodriguez told them in no uncertain terms, "No way."

But the two agreed on one thing: Patrick McCarthy was their man. Fortunately for them, Patrick could be hired to create almost anything, if the price was right. Unfortunately, Patrick wasn't working the faire that day. He was at home in his studio forging stock for the big, spring/summer faire.

But it wasn't a total waste of time. Patrick's competition was kind enough to give Savannah and her friends his phone number and studio address in the San Fernando Valley.

With Patrick's pertinent information tucked in her bosom and a roasted turkey leg in her hand, Savannah left the faire a far more cheerful maid than when she had arrived. On their way out, they encountered a number of bizarre characters: an old beggar dragging a "withered" leg and pleading for alms, an ominous-looking warlock in red-and-black robes with an inverted pentacle on his back who warned them to "beware the wrath of the ancient dragon's breath" or some such nonsense.

Savannah's favorite was the woman dressed in a Red Sonja skimpy, furry bikini costume who had the body of a seventy-year-old, two-hundred-pound-plus, couch potato. As the female strutted by, Savannah turned to Ryan and John. "I've got my information, food in my gullet, and for some strange reason, I suddenly feel svelte. It's enough. Let's go while the gettin's good."

Before taking the trip to the valley to check out Patrick McCarthy's studio, Savannah went home to change clothes, having had enough corset restraint to last a lifetime.

"Wow!" Tammy exclaimed as Savannah came through the door. "Now there's a couple of—"

"Can it. I've heard so many boob jokes today that my cup runneth over, if you don't mind. Any messages?"

"From Larry Bostwick. He wants you to return his call."

Savannah decided to call Lawyer Larry, even before the Grand Unlacing. Costume changes could wait.

"Did he say what he wanted?" From Tammy's hand she took the bit of paper on which she had scrawled his phone number.

"He wouldn't say, just that it was important."

Feeling her adrenaline level rising, Savannah punched in the number and wondered if it would be good news or bad.

"This is Savannah Reid, Larry. What's up?" she asked without preamble.

"Looks like the prosecutor is going to go for it," he said. "They firmly believe he did it, and they're out to show that they don't cut wayward cops any slack."

"Cut a cop slack. Now there's a novel idea." Savannah shook her head and sank onto her living room sofa. "What's next?"

"Bail. I've pulled a few strings, and it should be set this afternoon. I'm afraid it's going to be up there."

"How up there?"

He named a figure, and she thought it might as well have had a few more zeros tacked on to the end. It would be just as impossible either way. There was no way Dirk had money like that lying around.

"Call me as soon as it's set," she told him. "I'll see what I can do. And Larry . . ." She swallowed hard. "How is he?"

"He's holding up pretty well. Quiet. Rather resigned."

"Oh, shit, that's bad. Dirk's normally loud, obnoxious, mouthy, and full of attitude. Quite and resigned are bad. Very bad. We've gotta get him out of there ASAP."

"I'll do what I can, Savannah, but this is first-degree murder."

"Yeah, but it's Dirk Coulter who's being charged with that first-degree murder. Whatever you *can do* isn't enough. Do about twice that much."

"I will. Just don't get your hopes up."

"They're up. They're way, way up, and if you let me down, I'm going to be crushed, and I'll snivel and cry, day after day, right there in your waiting room and tell everybody what a worthless, overpaid, overrated mouthpiece you are. So don't you disappoint me, Larry. I'm not at my best when I'm disappointed."

"I'll take care of it, Savannah. I promise. I'll take care of him."

"Thanks. I know you will."

* * *

"If you hear anything at all from Larry, you give me a call. That second, you hear?" Savannah told Tammy as she headed out the door. In her camel slacks and matching sweater, she looked far less like a buxom ale-serving wench and more like a dignified private investigator. If, indeed, there was any dignity in the world of a P.I.

"I will, I will, I wi-i-i-i-ll, I swear!" Tammy promised. "In fact, if I even hear a weather report about whether it's going to rain in the county jail, I'll give you a ring."

"Don't be a smart aleck. I'm worried."

Tammy's look and tone softened. "I know you are, Mother Hen. Us little chickens are okay for the moment, even Feather-Brained Dirk. So, leave the nest already."

"I'm gone. Be back in a couple of hours."

She flew the coop.

Patrick McCarthy was definitely into his Celtic heritage. And viewing the incredible art that was displayed in the form of swords, daggers, poniards, and shields, Savannah felt a tug at her own Scotch-Irish genes.

Walking around the lobby of his studio, looking into the cases of magnificent, gleaming weapons, she could see why John had called the poniard left in Dirk's trailer gaudy. These pieces were far more intricately worked, covered in minute etchings and filigree, yet were classy beyond description. Precious metals inlaid with gemstones, twisting, turning, Celtic knotwork that metamorphosed into mythical creatures, benign and malevolent . . . all testified to the skill and vision of the artist.

"May I help you?" asked a voice behind her. The words had a softness, the lilt of old Ireland in them.

Savannah spun around and saw a young man with straw-colored hair, a ruddy face, and emerald eyes watching her. She could tell by the look of pride on his face that he knew how much his talent was appreciated.

"Gorgeous," she said. "Absolutely breathtaking."

"Thank you."

Driving to his studio, she had considered ruses to approach him. The old "will you make something like this for me" routine sprang to mind, but she discarded the lie. This man's openness, his innocent, yet appraising eye contact, made her feel she could dispense with the pretenses.

"I'm looking for the armorer, Patrick McCarthy."

"And what is it you'd be wantin' with ol' Patrick once you've laid eyes on him?"

"I need his help," she said, hearing the desperation in her own voice. "A friend of mine is in trouble, very bad trouble, and Patrick McCarthy is the only lead I have at the moment."

"Lead? You sound like a police lady," he said, wiping his blackened hands on his large leather apron.

"I'm a private investigator. But this is personal."

"I can see that by the look in your eyes," he said, his gentle brogue soothing on her ears and heart. "I'm Patrick McCarthy himself, in the flesh. How can I be of service to a bonny private investigator lady with a troubled friend?"

"You can tell me if you've ever seen this weapon before." She reached into her purse and produced the photo of the cobra-headed poniard.

He took the snapshot, gave it a quick look, and handed it back to her.

"Do I look like the sort of fella who would make a monstrous thing such as that?" he said with a coy smile.

"You look like a sensible fella with a practical side, who might make such a thing if the price was right. You probably have as many bills to pay as the next person."

He laughed heartily. "Ye've got that right. With a dozen sisters and brothers back in Dublin and a wife and two wee ones here in the States, I've an expense or two."

"Did you make that weapon, Patrick?" Savannah asked. "I swear I won't tell anyone . . . at least no one who would hold it against you."

"Aye. I'm the culprit you're looking for. Made it for a handsome fee. 'Twasn't my own idea to be sure. 'Twas custom-made for a turkey who wouldn't know a fine Celtic weapon from a pain in his arse."

"A turkey? I believe I've heard that term before . . . recently. What exactly do you mean by that?"

Patrick's ruddy complexion blushed a couple of shades deeper red. "Actually, it's ashamed I am to admit it . . . but it's a not-very-complimentary term we use at the faire to describe those who come to the faire without any notion of what it's about. They dress in bizarre, Hollywood-style clothes and carry strange weapons that never existed on God's green earth . . . until the turkeys dreamed 'em up."

"Not too concerned about authenticity, eh?"

"Not at all, at all. Now those of us who actually participate in the faire, we check everything, once, twice, even three times to make sure the design of a garment or a weapon is true to history, before we create it and use it at the faire. We're interested in the educational aspects of it all, not just the roarin' good time." He grinned broadly. "Though we enjoy that side of it, too."

"And medieval warriors didn't carry poniards adorned with cobra heads?"

"Most wouldn't have known what a cobra was if it had bitten them on the backside. Weren't a lot of cobras lurkin' in the hillsides of Ireland or Scotland in those days."

"So, you made this poniard this way for a turkey," she said, "someone with more money than taste or good sense."

He laughed. "You can say that if you please. I'll not be sayin' it about a payin' customer. And he did pay me plenty."

"Who?"

"The Snake."

"The Snake? That was his name?"

" 'Tis the manner in which he addressed himself. A bit bizarre if you ask me."

Savannah's heart sank. "Don't tell me that's the only name he gave you."

" 'Twas the only one he spoke. But don't let your chin drop so. I can give you a bit more help than that."

She brightened. "Really?"

He beckoned her over to the counter and cash register in the corner of the room. After rummaging around beneath the counter for a moment, he came up with a dark green, old-fashioned bookkeeper's ledger.

"Mr. Snake paid with a check, he did," Patrick said proudly as he scanned the rows of entries with one blackened fingertip. "And I always jot down the addresses and phone numbers off checks, to add to my mailing list. Then when I'm going to be at a faire, I drop my customers a postcard, informing them of my whereabouts.

"Ah, here's his real name, and his address as well. But before I give it to you, I'd like to know why you're lookin' for him? What's he done to you or yours?"

Again Savannah weighed the pros and cons of truth and lying. And decided to give Patrick McCarthy the benefit of the truth. "I think he may have killed someone, and my friend is being blamed for that murder."

Patrick's face blanched white beneath his freckles. "Mother of God," he whispered. "Tell me it wasn't with my poniard he did the deed."

"It wasn't."

"Really? Are you just sayin' that now to spare my feelings?"

Savannah gave him a reassuring smile. "If he did it, he did so with a gun, not your weapon."

"Thanks be to heaven," Patrick said, crossing himself.

"So, do I get the name and address, Mr. McCarthy?" Savannah asked, not daring to breathe.

He began to write on the back of one of his business cards. "You do, indeed. And I hope it will be of help to your friend. Nothin's worse in the whole, wide world than being blamed for what you never did."

No sooner was Savannah back in her Camaro, name and address safely in hand, than the lawyer representing the falsely accused man in question gave her a call.

"It's Larry," he said.

"Shoot."

"Bail's been set. There's no way he can make it."

"I'll be right there."

Dirk had no assets to speak of. And, while Savannah lived from one meager check to the next, and often didn't know where the money for next month's telephone bill would be coming from, she did have assets. They weren't exactly liquid, but bail bondsmen weren't picky. Money was money. Property was property.

Anything for a friend. And, especially, anything for Dirk.

CHAPTER ELEVEN

Even with a high-powered attorney like Larry Bostwick with a few tricks in his hip pocket, bailing a desperate criminal like Dirk Coulter, Ex-Wife Slayer, out of jail was not a quick and painless process. By the time Savannah had him home, sitting on her sofa, his feet on her coffee table and his mouth full of cheap pizza, she felt at least thirty years older. He had aged a few decades himself.

"Are you going to tell me?" he said, displaying a mouthful of mozzarella, pepperoni, and black olives. Not a pretty sight.

"No," Savannah replied, leaning over him and taking her second piece. He grabbed a fourth. The pizza never had a chance.

"I want to know."

"You don't need to know."

He washed down the slice—five bites' worth—with a

swig of beer. "What did you have to put on the line to bail me out? Tell me."

"What's it to ya?" she said, winding a string of cheese around her forefinger, then licking it off. "I pawned Tammy, okay?"

"Nope. They don't pay that much for bimbos at hockshops."

"I sold myself on the corner of Lester and Main to customers coming out of the porn shop."

Dirk shook his head. "Sorry, babe, but you're a bit past your prime. Those quarters just don't add up that quick."

She threw the beer-bottle cap at him, bouncing it soundly off his forehead. "Insult me again like that, buddy, and I'll hike your tail back to the pokey. Got it?"

She picked up the remote control, switched on the television, and found a game of *Jeopardy*. Cranking up the volume, she blurted out the first question, "Who is George Bernard Shaw?"

He snatched the remote out of her hand and pushed, MUTE. "Van, did you have to put your house up for collateral?" he asked.

"Why? Are you gonna take off for Tijuana?" She swallowed her last bite and added, "What are amethyst and citrine?"

"No, I'm not going anywhere," he replied, sounding slightly offended that she would even ask.

"Then it doesn't matter, does it? What is the Nile? Eat that last piece of pizza before it gets cold . . . as if you care."

He glowered at her for a few seconds, as he did when he didn't get his way . . . which was often with her. "You aren't going to tell me, are you? I can find out, you know."

"What is the *Book of Kells?*"

"I don't know why you like that stupid game," he growled.

"The game isn't stupid; you are. You don't like it because you don't know any of the answers ... I mean, questions. What is seven and a half?"

He choked on his pizza. Still gagging, he stood and walked into the kitchen. She heard the refrigerator door open. "Where's the beer?" he yelled. "I don't see any more here."

"You're cut off for the night," she said.

He marched back into living room. "Since when? I've only had one."

"And that's all you get. You're on duty."

He snorted. "In case you haven't heard, I'm *off* duty. Probably permanently."

"You're working, and so am I," she told him, "unofficially. I just figured I'd let you get 'assimilated' back into society before I sprang it on you."

"Sprang what?"

"We haven't exactly been slacking off around here while you were cooling your heels in the big house. The fine lads and lasses of the Moonlight Magnolia Detective Agency have got a lead on your case, big boy."

"Really? A good one?"

"Wait until you hear how good." She gave him a big grin. "You'll shout 'Howdy' and wet your britches!"

"Let's go pick him up, right now!" Dirk didn't need to change his briefs, but he was exuberant. "Gimme the bastard's name and address, come on, hand it over!"

Savannah calmly stood, picked up the empty pizza box and the dead-soldier beer bottle. "First things first," she said.

"I can certainly understand your enthusiasm, but we've got to think this through."

"What's to think about? The sonofabitch killed Polly, and I'm getting nailed with it. I'm gonna wring his neck with my bare hands and then deliver his head on a silver platter to Jeffries."

"How . . . Old Testament . . . of you," she said, walking into the kitchen with dinner's remains. "That's what I'd like to do to him, too. And that's exactly why we're not going to pick him up ourselves. If you hadn't noticed, you're the suspect in this case, not the investigator, and I'm not even a cop anymore. If we go waltzing in there—"

"Where? Where is he? I want to know right now!"

"—with guns a-blazin', you'll be in more trouble than you are now. And I'll be behind bars with you, and there'll be no one to bail out either one of us."

Dirk sat down hard on one of her dining chairs and let out a loud groan of frustration. She ignored him and continued to tidy the kitchen while he watched.

"McMurtry's green," he said. "He'll screw it up; you wait and see."

"No, he won't. We won't let him."

He cheered up, ever so slightly. "We'll be along?"

"Of course we will be."

"Do you think he'll let us come?"

"He will . . . or we won't give him what we've got. All of this will be handled in prenegotiation."

"So, in other words, we're gonna put the squeeze on him first."

Savannah smiled, but it wasn't a pretty expression . . .

more ominous than joyful. "If he cooperates, we'll go easy on him. If he doesn't, we'll squish him 'til the little bugger pops."

Newly promoted Detective Jake McMurtry looked like an eager Labrador puppy on his first hunting trip when he charged through the doors of the Chat & Chew Diner on Highway 101 and Main Street in west San Carmelita.

"I swear his tail is wagging," Savannah said as she sipped her coffee and took a big bite of the lemon meringue pie on her plate.

"Yeah, and he should roll his tongue back up and put it in his mouth," Dirk added, trying to stick his fork in her pie and getting his hand speared in the process.

"Get another piece if you're still hungry," she told him as Jake made his way toward their booth in the rear of the room.

"The waitress will think I'm a pig."

"Too late. It'll be your third piece of apple pie à la mode. She already knows you're a pig."

Savannah shoved her plate and cup to Dirk's side of the table and moved around to sit beside him. A united front.

As Jake slid into the booth across from them, the thought occurred to Savannah—not for the first time—that Jake had wanted so badly to become a detective so that he could come to work dressed in jeans and a sweatshirt, rather than his uniform. He had looked much better in his uniform. Apparently his promotion meant a daily shave was no longer a burden, and hair combing was optional.

Savannah didn't need to look at his bare ring finger to know there was no Mrs. Jake at home. No woman would have allowed her man out of the house looking like that.

He appeared to be dog tired, too. His eyes were bloodshot and had dark circles under their bags. He looked like she felt, and that wasn't good.

"Hey, Savannah, Dirk, I'm glad you called," he said as he motioned for the waitress to bring him coffee. "I was going to give you a ring first thing in the morning. I was going to give you the night off, Dirk, considering that you just got out."

"Thanks," Dirk replied coolly, "but I'd rather get this settled. Once I'm cleared, then I'll sleep."

Jake rubbed a hand wearily over his eyes. *Not promising,* Savannah thought. *What's going on that he doesn't want to see?*

"Maybe you'd better grab a nap or two along the way," Jake said. "It may be a while before we wrap this up."

"Oh, yeah. Well you don't know what we got."

Dirk looked smug as he said it . . . a look that always set off alarm bells for Savannah. She could hear her granny's voice quoting the proverb, "Pride goeth before a fall."

"What have you got?" Jake asked, without even a trace of enthusiasm or curiosity in his monotone.

"Actually, Savannah and her agency came up with it," Dirk said, giving credit where it was due. "I'll let her tell you about it."

He waved a hand in her direction and she took the floor. "You must know about the poniard that was found at the scene," she said.

"The what?"

"You don't know about the medieval weapon that was—"

"Oh, yeah. That thing. I didn't know what it was called, but, yeah, I've seen it."

"We figure the shooter left it there," Savannah said. "We

think he came into the trailer, intending to kill either Polly or Dirk or both with that weapon. Then she pulled Dirk's gun on him, he yanked it out of her hand—breaking her wrist—and turned the pistol on her."

"Yeah," he said, adding an enormous amount of sugar to his coffee. "I figured it might have gone down that way. So?"

"So, we traced the weapon to the armorer who made it, and we've got the name and address of the guy who commissioned it. We've got the killer."

Jake sighed. "You talked to Patrick McCarthy?"

Savannah nodded, feeling the helium begin to seep from her birthday balloon. "Yes, this morning."

"I talked to him half an hour after you did."

"No way. How did you find him? I didn't see you at the Medieval Faire."

"I don't know about any fair. I looked him up in the Yellow Pages under ARMOR."

Savannah's mouth popped open. "You dirty, rotten cheater! You didn't even have to dress up in those ridiculous . . ."

Jake was too tired to gloat. "Yeah, he told me you had been there. He gave me the same name and address he gave you."

"Leland Whitley? Twenty-four twelve East Lester, Apartment G?"

"That's it. It's fake."

"Don't tell me that. I don't want to hear that."

"There's no Leland Whitley in the state of California and the apartments at 2412 East Lester only go up to D."

Dirk visibly deflated and sank low in his seat. "Damn."

"Yeah, damn," Savannah whispered. "Double-dog damn."

"So, where does that leave us?" Dirk said, shoving his last bite of pie away, uneaten . . . a bad sign, indeed.

"It leaves us," Savannah said, "back at the Medieval Faire, looking for a dude who calls himself Snake and is probably bent out of shape over losing his poniard." She sighed. "Oh, well, I didn't have anything else to do tonight . . . like sleep, or anything boring like that." She turned to Dirk and nudged him in the ribs with her elbow. "Tell me, big boy, how do *you* look in a corset?"

An hour later, Dirk stood in Savannah's living room, an ugly scowl on his face, powder blue tights covering his legs, and the rest of him draped with a royal blue tunic. On her coffee table lay the satin waist sash and the Henry VIII-type, massive gold chains. He drew a line somewhere, and it was at the tights.

He shook his finger in Ryan Stone's face, sputtering and fuming. "Don't think for one minute that I don't know you and your . . . friend there"—he jabbed a thumb toward John Gibson—"did this deliberately."

"Now why would we want to do anything, deliberately or otherwise," Ryan said smoothly, "to upset you, Dirk?"

"Don't play innocent with me. You two had a good laugh putting this pansy outfit together, saying, 'How do you think Coulter would like this? Would he look cute in that?' I know how you are."

"And exactly how is that?" John said, raising his chin a couple of notches and looking down his nose with that aristocratic disdain perfected by the British.

"Never mind," Dirk said. "I just want you to know that

I'm on to you, that's all. And I'll tell *you* something. . . ." He turned on Savannah, who was trying unsuccessfully to stifle a giggle. Not to spare Dirk's feelings. But, laced once again in the accursed corset, she was afraid she might pass out if she did anything that required extra oxygen . . . like laugh.

"Yes, dearest," she said. "What wouldest thou say unto me?"

"If I'm the only horse's ass there wearing a getup like this one, I'm gonna—"

"Don't worry, sweetheart," she said, taking him by the arm and leading him toward the door. "You won't be the only one there dressed in blue tights, but you might be the only horse's ass."

She turned to Ryan and John. "Thank you, once again, for wardrobing us so handsomely."

"It was our pleasure," Ryan said with a chuckle.

"I'll just bet it was," grumbled Dirk as he headed out the door.

"Are you sure you don't want the two of us to come along?" Ryan asked.

Savannah watched Dirk stomping across the lawn in his leather slippers with their cute little pointed toes. "I don't think you two should be within spitting distance of Dirk for a while. Tights, really? Did you have to?"

Ryan laughed. "John wanted to bring the hot pink ones. But I put my foot down. Didn't want to send the old boy over the edge."

Savannah shook her head. "Are you kidding? For years now, Over the Edge has been Dirk's legal address."

* * *

"What color are the tights they brought for Jake?" Dirk grumbled as she got into his Buick and he peeled out of her driveway.

"Tights? Jake?" She thought of the wizard's costume tucked into the bag at her feet and thought it best to avoid the question for the moment. "Um . . . I don't know . . . exactly. I saw some purple in the bag . . . and red."

Dirk grinned. "Purple and red, huh? Cool. He'll look pretty stupid in that."

Savannah covered her mouth with her hand and coughed. Once she got her hacking fit under control, she gave his shoulder a comforting, companionable pat. "Like I said, darlin', you've got nothin' to worry about," she told him. "You're bound to be the best-dressed horse's ass there."

CHAPTER TWELVE

By nine-thirty that evening, Dirk, Savannah, and Jake were pulling into the parking lot of the Medieval Faire, which was nothing more than a hard-packed field of dirt, surrounded by bales of hay to mark its perimeters. Compared to their previous visit, there were hardly any automobiles there. Only the moonlight illuminated the lonely scene. A few campfires glowed, dots of red scattered across the hillside, and a couple burned in a valley below.

"I told you it would be closed," Dirk mumbled, still disgruntled about the distribution of the costumes. He was even less happy now that he had seen Jake's regal, wizard's attire. "There's not gonna be anybody here who can tell us what we need to know."

"Quite the contrary," Savannah said. "The ones who stay and camp out overnight in the tents and pavilions are the people who work here, who are true devotees. They're far more aware of what goes on than the guests who only visit in the daytime. Ryan says it's a close-knit community, and everybody knows everybody. That's why we had to dress up, so that we'll fit in."

"If everybody knows everybody," Dirk argued, as they climbed out of his Buick and headed down the moonlit path toward the encampments, "they'll know that we ain't nobody."

"Yeah, that's what I was thinking," Jake said. "We'll stand out like sore thumbs."

"Naw. You guys worry too much. Ryan says they frequently have visitors at night, like groupies who hang out after hours. That's who we are."

"Well if *Ryan* says it, it must be true," Dirk snapped. "He's certainly never led us on a wild-goose chase or dressed us up in dumb-ass outfits just to—"

"Oh, stop your complaining. I've heard just about enough bellyaching out of you for one night. If we catch Polly's killer, it'll all be worth it, right?"

He mumbled an incoherent response and trudged a few steps behind Savannah and Jake as the path narrowed. Savannah wanted to yank him bald, but decided to cut him some slack, considering all that was going on in his life at the moment. A guy couldn't be at his jolly-self best all the time.

Besides, he didn't have enough hair to make it worth her while.

"How do you want to handle this?" she asked Jake, keeping a low tone. Dirk wouldn't approve of her deferring to Jake, but he was the only one with a badge and valid, legal authority at the moment. Besides, when push came to shove, she'd do whatever she wanted anyway. So, she might as well give the guy the illusion of control . . . a trick most women knew, but men like Dirk failed to comprehend or appreciate the advantages of.

"I think we should split up, cover twice as much ground," Jake said.

He was already starting to pant a bit, even though they had only walked about a quarter of a mile from the parking lot and down the dirt path toward the encampments. Savannah noted his burgeoning waistline and lack of conditioning and momentarily seethed at the thought that she had been fired from the police force under the feeble excuse that she was "overweight" and "out of shape." Of course, it had been hogwash, but that was the reason etched in black and white on the documentation, and she was still irked. Just couldn't help it.

Of course we'll split up . . . duh, she thought. They wouldn't go traipsing around like the King's Army, making themselves ridiculously obvious. But she bit back her words and let Jake continue.

"I don't want him alone," he said, nodding back toward Dirk. "If he gets into any sort of trouble, somebody needs to be around to witness what goes down. I mean, he's not armed, but . . . still, you never know."

Not armed, huh? Savannah flashed back on her slipping Dirk her Ruger .22 just before they left her house. Of course, he had been forced to surrender his badge, and his own gun was still with ballistics, the murder weapon in a case. He wouldn't be getting his hands on it anytime soon, if ever.

Sure, her butt would be in a major sling if anyone found out she had loaned him the Ruger, but she wasn't going to let him run around unarmed, virtually naked, after a killer.

"So, what are you saying?" she asked Jake. "You want me to stay with Dirk?"

Jake thought carefully before answering. "No, I think I should be with him. But will you be all right on your own?"

"If I need you, I'll fire three shots into the air," she said. When a look of horror crossed his face, she quickly added, "Just kidding! I'll holler. It's not that big a place; you'll hear me."

He looked doubtful but nodded anyway. "Okay, I guess. But don't take any unnecessary chances. If, by any stretch of luck, somebody tells you that he's here tonight, don't go after him yourself. Come get us."

"No problem," Savannah said, knowing that, like any other cop, Jake's motivation lay more in collaring the killer himself than in her safety. But, what the heck, she played along. "I'll let you know if I get anything at all. And you guys do the same."

"We will. Have you got your copy of the picture . . . the one of the knife?" he said.

"The poniard," she corrected him.

He shrugged. "Whatever."

"No, not whatever. This crowd knows the difference, and you should, too, if you're going to be mingling."

"Okay. Poniard."

"Yes," she said, "thanks for asking. I have the picture here in my purse or pouch or whatever this leather thing is that Ryan gave me. But I'm not going to be showing it unless I have to."

"Why not?" Jake asked, so innocently that it scared her. This was the investigating officer in whose hands Dirk's life rested. Scary stuff.

"Because it looks like an evidence photo. The weapon is lying there on a stainless-steel table with a ruler next to it. You know, people watch Court TV these days. They're smarter than they used to be."

Dirk picked up his pace and caught up with them. "And," he added, "thanks to *NYPD Blue*, they know that we tell them bald-faced lies to get the truth outta 'em, too. Bein' a cop ain't what it used to be."

"It never was," Savannah replied.

"Huh?"

"Huh?"

"Never mind."

They had just about reached the encampments. The smell of roasting meat, fresh coffee, and strong ale tantalized their noses, in spite of their large dinner and later pie indulgences.

"So, you guys are going together and I'm gonna go off on my own," Savannah said, giving Jake a questioning look.

"That's right," Jake replied. He glanced at his watch. "Why don't we meet over there by that big rock in, say, half an hour?"

"Wait a minute," Dirk said, his feathers highly ruffled. "Since when are we splittin' up like that? I go with Savannah; you're on your own, buddy."

"No. That's not how it's going," Jake said, bristling a bit himself. "I'm in charge here and—"

"Hang on, hang on," Savannah said, grabbing Dirk's arm and turning him toward her. She could see the evening diving into a bucket headfirst. "I want it this way. A female can get a lot more information out of a male without another male hanging around."

Dirk looked doubtful.

She pointed to her bodacious cleavage. "Especially when she looks like this. See y'all in half an hour. And I'm betting you, I'll do better in my corset then you two will with your tights and oversize codpieces."

"I'm looking for a man with a twelve-inch poniard."

"So, who isn't?" replied the lusty wench who was ladling a wicked-looking amount of dark ale from a wooden keg into a huge pewter mug.

Savannah laughed. "Not just any man, and not just any twelve-inch poniard."

"Ah, a lady of discriminating tastes," the lass replied, one eyebrow lifted. "Now there's where we differ. Any poniard of such hearty proportions is worthy of a maiden of ill repute, such as meself."

She offered the foamy-topped tankard to Savannah, who graciously refused. The self-proclaimed strumpet took a hearty draught herself. "And what sort of . . . blade is it you're searching for, m'lady?"

Savannah sat down beside the young woman on a bale of hay that had been covered by some roughly woven blankets. A dry, night wind caught the canvas flap of a nearby tent and fluttered it. Over their heads, flags bearing crests also snapped and popped in the breeze. A campfire about ten feet away sputtered and showered tiny, glowing ash into the air. The mystery meat that was roasting over it on a spit smelled incredible.

"I saw this poniard the other day here at the faire," Savannah said, "and I want to either buy it or find out where I can get one just like it. The hilt was a cobra's head with red stones in the eyes."

"Why would you want something like that?" The woman pulled a dagger from her leather belt and handed it, hilt first, to Savannah. "Now here's a fine piece, to be sure, with authentic rune symbols on the handle. 'Tis much finer than any cobra nonsense. Besides, the fellow who carries it is a lad of low degree, and you'd best not venture into his vicinity if you can avoid him."

"A maiden of ill repute rates him a lad of low degree," Savannah said with a smile. "Not a high recommendation."

The maiden licked the foam off her upper lip. "That fellow crawls lower on his belly than the cobra on his poniard. Cut a wide path around him, if you know what's good for you. His name is Snake, and it says far more about his conduct with ladies than it does about his . . . weapon."

"Where is Sir Snake?" Savannah asked. "So that I can avoid him, that is."

The maiden shook her head and chuckled. "My warning has fallen on deaf ears. You're so smitten with his vulgar poniard that you won't heed my words of wisdom. Ah, well . . . it seems the stars are against you, m'lady. The knave you seek is here this very night. He's down near the river among the gypsies. They're the only ones who haven't banished him . . . yet. I wager they will, once they've relieved him of his poniard and other valuables."

"Thank you so much," Savannah said, rising. "And exactly where are the gypsies camped . . . so that I can be sure to go the other direction, of course."

"Of course. " She pointed in the distance, where a large bonfire lit a copse of oaks near a narrow creek that glimmered, a thin silver ribbon in the moonlight. "That's where you'll be most likely to . . . not . . . find him."

* * *

At the edge of the gypsies' camp, Savannah ran into Dirk and Jake, who were hurrying down the path in the same direction.

"I understand our guy is here tonight," she told them.

"Yeah," Dirk said, panting slightly, "that's what we heard, too. I can't wait to get my hands on the—"

"Now, now . . . none of that vigilante nonsense," Savannah said, cutting off Jake, who had opened his mouth to say the same thing. "You're just here to identify the guy, and I'm here in case Jake needs somebody to help knock the stuffin' outta the little weasel."

As they approached the camp, they heard the classic sounds of a violin and an accordion, as well as some hearty singing, clapping, and tambourine jingling. Near the large bonfire, a couple of young women and a man performed a feverish dance, whirling and spinning in brightly colored costumes to the musicians' merry tune.

A red-and-blue-striped caravan had been drawn close to the fire, and food and drink were being generously dispensed from the back of the wagon. When it came to merrymaking, it seemed the gypsies were even more experienced than their counterparts higher up the hill.

"You guys hang out here for a minute," Savannah told them. "It'll be better if I ask about him."

"Let her," Dirk said. "She's good at wringin' information outta people and them not even knowin' they're bein' squeezed."

"All right, I guess." Jake pouted a little, like a kid who wasn't getting to play the captain of the football team. "But hurry back."

Savannah gave him a half-lipped sneer and walked off toward the caravan. Several young fellows in their twenties were chewing on ears of corn and rows of spare ribs, dripping with a fragrant sauce. They had been laughing and talking, but when they saw Savannah approach, they stopped and exchanged lascivious, knowing looks.

"Good evening, m'lords," she said, trying to turn a Georgian drawl into a crisp, old English accent. What came out was a strange mixture of both. The gypsies chuckled.

"Good evening to you, fair maiden," said one as he flashed her a grin that probably would have been sexy, if bits of corn hadn't been stuck to his chin. "Shall I read your palm and tell you what wonders await you . . . this very evening."

"Let me guess," she said, sizing him up. "You'll predict a meeting with a tall, dark, handsome stranger . . . or maybe two strangers."

Gypsy Number Two laughed and nearly dropped his rack of ribs. "I see you have the gift of second sight yourself, m'lady."

"Not at all," she said. "But I've had more than one lecherous lad cross my path at this faire, and I have a feeling that if you were to tell me my fortune, the cards would be stacked in your favor."

"A fine lady like yourself could do worse than a couple of free-spirited gypsies," Corn Face said, flashing white teeth.

"Speaking of worse," she said, "I'm looking for someone much worse than either of you, I'd bet. He's a fellow by the name of Snake. Do you know where I might find him?"

The rib-eater turned to his friend. "Snake has his problems with the ladies. One damsel cannot rid herself of him, and another cannot find him."

"If I were Snake," the second one said thoughtfully, "I'd

choose this second one. She's more comely and far friendlier. Should we point her in his direction?"

"If we do, our friend Snake will be forever in our debt."

"Indeed." He waved his corncob in the general direction of a path that led away into the trees. "The last time we saw him, Snake was hastening yonder, trying to catch up to a belly dancer who had slapped his face and told him to mind where he placed his lips."

"I think," said the other one, "that he was determined to give her a second chance to appreciate his . . . talents."

"Whether she wanted that chance or not?" Savannah asked.

"I think her reluctance was half her charm," he replied.

Savannah raised an eyebrow. "I see. And would you pursue a woman who had slapped your face and told you to take your lips off her?"

He laughed and glanced approvingly up and down her figure. "I have never suffered such a fate, lady. My lasses beg for more."

"Oh, I doubt they have to beg," she replied. "Thank you for your help, gentlemen. Enjoy the rest of your evening."

"If you don't find that knave, Snake, come back and enjoy the moonlight with us," one of them called after her.

She waved good-bye and hurried back to Dirk and Jake. "He's gone down that path into the trees, after some gal who refused to pucker up."

"A real charmer with the ladies," Dirk said, a depth of anger in his eyes that Savannah had seldom seen before. "Let's get him."

"Yeah . . . let's," Savannah said, heading for the path. "Don't forget it's a team effort, buddy."

He replied by muttering unintelligible obscenities under his breath as he followed her.

"We don't want to kill the only other witness to your wife's murder," Jake added, rushing to catch up with them.

"You two can just shut up now," Dirk snapped. "I'm not stupid, you know. I'm not going to shoot the only guy standing between me and a murder rap."

Jake stopped abruptly and grabbed Dirk's arm. "What do you mean, 'shoot the guy'? Are you carrying a weapon?"

Savannah gave Dirk a warning look, which Jake intercepted.

"No, of course not," Dirk grumbled. "Why would I want to be carrying a gun to defend myself when we're trying to nab a cold-blooded killer? Who'd want personal protection at a time like that? Certainly not me. I just figured I'd spit in his eye."

Jake stared at him for a long moment, weighing whether to push any further, then said, "Let's just find him. We'll play it by ear from there."

As they approached the stand of oaks, the path split, the left leading deeper into the trees, the right around the edge of the miniforest and down to the riverbank.

"Since there's two of us," Jake said to Savannah, "we'll go into the trees. You take the one leading to the river."

"No way," Dirk said. "This guy's already killed one woman. We're staying together. Or you go off by yourself, McMurtry."

"Nope." Jake shook his head. "I'm not taking my eyes off you, especially if you've come armed . . . with a mouthful of spit," he added sarcastically.

"Thanks for your concern." Savannah slapped Dirk on the shoulder. "But we'll cover twice as much ground this way. I'll give a yell if I need you."

Dirk muttered a few more objections, but Savannah left them and headed toward the river, which sparkled in the moonlight as though it had been liberally sprinkled with fairies' dust. The smell of wild sage filled the moist night air, along with the smoke and cooking aromas from the campfires.

Such a romantic place, she thought, *to be looking for a killer*.

She hadn't expected the burbling of the water to be so loud. She wondered if she would be able to hear anyone, even if they were near. Her eyes searched the shadowed brush that lined the bank, and her skin tickled along the back of her neck. It was a sensation she often experienced when danger was close. Long ago, she had learned not to dismiss it.

Normally, she didn't pull her weapon unless she intended to use it. But as her intuitive anxiety mounted, she reached inside the leather pouch Ryan had given her for a purse and pulled out the Beretta. She even switched the safety off.

When she saw the path crook away from the river and into the back edge of the woods, she felt even more apprehensive. Without a flashlight, it was going to be pretty dark under the trees. She reminded herself that if she wasn't careful, she could even get spooked and wind up shooting Dirk or Jake ... or vice versa.

Dry leaves crackled beneath her feet as she walked slowly among the trees, each step taking her deeper into the darkness. If she had wanted to sneak up on someone, they would certainly hear her steps. But then, she reminded herself, she would hear theirs, too. From here the sound of the river flowing was muted.

She couldn't see worth a tinker's damn, but she could at least hear again.

The shivers along the back of her neck intensified so much and so suddenly that she stopped still and waited, holding her breath and feeling her pulse throb in her head.

In some bushes off to her left, she heard a rustling, but the sound was small, like that of a bird or maybe a rabbit. The sound to the right was much bigger.

Her finger moved to the gun's trigger as she lowered the barrel. "Freeze," she said to the mass of shapeless shadow. "I can see you, and if you make another move, I'm going to blow your brains out."

Of course, she couldn't see them. She couldn't see a blamed thing, but they didn't have to know that.

"All right," she said, taking one step forward, closer to a tree, in case she needed to duck for cover, "walk toward me . . . slowly . . . your hands in the air."

She wasn't that surprised when no one came forward. In all the years she had tried it, the ploy hadn't worked a single time. But for some reason which only she could explain, she thought it was a pretty good one, at least theoretically. She was determined to keep trying until somebody fell for it.

"I told you to get over here," she said. "Unless you wanna get yourself shot, you'd better get to gettin'!"

Silence.

Okay, plan two? she thought. No plan two came leaping to mind. Or three. Or four. *You've gotta stop trying that foolishness,* she told herself. *It never works and you never know what to do when it doesn't.*

"All right, you asked for it. Now you're gonna get—"

She heard a whooshing sound, then felt the tree trunk reach over and smack her hard on the upper left arm. Of course, trees didn't attack people, but that was what it felt like.

And she couldn't move her arm. It was stuck to the tree. Pinned.

She jerked it away from the trunk and heard and felt her shirtsleeve ripping. Reaching for the tree with her left hand, she felt something protruding from the bark. A small rod . . . a shaft. An arrow shaft.

Someone had just shot at her with a bow and arrow!

Then there was a second swoosh . . . but, thankfully, this time she felt nothing.

"What the hell? What do you think you're doing?" she yelled as she ducked behind the tree. "You're playing cowboys and Indians out here in the woods? I got the gun, you moron! You're gonna lose!"

But not if he saw her first. He had been able to at least get a shot off and nail her, which was more than she could have done to him.

"Now get out here before I have to shoot you dead! Right now, sucker!"

She heard a rustle, then more movement. She couldn't believe it! Somebody was actually walking toward her. Small, shuffling steps, but they were doing it!

It worked! Glory be! It worked! her mind shouted. *Finally!*

And he was walking into a patch of light. Well, not exactly light, but less darkness. It was a man, dressed in medieval garb, and he seemed to fit Dirk's general description:

medium height, medium weight. Just pretty darned medium all the way around.

She looked at his hands to see if he was carrying a weapon, but they seemed empty.

"Put 'em up!" she yelled, stepping halfway from behind the tree. "Stick your hands up in the air right now!"

She thought she heard another sound, someone deeper in the trees behind him. "Dirk?" she called. "Jake? Over here."

No one replied. The guy took another two halting steps toward her. His hands weren't exactly raised; one hung limply at his side, the other out in front of him, as though he were feeling his way through the darkness.

She walked toward him until they were about twelve feet apart. "Get down on the ground," she said, training the pistol on him. "Shoot me with an arrow, huh? Get down, now!"

His face was in shadow, and she couldn't see his expression. But he dropped to his knees. Hard.

"On down," she said. "And spread your arms out to either side."

He did exactly as she said. Except for the arms part. Suddenly, he plunged forward and did a dramatic face dive, right onto the ground.

She couldn't believe it. This was working too well. Since when did a suspect obey to this extent?

Where he was lying, a bit of extra moonlight illuminated most of his body . . . and the reason why he had been so cooperative.

Sticking straight out of his back was a second arrow. The source of the other whooshing sound she had heard.

If this was, indeed, the guy named Snake, the one who

had killed Polly Coulter . . . he wasn't groveling just to please her. He hadn't fallen on his face because her marvelously brilliant ruse had finally worked.

As much as Savannah hated to admit it, the Snake had hit the dirt because . . . he was dead.

CHAPTER THIRTEEN

"You killed him! Damn, Van, what'd you go and do that for?" Dirk stood over Snake's body, looking, if possible, more distressed than the corpse.

"I didn't kill him, you dork," she said. "Do you think I traded in my Beretta for a bow and arrows?"

"So, what happened?" Jake said, shining his flashlight on the shaft that protruded from the body's back.

"You had a flashlight?" Savannah asked, indignant. "And you didn't offer to share it?"

Jake looked only slightly ashamed. "Hey, *I* remembered to bring one. If you forgot, that's not my fault. Besides, we were going into the dark woods and you—"

"And as it turned out, I did, too. I even got shot!"

"Shot?" Dirk grabbed the light away from Jake and shined it in the region of her chest. "Where? Are you all right?"

"Yeah, just a shirt wound." She pointed to her torn sleeve. "I don't know how I'm going to explain ripping the costume to Ryan."

"Eh, he knows better than to lend you undercover clothes. You're always getting shot at or something." Dirk shined the light back on the dead man. "I'm the one with the problem here. My only witness to the murder, the killer himself, is dead."

Jake groaned. "I'm the one who has to call this in. I mean, we'll have to get the medical examiner's team out, cordon off the area. We've got a homicide scene here. And I've got to write up a report and to explain to Jeffries and Hillquist why I let you two come along. I knew better, but I let you talk me into it, and now look at the mess I'm in."

Savannah nodded toward the body. "Of all our problems, I think that guy's is the worst."

"Naw," Dirk said, "he's got no worries. He doesn't even have to come up with next month's rent."

Savannah took the light from him, knelt beside the corpse, and shined the beam on the dead man's face. "Are you sure he's the one who was in your trailer?"

Dirk nodded. "Positive. He's the one who killed Polly, the guy I fought with."

Savannah stood and flashed the light among the trees and bushes around them. They had checked before and seen no one. There was still nothing to look at but foliage. Nothing moved. She sighed. "Now all we have to do is find the dude who thinks he's Cupid."

"Maybe we'll luck out," Jake said. "After all, how many people are running around here with bows and arrows?"

* * *

"Oh, a lot of people here have bows and arrows," Tony Rodriguez, the armorer, told Savannah and Dirk an hour later. "Crossbows were a common weapon during medieval times, and they're very popular here at faire."

"Peachy," Savannah said. "That is *not* what we wanted to hear."

"Yeah, thanks for nothin'," Dirk grumbled.

Tony continued to polish the dagger blade he had been working on when they had approached him at his campsite. He hadn't heard about the murder in the woods yet, and he seemed to be taking the news with remarkable nonchalance. More than half of the faire workers and performers had congregated in a noisy, rambunctious mob at the wood's edge, making a nuisance of themselves as Jake, several other cops, and Dr. Liu's team processed the scene.

But Tony just sat on his bale of hay . . . polishing.

"Pretty weird, that guy getting shot like that," he said, dropping his pseudo-old English accent. "And in the back, too. Pretty bizarre."

Savannah thought of Snake lying there, blood oozing from the wound in his back. He had died quickly, but he had seemed to be in considerable pain from the time he hit the ground until his speedy demise.

"Bizarre, yes," she said, "but not pretty. Not at all."

"Yeah, Tony's right. Everybody's got a crossbow," a dainty, rather empty-headed, heavy-lidded lass told Savannah and Dirk. Savannah had previously seen her selling flowered wreaths for ladies' hair, but now she lay sprawled across a rough-woven rug, holding a pipe in her hand that smelled suspiciously like a combination of skunk and oregano. "Well, not everybody," she added, "but a lot. Everybody's got daggers. We eat with them, you know."

She, too, had dropped her accent the moment she had been told about the killing, and shrieked, "Oh, like . . . oh my God!" in distinctively valley-girl fashion.

"I don't care about daggers," Dirk snapped. "Did I ask you about friggin' daggers? Did I ask you what you crazies eat with out here when you're playing knights and ladies of the Round Table?"

Savannah could practically see the flower wreath on the woman's head wilt beneath the onslaught of the dragon's breath. The girl whimpered as though she had been struck. "Well, like, you don't have to be rude about it," she said. "I was just trying to, like, help you and . . ."

Dirk walked away in disgust, muttering something about, ". . . bimbos . . ." leaving Savannah to appease the emotionally wounded weaver of daisies.

"He's a bit of a curmudgeon," she tried to explain, but the girl just looked confused. "You know, cranky, cantankerous," she added. "He can't help himself. See, his mother dropped him on his head."

The lass's eyes widened ever so slightly. "You mean, like, when he was a baby?"

"No, last week." Savannah followed Dirk, shaking her head. "Bimbos . . ."

Dawn broke over the dark hills and, bathed in the pink-and-lavender light of the new day, the medieval campsite looked even more authentic than it had by moonlight or in full sun. Savannah had scored a couple of sticky buns and some hot coffee, which she brought to Dirk, hoping the nourishment would raise both their spirits along with their blood sugar level.

He was standing at the edge of the woods; Jeffries had hotly ordered him and Savannah to stay at least a hundred feet from the actual murder scene. And whatever threat the lieutenant had used on Jake McMurtry had been most effective. As soon as Jeffries had left, Savannah and Dirk tried to cross the tape and Jake had barked and shown his teeth at them. Worse, he said he would arrest them both if they did, and he looked like he meant it.

So they were relegated to the proverbial bench, watching the game of criminal investigation continue without their participation. Neither were good at bench sitting.

Savannah found a makeshift seat on a dew-damp log and motioned for him to sit beside her. As they unwrapped their sticky buns, the aroma of the cinnamon and freshly baked dough made her realize how hungry she was, how much energy she had expended in the past twelve hours.

She had to stop missing entire nights of sleep like this. She was too old for that sort of deprivation; even one night of tossing and turning meant she would be grumpy and out of sorts for at least five days, more grumpy than usual.

"Do you think Jake's come up with anything?" she asked as she watched the young detective wandering about like a Thanksgiving turkey who had been relieved of his head.

"Nope. He's got nothin'," Dirk said, gnawing at the sticky confection.

"How can you tell for sure?"

" 'Cause he looks like I feel when I got nothin'. He looks like I feel right now. Lousy."

"Part of that is because you haven't had a good night's

sleep in ages," she told him. "What do you say I take you home and tuck you in for a nice long nap? Then we'll come back out here later if we need to and pick up where we left off."

She was afraid he would say no. Dirk was a real bulldog when he was on a case. Any case. Let alone one that concerned his own life and freedom.

"All right. For a little while," he said.

He really *was* as tired as he looked. She decided to get him back home and in bed, as quickly as possible. Even if that meant stranding Jake McMurtry out here with no ride home.

Oh, well, he could always hitch a ride with Dr. Liu and the corpse in the coroner's wagon. She had done it often enough. It was part of the job, the joys of working with dead bodies that had, until recently, been live people.

Not for the first time, Savannah wondered why she or anyone else would want to be a cop or a private detective.

Oh well, somebody had to do it. The bad guys couldn't be allowed to win 'em all.

When Savannah and Dirk arrived back at her house, they found Tammy at the computer, her ubiquitous glass of mineral water and a plate of veggie munchies sitting beside the keyboard.

"Pigging out again, I see," Savannah said as she walked past Tammy and her assortment of carrot sticks, radish roses, zucchini slices, and broccoli florets. "You're positively hedonistic," Savannah told her, "stuffing your face with junk food like that. Where are your chocolate, cream-filled cupcakes? Or your nacho cheese chips? What about those all-important nutrients: sodium, sugar, artificial flavors?"

"I prefer to eat things that have some life in them," she replied haughtily, hefting a leafy celery stalk and chomping into it.

"Smear some onion-flavored cream cheese on that thing, and it'll taste a helluva lot better," Dirk added as he walked over to the sofa, kicked his sneakers off, and sank into the overstuffed cushions. With his Nikes under the coffee table, his medieval ensemble looked a lot more authentic.

"You two are dietary nightmares," Tammy said, shaking her head. "When I'm eighty-nine, I'll still be in great shape, and you'll be on your fifth quadruple bypass and—"

"Eh, a bus could run over you tomorrow," Savannah said. "You'd be squashed flatter than a flitter all over the road, and then who'd care whether your arteries are clear or not?"

"I've been meaning to ask you"—Tammy quirked an eyebrow, a gesture Savannah recognized. Her right eyebrow wriggled when she was about to be a smart aleck—"exactly what is this *flitter* thing that you're always saying I'm going to be mashed flatter than?"

"It's a highly technical term used south of the Mason-Dixon line, one that I've explained many times to you. But, sadly, you don't have sufficient additives and preservatives in your system for your brain to retain the information. Why should I bother to tell you again?"

"*Don't* bother." Tammy tossed her head, sending her blond ponytail swinging. She turned back to the computer. "It's hard to take you seriously anyway when you two are dressed like Maid Marian and Robin Hood."

"Watch it, bimbo," Dirk said, tucking one of Savannah's fringed throw pillows under his head. "I'm startin' to like these tights things. They're more comfortable than jeans. I think I'm gonna wear 'em all the time."

Savannah grabbed one of Tammy's radishes and popped it into her mouth. "Anything new?"

Tammy shot Dirk an uncomfortable look. She cleared her throat. "Well . . . we finally got a check from that old codger who had us investigate that young chickie-pooh he was dating."

"The girl who had served time for prostitution, grand larceny, and embezzlement?"

"That's the one." Again she glanced uneasily over at Dirk, who had closed his eyes and looked as though he might be dropping off to sleep.

"Anything else?" Savannah said, almost afraid to ask.

"You got another message from that Macon person." She held out a slip of paper. "I printed it out for you."

Savannah took the paper from her, but quickly folded it and stuck it in her pocket unread. She stepped closer to Tammy and lowered her voice. "What else?"

Tammy looked up at her, sadness in her eyes. "And *they* called," she whispered, nodding toward Dirk. "Wanted to talk to him about . . . you know. . . ."

"They? Who are they?"

"And what did they want with me?" Dirk asked, sitting up, fully alert.

"The . . . um . . . the funeral home," Tammy said. "It seems the medical examiner is all finished with the autop . . . well, you know, Dr. Liu is done examining your former wife, and it seems no one has claimed the body and . . ."

"Oh, that." Dirk's face seemed to turn from a tired white color to an exhausted, ashen gray. "Polly doesn't really have many family members. And the sorry few she did have told her to kiss their lily-white asses years ago. I'm not surprised they're not volunteering to come forward and claim her now. They wouldn't wanna risk gettin' stuck with the funeral expenses."

Several thoughts on the subject filtered through Savannah's mind, but she decided to keep them to herself. She, too, wasn't surprised . . . that someone would tell Miss Polly Freeloader to kiss off. As far as she was concerned, Dirk should have done the same thing ages ago. If he'd done so, he might not be sitting on her sofa in strange, medieval garb, facing possible murder charges.

Dirk sighed and reached for his sneakers. "I guess I get to do this, too. Not that I mind, but—"

"But you're dead tired, and it can wait for a few more hours," Savannah said, snatching the shoes out of his hand. "You're going to hike your tail upstairs, get out of that goofy outfit before you decide you like wearing it *too* much, and lie down on the bed. I want your toes pointing skyward in the next three minutes. Hear me?"

"But I . . ."

"No buts. Not a one. Away with you."

She yanked him to his feet and shoved him toward the stairs.

As he passed by Tammy's desk, she turned around in her chair and put her hand on his arm. "Ah . . . Dirk," she said, her face flushing beneath her perfect golden tan. "Do you know how Polly wanted to be . . . ah . . . taken care of after . . . ah. . . . Did she want to be buried or—?"

He paused and thought for a long moment. "Cremated," he said. "I remember when we were still married, one of her biker friends wiped out on his Harley and croaked. We went out on a boat—I got sicker than a dog—and we dumped his ashes in the ocean along with his leather jacket and gloves and some stuff like that. I remember she said something about that being a cool way to go. I guess that's what I'll do."

Tammy stared down at the floor, but she gripped his sleeve harder. "You know," she said, "I've done that sort of thing before, when my grandparents and one of my elderly aunts passed away. Made arrangements I mean. Can I do that for you? I mean, I'd like to, if you don't mind. I know you've got a lot on your mind right now, and . . ."

Dirk swallowed hard, and Savannah could have sworn she saw tears in his eyes. His and Tammy's history had been stormy, to say the least. Both had claimed to hold only contempt for the other, though Savannah had always wondered how deep that animosity went. She had suspected it was pretty shallow, something more akin to sibling rivalry than genuine dislike.

"Well," he said, "if you're sure it wouldn't be too much to do, I'd appreciate it."

"No problem," she replied, releasing his arm and turning back to her desk. "Besides, I'm going to be doing it on Savannah's time, so you'd better thank her."

"Don't tell me that," he grumbled. "She'll probably send me a bill."

Savannah chuckled. "I only pay her a nickel an hour, so the grand total won't be more than a dollar. Even a tightwad skinflint like you can afford that."

As Savannah watched Dirk disappear up the stairs, she walked over and put her hands on Tammy's shoulders.

"Thanks, sweetie," she told her. "That was really nice of you, especially considering how you feel about the old fart."

"He's your friend," Tammy said matter-of-factly. "And he's not so bad. We're sorta like a family around here. A highly dysfunctional family, but . . ."

Savannah fingered the piece of paper in her skirt pocket. Speaking of dysfunctional families, she needed to decide what she was going to do about hers.

"I'm going to change out of this outfit. Unlike Dirk, I'm *not* getting used to the comfort of being laced up like a Thanksgiving turkey. Then I'm going to fall onto some horizontal surface and faint dead away, like the delicate buttercup that I am."

"Shall I call you if I need you?" Tammy shouted up to her as she climbed the stairs.

"Only if the extinguisher won't put out the fire and the tourniquet won't stop the bleeding."

Hours later, when Savannah had finished her nap and changed into modern attire—a sweatshirt and jeans—she came back downstairs to find that Tammy had left for the day. She stood beside the desk a long time before finally sitting down and turning on the computer.

Feeling a strange mixture of pain and numbness, she accessed her e-mail and began to compose the short note:

> Macon,
> Received your message. If it's really important, I
> suppose we could meet. When? Where?
>   Savannah

She typed in the e-mail address he had given and pressed SEND with a note of finality. The instant she saw the message YOUR MAIL HAS BEEN SENT splayed across the screen, she wanted to take it back. Why open a door left closed for so long? Let sleeping dogs lie and all that.

After all this time, she had nothing to say to this man who had been her father, biologically and in name only. It had been years since she had cursed him mentally and rehearsed the hard words she would use to express her hurt. It had also been years since she had wanted to express any kind of affection.

No, she had nothing to say to Macon. No words of love or hate.

What could he possibly have to say to her? Whatever it was, she was pretty sure she didn't want to hear it.

Yes, she definitely wished she could "unsend" that message. But like most things between her and Macon Reid, it was too late.

CHAPTER FOURTEEN

Savannah and Dirk waylaid Jake McMurtry the moment he stepped out of his apartment door the next morning. Neither really wanted to show their mug at the police station, but they wanted to know what, if anything, was happening with the investigation.

"Get in," Jake said, motioning to his new Mitsubishi. His eyes were bloodshot, his hair uncombed, his clothes rumpled, his face still sheet-creased. He looked better than they felt.

"You two look like hell," he told them.

"Yeah, and your mother wears combat boots, and she dresses you funny," Savannah replied as she slid into the passenger seat. "But we love you anyway. What have you got?"

Dirk climbed into the back. "Yeah. Who was this Snake dude and who killed him?"

"Hell, you don't ask for much," Jake said. "I'm supposed to have it sewn up already?"

"Damned right." Dirk told him. "It's my butt in the wringer here; you'd better wrap it up quick. I've got the DA breathing down my neck. Indictment's right around the corner, staring me in the face."

Savannah nudged Jake in the ribs with her elbow. "Dirk frequently mixes his metaphors, but you can't blame him for being upset . . . considering the circumstances."

"Hey, I understand, but I'm only one guy."

Dirk leaned over the console, his nose almost in Jake's right ear. "Yeah exactly why is that? Why doesn't my case rate more than one detective, and—no offense—but a rookie detective at that?"

Jake gave Savannah a wry smile. "Ever notice how people always say, 'no offense' just before they say something really offensive?"

She nodded. "True. I've noticed that myself. And when they say, 'I like you, or whatever, *but* . . .' you can just forget everything they said before the 'but'. It's what they say after the 'but' . . . that's what's really on their mind."

Dirk sighed and fidgeted like a kindergartner who needed to visit the little boy's room. "When you two get done blabbering about worthless shit, could we get back to my case?"

"Sorry," Savannah said, turning suddenly businesslike. "Exactly who *is* this Snake dude and who killed him?"

"I got the first part," Jake replied. "I'm working on the second."

He leaned across Savannah, opened his glove box, and took out a pack of cigarettes. Before he even had one out, in his mouth, and lit, Dirk was puffing away in the backseat.

Savannah quickly rolled down her window. Normally, she would have complained, but considering the stressful circumstances, she decided to let it slide.

"So, give us what you've got," Dirk said, blowing smoke out his nose and settling back in the seat.

"Snake was a charming nickname—"

"Well, I figured Mama Snake didn't name her sweet newborn baby something like that," Dirk said.

"No, she didn't," Jake agreed. "She named him Maximillian. Maximillian Fernando Schneider."

Savannah sniffed. "No wonder he changed his name to Snake. Imagine how the other kids would beat the crap out of you at recess with a name like Maximillian Fernando Schneider."

"Yeah," said Dirk, "but Snake Schneider ain't all that easy to wrap your tongue around either. Did he have a record?"

Jake nodded and took a deep drag. "Yep. Long one. Grand theft auto when he was a juvenile and several break-ins. Drug charges. Aggravated assault on a convenience-store clerk who wouldn't sell him booze. Domestic violence with girlfriends."

"Nice guy," Savannah said. "But it's not too surprising. Most people don't begin their criminal careers with first-degree murder. Usually they sorta work up to it."

"How much time had he served?" Dirk asked.

"Six years total. That's quite a bit, since he was only twenty-eight. He spent more of his adult years inside the system than out."

"A local boy?" Savannah asked.

"Born and bred San Carmelitan. Mostly worked construction jobs, here and there, nonunion, under the table."

"Any obvious connection to me?" Dirk said, flicking ash out the window.

"I was hoping you'd tell me. Did you ever bust him or—?"

"Hell no. If I'd busted him, I would have remembered him, and I would have known who he was all along."

"Hey, don't jump down my throat." Jake held up one hand like a school traffic monitor. "You've busted a lot of people; I figured you might have forgotten a face or—"

"I never forget a face, and I'd never seen that guy's ugly mug before . . . except the night he murdered my ex-wife. I'm asking you if there's any other connection to me, something you might have uncovered yourself, razor-sharp detective that you are."

Savannah discreetly reached back, laid a hand on Dirk's knee, and gave it a cautionary squeeze. It wouldn't help his situation any to piss off the only detective working the case.

"What Dirk means is . . ." she quickly inserted, ". . . did you check this Schneider's locations—work, home, spare-time activities—against Dirk's places, like his home, the police station, etc."

"Yeah. I did." Jake sounded slightly wounded. "Nothing that I could see."

"And connections to Polly?" Savannah asked.

"No." Jake shook his head. "Nothing there either. I don't know what he would have had against either of you."

"And how about his killer?" Savannah asked. "Have you got any leads on who shot that arrow?"

"Not really. Dr. Liu wrote up a description of the arrow for me and gave me a snapshot of it. I'm heading out to the faire this afternoon to show it around. Whoever it was, he was a pretty good shot. The doctor said it got Snake right in the heart. Just like he got Polly."

Savannah grimaced. "He died so quick, I figured it was through the heart."

"I understand," Dirk interjected, "that it's not that hard to be accurate with a crossbow. They're almost as deadly as a gun. Even more if you consider how quiet they are." He looked at Savannah and grinned. "Maybe I'll start packing a crossbow and a quiverful of arrows until they give me my Smith & Wesson back."

A buzzing sound startled all three of them until Savannah reached into her purse and pulled out her cell phone. "No rest for the weary," she said as she punched the appropriate button and put it to her ear. "Yep, I'm here."

The caller was Tammy, and she sounded excited. But then, Tammy was usually thrilled about something. It was her charm . . . and her downfall.

"Somebody called you," she said. "I think it's a lead. A cool lead!"

"Great. Who was it?" Savannah asked.

"Who? Oh, yeah . . . well, he didn't give me his name."

Savannah sighed, momentarily deflated. "Tam, most really cool leads generally leave a name."

"He didn't say who he was, said you gave him your card at the faire and told him to call if he heard anything. He acted like you'd know who he was."

"I gave about twenty people my card," Savannah said . . . wanting, hoping, but doubting. "Did he leave a phone number?"

"No, but he wants to meet with you. He says his crossbow

is missing . . . or at least it was for a while . . . and he knows who took it."

Savannah smiled and gave the acutely interested, eaves-dropping Dirk and Jake the thumbs-up. "You're absolutely right as rain, Tammy, my darlin', that *is* a cool lead. Tell me all-l-l-l about it. Where and when? We'll be there with bells on."

"Are you sure this was the third dirt road on the left after we crossed the bridge after the sulfur started stinking?" Savannah asked as the three of them trudged down a dusty path that wound through a woods and eventually led—at least in theory—to some water holes, where—or so they had been told and were fervently hoping—their cool lead would be waiting for them.

The directions had been: Take Santa Lucia highway into the Los Lobos National Park, turn left on Sulfur Hill Road, and wind around the base of the minimountain until the stench of the sulfur-rich, natural springs was strong enough to gag you, cross the stone bridge, and hang a left . . . or was it a right . . . at the third dirt road and hike back to water holes. The disgruntled owner of the missing crossbow was supposed to be there, waiting for them.

"He'd better be there," Savannah said, as the path narrowed and dry, brittle bushes scratched her legs, even through the linen of her slacks. She was wearing loafers, not boots, as the path might have dictated. Of course, she'd had no inkling when she'd dressed that morning that she'd be marching to Tipperary before the day was over.

"This is probably a setup," Dirk said, huffing and puffing along behind her as the Southern California winter temperatures took a nosedive to a bone-chilling seventy-nine degrees.

"We're probably going to get an arrow through the back any minute now."

Savannah stopped so abruptly that he ran into her. "Do you mind? I've got other things to think about right now, like dying of thirst, hunger, rattlesnake bite or grizzly bear attack. I'm so hungry right now that an arrow through the back would be a mercy killing. I should be home right now, sitting in my easy chair with my cats at my feet and a red heart-shaped box of chocolates on my lap."

"Eating and sitting . . ." Dirk muttered, ". . . that's your calling."

She glared at him. "And this from a guy whose greatest talents are lying on *my* sofa, swigging *my* beer and watching the fights on *my* HBO."

Dirk shrugged, mumbling something about "the price is right" and continued to drudge down the path. Savannah followed suit.

At the head of their short, motley column of foot soldiers was their ranking officer, Jake, looking as out of sorts as they did. "Why couldn't this dude just meet us at Mama's Cafe on Lester Street for breakfast, like any other snitch?" he said. "What's with the Nature Boy routine, setting up a meet out here in the sticks?"

"I told you," Dirk said. "He's gonna kill us."

Savannah sighed. The hike wasn't bad enough; she had to put up with Tweedledee and Tweedledum. "And since we have no idea who he is," she said, "and therefore, couldn't bust him if we had to, he has absolutely no motive whatsoever to kill us."

"For all we know, Snake didn't have a motive to kill

Polly, either," Dirk said dryly, "but, even as we speak, she's probably getting baked to a crispy critter."

Savannah winced and looked over her shoulder at him. Even for Dirk, that was a pretty dark joke. Having one's former spouse cremated wasn't a laughing matter for almost anyone.

But his face was stoic, telling her nothing.

Dirk was a weird duck, no doubt about it. And he was probably her best friend in the world. She didn't really want to think what that meant about her.

"Hey, I think I hear a creek," Savannah said, identifying the charming, burbling sound in the distance.

Jake pointed to a spot farther ahead where the path seemed to dip and disappear. "There it is," he said. "Not much water in it."

"Good," Savannah replied, "because we're going to have to cross it, and I didn't bring my snorkeling gear."

As they drew closer, they saw that others before them had utilized a large tree trunk, cut in half lengthwise, as a makeshift bridge. They did the same, and around the next bend, found that they had arrived at their destination. Three water holes—not that deep, muddy, and stinking of sulfur— were nestled at the base of a thirty-foot cliff. A small waterfall trickled down the moss-covered drop, feeding the holes. It would be larger when the March rains came and would probably disappear completely in the late-summer months.

Water beetles and mosquitoes buzzed across the surface of the miniature pond, along with a couple of dragonflies, shimmering, iridescent in the sunlight. Savannah made a mental note to maybe come back here sometime for a roughing-it type of picnic ... with plenty of mosquito repellent and sunscreen in the picnic basket along with the fried chicken, potato salad, and a bottle of wine.

At the moment, not knowing who might be sitting on an overhanging oak limb, a crossbow aimed at them, it was a bit difficult to enjoy the ambience.

"Look sharp, you two," Dirk said as he glanced around, apparently thinking the same thing. "Anybody who'd want to meet out here is missing a few nuts and bolts."

"Or maybe he just wants to make sure nobody sees him talking to you," said a voice behind them. They spun around to see a skinny kid, not more than sixteen or seventeen years old. He was dressed in an enormous black Metallica T-shirt that hung like a limp tent around his thin frame. Knobby knees and bony legs protruded from equally oversize shorts.

"I remember you," Savannah said, talking a few steps toward him. "I talked to you at the faire, only you were a juggler then, in a jester's Harlequin outfit."

But at the moment, he didn't seem to be in a jesting mood. In fact, he looked downright scared to death. His blue eyes were large in his gaunt face, looking through a mop of dirty blond hair, but now they were enormous. His skin was so pale that his freckles seemed to stand out in bas-relief.

"I wondered if you'd remember," he said. "You said that guy at faire was killed with a crossbow. You were wondering who had one and all that."

"Have you got something for us or not?" Dirk asked, far too aggressively. Desperation was going to be his undoing.

The kid winced, and for a moment, Savannah thought the frightened kid was going to pull his head into his T-shirt shell like a turtle and disappear.

Jake stepped forward and flashed his badge at the boy.

"I'm Detective McMurtry, son," he said in what sounded like a lousy John Wayne impression. "And if you've got information that would help me with this case, you should volunteer it now."

Savannah was afraid the teenager would react badly to Jake's clumsy approach, but he seemed comforted by the sight of the badge. "You're really a cop?" he said. "Like you could arrest somebody and make sure they stayed locked up?"

"Well, I can take somebody into custody," he replied. "It's up to the courts to say whether they stay in jail."

The boy looked disappointed. "Oh, yeah. Well, if you had good enough evidence you could make it stick, huh? I mean, if I helped you as much as I could, you'd make sure the guy didn't come after me, right?"

Savannah saw the trust in the kid's eyes and wished that she could be more certain of the law's ability to protect the innocent. So many times she had seen it fail in that regard; she was reluctant to make any promises.

But Jake was new to the game. And he had no problem giving reassurances. "Sure, I will. No problem. You tell me what you've got, and we'll go get the guy. Nothing bad will happen to you if you just tell the truth."

Savannah walked over to the boy, took his arm, and led him over to a large, smooth boulder. "Here," she told him, "take a load off. Have a seat and tell us all about it . . . starting with your name."

CHAPTER FIFTEEN

The teenager who had identified himself as Nathan — aka Nat the Juggling Computer Nerd—began to relax as Savannah sat on the sun-warmed rock beside him and nudged answers out of him. Neither Dirk nor Jake was nearly so mellow-minded; they paced up and down the edge of the pond, listening anxiously. Jake jingled change in his pocket and smoked liked a salmon in a hothouse. Dirk just paced and smoked.

"The belly-dancer girl," Nat was saying, "the one who wouldn't let Snake kiss her . . ."

"The girl who slapped him and took off down the trail?" Savannah offered. "The girl we never found?"

He nodded vigorously. "Yeah, her. I think she had something to do with what happened to him later."

"Oh, yeah?" Savannah's left eyebrow lifted one notch,

an accurate barometer of her interest level. "What do you think she had to do with him being killed?"

"Well, it wasn't her fault, or nothing like that," he quickly added. "I mean, if she did do it . . . come on to him and then slap him and get him to follow her into the woods . . . she didn't mean to. That is, she didn't do it to get him killed. She would've just done it because . . . well, because her boyfriend wanted her to. That's all."

Savannah studied his face, the blue eyes so full of fear. "Sounds as if maybe you like her a little, maybe you want to protect her even though you know she did something wrong."

He shook his head. "No. She didn't do anything wrong. And I don't like her. At least, not that way. She's . . . well . . . she's my older sister. I'm just telling you this because I'm worried about her."

Dirk stopped pacing for a minute. "You'd *better* be worried for her. If she lured that guy Snake into the woods to get him killed, she's in big trouble."

"Yeah!" Jake agreed. "And you'd better not protect her, because then you'd be an accessory, too."

Savannah gave them both scathing looks. "If you two don't mind. Nat and I are talking. You two are pacing and smoking and acting like jerks. We all have our gifts, and it's best if we stick to what we're good at."

She turned her attention back to the boy. "You said she would have done it because she was told to. Who would want her to do such a thing?"

"Her no-good, bum boyfriend, Kevin Donaldson. He's a really bad dude."

The kid's fear intensified, and Savannah realized the source of his anxiety and why he had requested such a private, out-of-the-way meeting place. He was scared to death of this bad dude. But he still had the courage to come forward out of concern for his older sister. She had to admire him for his moxie and loyalty to his family.

"What makes you think this Donaldson is so bad?" she asked him. "Have you seen him do anything or—"

"I've seen him smack my sister around. And he kicked our dog a couple of times, really hard, and she wasn't even doing anything wrong. And, one time when he was really drunk, he said that he had burned some people's house down. Said he did it with another guy for money. That's how he bought his Corvette."

"Did he say who those people were . . . the people whose house he burned?"

"No. And I didn't ask him either. I was afraid that the next morning he'd sober up and remember he told me about it and kill me."

"Probably smart on your part. What else?"

"And he was asking me all about my crossbow, how to use it and stuff."

"Did you tell him?"

"Yeah. I was afraid not to. He even made me take him out into the woods, and he practiced shooting at trees and then birds."

"How was he?"

"Pretty good! He shot a crow out of a tree, first try."

Savannah gave Dirk and Jake knowing looks. They had stopped their restless wanderings and were listening attentively to every word.

"He was all proud of himself that he'd shot it," he continued. "It was lying there all dying and bloody, its wings twitching. And Kevin was laughing, bragging that he'd got it right through the heart."

"Where is your crossbow right now?" she asked.

He shrugged. "Don't know. I put it back after we'd been shooting in the woods. I kept it under my bedroll in our tent. But when I looked for it this morning, it was gone. My quarrels, too."

"Quarrels?"

"Sorry. That's what they used to call the square-headed arrows used with a crossbow."

"Of course. I'm a little rusty on my old English. Did this Kevin guy know where you kept your bow?"

"Sure. He saw me get it out before we went shooting, and he saw me put it back under my bedroll."

Dirk walked up to them and sat on a nearby rock. His face softened as he dropped the tough-guy routine and became the man Savannah had always found endearing.

"I'm sorry I was a jerk a few minutes ago," he told Nat. "I'm just really worried about this case and mad, too. See, that guy Snake murdered my ex-wife, right in my own home. Shot her with my gun."

Nat's eyes bugged. "No way!"

"It's true," Savannah assured him. "And now Snake's dead, too, and we don't know why."

"Do you think your sister might have lured Snake into the woods so that Donaldson could shoot him with your crossbow?" Dirk asked.

The kid's blue eyes quickly filled with tears, but he blinked them away. "I think so. I heard them arguing just before. She was saying, 'Why? Why do you want me to do it? I won't do it unless you tell me why.'"

"Do you think he told her?" Savannah asked.

"No. I listened, and he didn't. He just hit her and told her to do it or else she'd be sorry. And he told her to keep her mouth shut about it, too."

Jake had sat down on the rock near Dirk and lit up another smoke. "Did you hear him tell her what she was supposed to do?"

"No, but it was right after that happened that she went out and found Snake and was making eyes at him, coming on to him and stuff. Then, when he decided to go for it, he tried to kiss her, and she slapped him. My sister Lynn isn't that kind of girl. She doesn't go around teasing guys. And she didn't like Snake at all. She's just into Kevin; I don't know why."

Savannah gave him a sympathetic nudge with her elbow. "Sometimes girls get involved with a bad guy before they realize what's up. And then, they're afraid to walk away. Your sister's probably caught in that sort of situation. But now that you've come forward, I think we can help her. You did the right thing, Nat."

"Yeah, and we really appreciate it," Dirk said. "*I* really appreciate it."

"Will you come down to the station with me," Jake asked, "and put this on paper?" When a look of horror crossed the boy's face, he quickly added, "I'll keep you safe. I promise. I won't move on this Donaldson until I'm sure I've got him. We'll do it right. Trust me."

Savannah gave Jake a You'd Better Not Screw This Up Or You're Dead look. Then she turned to Nat. "They're going to do it right. Promise. We have to take good care of folks who do the right thing; there aren't enough of them in the world as it is."

* * *

Savannah licked the edge of the Very, Very Berry and Chocolate Supreme Decadence, double-scoop ice-cream cone and decided that maybe, just maybe, life was worth living after all. How many occupations allowed you to indulge in such culinary hedonism . . . all in the line of duty? And every dieter knows that food eaten on the job has no calories, as well anything consumed standing up or riding in a car, or bites stolen from someone else's plate in a restaurant, as those calories rightly belong to the person who ordered the dish in the first place. Guilt-free goodies . . . one of life's greatest treasures.

The girl who had scooped this bit of heaven on earth for Savannah was none other than Nathan the Juggler's wayward older sister. Though it was difficult to imagine her belly dancing in a medieval gypsy village. At the moment, she was a study in boredom, standing behind a counter that held more than twenty flavors of ice cream, dressed in a pink-striped smock and wearing a pink scarf to hold her blond curls away from her face.

She had served Savannah with only minimalist grunts and a mumbled, "Two-fifty." Savannah decided that her somewhat surly attitude might be due to her blackened left eye and her busted lower lip. Either Nathan's sister, Lynn, had a self-destructive habit of walking into doors, or old Kevin had been using her for a punching bag again.

Retreating to the card section of the large drugstore, Savannah stood behind a rack of red, pink and white Valentine cards and watched Lynn as she mechanically performed her duties of scooping and collecting money. The young woman looked intensely unhappy. There was a heaviness about her actions that indicated something was crushing her spirit.

Savannah had seen the look on far too many women, young and old. And many of those had been truly kind, loving people . . . all the more easily taken advantage of because of their gentle natures.

She found it hard not to hate the abusers who mistreated these women simply because they could. They were cowards who chose those females as targets for their rage and feelings of impotence, rather than stronger, less kind and generous souls. For the most part, bitches didn't get whacked around. Nice ladies did. It was a cruel irony that Savannah despised.

And Nat's sister, Lynn, looked like she had once been a nice, sweet young lady. Now she just looked empty, used up.

Savannah killed time, shopping for a Valentine for Tammy, until another ice-cream server relieved Lynn, and she walked outside the store for a cigarette break.

Savannah followed and found her leaning against an empty bicycle rack, lighting up.

"Hi," she said as she approached her, trying to look as casual as possible. It wasn't easy, considering that Jake and Dirk were anxiously watching every movement she made from Dirk's old Buick Skylark, parked in the rear of the lot near the road.

Lynn gave her a suspicious half scowl that made her black eye look even more ominous than before. She didn't reply . . . only grunted.

"I know something about your boyfriend, Kevin," Savannah said, leaning against the rack herself, watching traffic whip by on the busy, palm-tree-lined Lester Street.

"So?" She was like a trout who was obviously interested in the worm on the hook, but wouldn't bite.

"So . . . I know that he killed that guy, Snake, at the

faire. And I know that you helped him by getting Snake to follow you into the woods."

There! That had the desired effect! Miss Cool Hand Lynn's mouth sagged and even her bruised, swollen eye opened wide. Savannah loved dropping bombs on people, especially deserving folks who had done nasty deeds like helping to murder another person.

Lynn sputtered and spewed, but no articulate words came out.

Savannah continued. "I also know that you didn't really want to help him, that he bullied you into it. Which means, that if you come forward right now and tell the authorities everything you know, you won't be in nearly as much trouble as you will be if you wait until they come after you."

Lynn's fingers were trembling so badly that she could hardly bring her cigarette to her lips. "Are you . . . are you a cop or something?"

"No. I'm not a cop. I'm a private investigator." She pointed to Dirk and Jake, sitting in the car near the street. "But *they* are. And they know everything that I know."

Lynn choked on her smoke. "So . . . why haven't they arrested me yet?"

"They were going to. I talked them out of it, said I wanted a chance to convince you to give up Kevin and save yourself."

Throwing the cigarette onto the ground, the young woman began to cry. Savannah reached into her purse, pulled out a tissue, and handed it to her.

"Why would you do that?" Lynn said between sobs. "Why . . . did you want to help me? You don't even know me."

"Oh, I know you. I know you all too well," Savannah said, wrapping her arm around the girl's shoulders. "I've known literally hundreds of women like you, young and old, rich and poor, black, white, and all the colors in between. And I know that the best thing you can do to be rid of this bastard, once and for all, is to help the cops put him away."

Savannah shook her gently, wishing she could literally shake some sense into her. But there was so much fear in the young woman's eyes. And, often, fear overrode common sense.

"He's a killer, Lynn," she told her, "and he's incredibly selfish. He'll kill you, too, if he decides it's what's best for him. Don't think for one moment that he won't. In spite of what he tells you when you're having sex, you aren't that special to him. Believe me, no one is truly special to someone like him."

Tears streamed down the young woman's face, causing her mascara and eyeliner to run in black rivulets down her cheeks. Savannah could tell that her mind was racing as she tried to make what was probably the most difficult decision of her life.

"He murdered somebody, Lynn," Savannah added softly, trying to tip the scale to the right. "He killed someone in cold blood. And worse yet, he used you to do it."

Lynn blew loudly into the tissue and dabbed at her eyes. "Snake was a jerk," she offered feebly.

"I'm sure he was," Savannah agreed, "but that didn't give Kevin the right to stalk him with a crossbow in a dark woods. He died in a lot of pain; I know, I was there. And you know as well as I do that this wasn't the first time Kevin has done something illegal."

It was a shot in the dark, but this particular quarrel had found its target. Lynn looked shocked that Savannah seemed to be so knowledgeable on the subject of Kevin Donaldson's exploits.

"And Snake isn't the first person that Kevin had hurt either," Savannah ventured. "There was that house that he burned and heaven knows what else. Somebody like that can't be allowed to walk around free, hurting more and more people. Next time it could be you, Lynn, or somebody in your family, someone you love."

Lynn nodded, looking positively miserable. "Last night he hinted that he was going to do something to my little brother, Nathan. Said he thought Nat might get him into trouble, you know, about the crossbow."

"What about the crossbow?" Savannah asked with conjured sincerity.

"It was my little brother's crossbow that Kevin used to shoot Snake. And Kevin's afraid that Nat noticed it missing. I told him if he touched my brother, I'd turn him in or kill him myself."

"Let me guess," Savannah said dryly. "That's when you got the shiner."

"Yeah. I didn't sleep at all last night, worrying about my little brother." She started to sob again, even harder than before. "If anything happened to Nat, I don't think I could stand it."

Savannah patted her back soothingly, just as she would have any one of her own younger siblings. "That's why you have to talk to them, Lynn," she said, pointing to the car where Jake and Dirk sat, watching. "You have to tell them everything you know so that they can make sure they have a case against him. Are you willing to talk to them right now? I'll walk you over to the car and introduce you. Then I'll go back into the store and make it right with your boss. I'll tell them that you have a serious family problem and had to go home. Okay?"

Lynn blew her nose again, squared her shoulders, and nodded. "Okay."

"Good girl! That's one of hardest, smartest things you'll ever do. I'm mighty proud."

CHAPTER SIXTEEN

An hour and a half later, Lynn was sitting in Savannah's Camaro in the middle of the drugstore parking lot, crouched down in the seat, so that she could barely see out the car window. Savannah sat in the driver's seat beside her, cell phone in her hand.

"How's she doing?" Dirk asked over the phone. He and Jake were still in Dirk's Buick, but they had pulled the car to the front row, near the store's door.

"She's fine ... considering," she replied, looking down at the frightened young woman in the pink smock beside her.

"Isn't this about the time Donaldson usually picks her up from work?" he asked.

She turned to Lynn. "Your shift is over at five, right?" she asked her. "And that's when he arrives to drive you home?"

Lynn's teeth were chattering, her arms crossed tightly

over her breasts, as though she were afraid her heart was beating so hard it would fly out of her chest at any moment.

"He's usually here about ten minutes early," she said, "to make sure that no other guy is hanging around. He's really jealous."

"Yeah, he's jealous. His kind always is. They're also the sort of jerk who fools around on a girl. It never fails."

She lifted the phone back to her mouth. "She says he's often early, so it's anytime now. You two ready?"

"Chomping at the bit, fit to be tied, and rarin' to go . . . as you would say."

Savannah grinned. "Why, I'll make a righteous Rebel out of you yet, Yankee boy."

Dirk just growled.

Suddenly, Lynn gasped, reached over, and grabbed Savannah's thigh. "That's him, there in the new black Corvette."

A sleek, perfectly polished Corvette slid into one of the parking spots near Dirk's Buick and came to a stop.

"Heads up, lawman," she said. "That there's your guy . . . the scrawny-assed yahoo crawlin' out of the black 'Vette."

"They'd better be careful," Lynn said breathlessly, as they watched Dirk and Jake approach their suspect from the rear as he walked across the lot toward the store entrance. "Kevin's really strong, and he's mean, and he knows a lot about fighting. He might hurt them and get away."

"He's like all the rest of the lily-livered bullies," Savannah said. "He's a big shot when he's beating up on women and other innocents, or when he's stalking somebody in the dark. But let's see how he does against a couple of really tough guys. How much you wanna bet he folds like a cheap playing card?"

Lynn had started crying again, hugging her arms even

tighter across her chest. "No, you don't understand. He's really—"

Her words ended the instant that Dirk and Jake grabbed him from behind and threw him up against the store's cement-block wall. He struggled a moment, but gave up quickly as Dirk twisted his arms behind his back and Jake slapped cuffs on him.

Savannah and Lynn couldn't understand the words they were saying to him, but their no-nonsense tone was unmistakable. Kevin Donaldson was being read his rights.

When all three turned around and headed back to the Buick, Dirk gave Savannah a smile and a discreet thumbs-up. Savannah had pushed Lynn's head below the dash, but now she coaxed her to sit up. "Look at big, bad Kevin," she told her. "He can dish it out, but he can't take it. He's bawling like a scalded hog."

She looked over at Lynn and saw something new on her face, the trace of a smile.

"I guess I should feel bad," the young woman said. "I mean, he is my boyfriend, and I've just caused him to be arrested for murder. Yeah, I should feel really bad."

"Why the hell should you feel bad?" Savannah asked. "A sonofabitch who's made your life miserable, who's threatened to hurt or even kill members of your family, who's blacked your eye and busted your lip ... you're supposed to feel bad that he's getting locked up? Bull puckey! Are you over twenty-one?"

"Turned twenty-two last month."

"Good!" She slapped her on the back. "Let's celebrate. We'll go to Tijuana Rose's Cantina and order a couple of margarita grandes big enough to take a Jacuzzi in!"

* * *

Savannah and Dirk stood on the window side of the two-way mirror and watched Kevin Donaldson sweat as Jake interrogated him in the "interview" room next door. Jake had allowed them to sneak in before the questioning with plenty of threats about "disavowing any knowledge of their actions should they be caught or killed."

Jake had only been at it for fifteen minutes, and Donaldson was already starting to crack.

"The kid's better at this than I thought he would be," Savannah said, watching how Jake stayed behind Donaldson, just out of his line of vision, and leaned over him, practically breathing down his neck when he wanted to score a major point.

"He is," Dirk said. "But not as good as me."

"No one's as good as you, sugar," Savannah cooed.

"If only you meant it when you kiss up like that," he replied dryly.

"Yeah, wouldn't it be nice, if I were being sincere instead of just a smart aleck when I tell you how wonderful you are?"

Dirk snorted. "You wanna shut up now so that I can hear what's going on next door?"

She laughed. "Sure. Let's turn it up a notch." She reached over and twisted a knob that was next to the light switch on the wall. Instantly, the conversation in the adjoining room was twice as loud.

"We have the weapon," Jake was saying. "You, know, the crossbow that you 'borrowed' from your girlfriend's little brother."

"No way," Kevin said, enraged and not a little worried.

"Way. We dug it up from where you buried it there by that tree."

Savannah nudged Dirk. "Is that true? Do you guys have it?"

"Naw. It's bullshit. Lynn told us that he buried it under a tree down by the river, but we haven't had time to get it yet."

"And not only that," Jake continued, "but it's got your fingerprints all over it."

Kevin shrugged. "So . . . I never said I didn't touch the brat's bow. I've shot it lots of times. But just at trees and birds and shit like that. I didn't shoot that asshole Snake. Somebody else must've done it."

"Like I said," Jake continued coolly, "the weapon has your prints all over it. And that's not all." He walked around in front of Donaldson and leaned across the table until he was squarely in his face. "And we know it was *that* crossbow that killed him."

"How? How would you know something like that?" Donaldson was starting to sound a bit desperate, as if he could see the old jail door swinging shut in his face.

"Are you familiar with the concept of ballistics testing on bullets to prove that they came from a certain firearm?"

"Yeah . . . I guess so. But it ain't the same with bows and arrows."

"Oh, yeah? A lot you know. It's not that way with a regular bow and arrows, but a crossbow is different. Every individual crossbow leaves distinctive markings on any arrow that's shot from it . . . just like a gun barrel scores a bullet that passes through it. That's the beauty of this whole thing. The arrow that killed Snake . . . was shot from the crossbow that has your fingerprints on it."

Savannah snickered. "What a load of bullshit. Let me get out my hip boots."

"Yeah, I'm jealous," Dirk replied. "I thought I was the best b.s. slinger on the force. But the kid's got me beat."

"That's the beauty of it all," Jake told his increasingly more uneasy interviewee. "We've got you by the balls, brother. Can't you feel the squeeze? You're practically singin' soprano!"

Kevin Donaldson could feel it. You could tell by the look on his face. Savannah knew the satisfaction that Jake was feeling. It was an almost orgasmic experience, watching a bad guy start to go down like a felled oak, and you standing there with the ax in your hand yelling, "Timber!"

"There's no question that you did it, Donaldson," Jake said. "That's been established. The only blank that needs to be filled in is: Why? What did you have against the old Snake boy that you'd hunt him down and shoot him dead like a deer in the woods? If you've got a good enough reason, maybe you won't be lying strapped to a table while they shove needles up your arms. I hear you don't like needles, Kevin. That's why you either smoke or swallow your dope. No shooting for you."

Jake had hit a main nerve with that one. Donaldson's face blanched, and he looked like he was about to throw up.

"Snake wasn't that great of a guy," Jake continued, almost companionably. "He had a helluva rap sheet, and everybody I talked to said he was an ass. He helped you burn down that old couple's house and he killed that lady . . . the cop's ex-wife. You probably had a good reason for taking him out. What was it?"

"I . . . I didn't. I mean, I . . ."

"Yes . . . yes . . ." Dirk murmured. "Come on, spill it."

But Kevin's possible confession was cut short when the door to the interrogation room opened and Lieutenant Jeffries rushed inside.

Savannah groaned and Dirk mumbled, "Talk about shit timing. . . ."

"Is this him?" Jeffries asked, pointing an accusing finger at Donaldson. "Is this our crossbow shooter?"

"It's him, all right," Jake replied. "He's already confessed, I—"

"Did not! I didn't either confess nothin'!" Donaldson shouted. "I didn't do nothin'. Didn't confess nothin' neither."

"Ever notice," Savannah said, "how frequently criminals use double negatives? I wonder if they've ever done a study on the correlation between bad grammar and the criminal mind."

"No, I ain't never noticed nothin' like that," Dirk replied.

"Oh, well . . . it was a thought."

They watched and, within moments, Lieutenant Jeffries had sent Jake out of the room, supposedly to get a copy of Donaldson's rap sheet. And Jeffries himself was interrogating the suspect.

"What did you tell him?" he demanded in low tones as he stood over Donaldson, his fists clenched at his sides.

"Nothin'. Nothin' at all," Donaldson sputtered. "I told him I didn't do it, but he says he's got the crossbow and it's got my fingerprints on it and he said the tests showed that it shot the arrow that killed him and . . ."

"He's lying to you, you stupid jerk," Jeffries said, slamming his fist down on the table.

Savannah reached over and grabbed Dirk's arm. Neither of them breathed.

"He's got nothing except your girlfriend's statement. That's it. Now if you . . ."

Jeffries's words trailed away as he seemed to realize where he was. He stared straight through the glass at Savannah and Dirk, as though he could see them standing on the other side of the mirror. They knew he couldn't, but it was a creepy feeling all the same.

"You got nothin' to worry about," Donaldson said. "I never told him that—"

"Shut up!" Jeffries held up one hand,. "Don't say another word."

The lieutenant walked over to the wall that separated the two rooms and flipped a switch mounted next to the mirror. Instantly, the speaker in Savannah's and Dirk's room crackled and went dead. Then Jeffries reached up and pulled a heavy shade down, over the mirror, and they were left in darkness.

"Do you think he knows we're in here?" Dirk whispered.

"No, he's just being careful. Can you believe it? Old company-man Jeffries?"

"No, I don't believe it, but . . ."

"Shh-h-h-h," Savannah said, carefully leaning her ear against the glass.

"Can you hear anything?"

"If you'd hush, I might."

Dirk took the hint and was silent. Savannah strained to listen for a minute or two. Then she peeled herself away from the glass and grabbed Dirk's sleeve. "Come on!" she said. "We've gotta get out of here."

"Why?"

"Jake's come back in and it sounds like Jeffries is leaving. He might check in here."

They scurried out of the room and had barely closed the door behind them, when they heard the door to the interrogation room opening. They quickly ducked into the small, one-toilet men's room across the hall. Leaving the door cracked, they watched as Lieutenant Jeffries did, indeed, stick his head into the room where they had just been, flip on the light, and look around. Satisfied, he closed the door and returned to the interrogation room.

Savannah closed the rest room door and turned on the light. Dirk's face registered her own shock and disbelief.

"No," she said, shaking her head. "Jeffries involved in Snake's murder? How? Why?"

Dirk's expression grew hard, his jaw tight. "What I want to know," he said, "is what did Jeffries have to do with Polly gettin' killed."

CHAPTER SEVENTEEN

Savannah's dragonfly Tiffany lamp lent a cozy glow to the scene as the members of Moonlight Magnolia—official and unofficial—sat around her table, pooling their assorted talents and resources. But the conversation was anything but cozy. Deciding the best way to nail a crooked cop, especially a lieutenant, was somber business.

Jake McMurtry had joined them tonight. His misery was palpable, his position being more tenable than anyone else's at the table . . . except for Dirk, who was equally out of sorts. He had received word an hour before that the DA was proceeding with the charges against him, in spite of the new developments in the case.

As usual, Savannah had provided the munchables and potables for the occasion: Beck's Dark beer for Dirk, Earl Grey tea for John Gibson, sparkling mineral water for Tammy, a glass of Chardonnay for Ryan, a Coke for Jake, and a cup of strong coffee laced with cream for her. More hot-from-the-oven Valentine cookies were piled on a plate in the center of the table, along with a platter of Brie and English wheat crackers. No one died of starvation on Savannah's watch.

"As if that weren't enough," Savannah said, after she and Dirk had told them everything they had witnessed earlier that evening during the interrogation, "wait until you hear the other little tidbit of info we have for you."

Savannah took a long drink of coffee, building the suspense for her listeners. "After Jeffries turned off the sound and dropped the shade, I put my ear to the glass and . . ."

"What did you hear?" Tammy asked, more impatient than the rest.

"Not much," Savannah admitted. In unison, her audience sighed and deflated a bit. "Just one name."

Ryan's eyes sparkled with anticipation. John toyed with the corner of his silver mustache.

Jake was wriggling all over his chair, like a kid who needed to pee. "Well, what name?"

"Cooper."

"Cooper?" Jake said.

"Cooper who?" Ryan added.

"Cooper what?" Tammy asked.

"My dear," John Gibson said, more patiently than the rest, "you were quite right in your original assessment of this new lead. It simply isn't the grandest one might hope for."

Savannah batted her eyelashes and gave them her best, dimpled grin. "I have total confidence in you all," she drawled. "We here at Moonlight Magnolia Detective Agency have produced miracles with far less. I see no reason we can't do it again."

She reached across the table and helped herself to a cookie that was liberally sprinkled with red and pink sparkles. Turning it this way and that, she admired her handiwork, while savoring the anticipation. "Now, who's gonna do what?"

Hours later, when everyone had left, except Dirk, and he was tucked into bed, Savannah sat on the edge of her own bed, still fully dressed, a pink WHILE YOU WERE OUT note from Tammy in her hand.

She stared at the number. A local number. The number of a local motel that truckers often patronized. It was right off the freeway, with easy access and an oversize parking lot to accommodate big rigs. Next door was a diner that specialized in down-home, Southern-style cooking.

And that was where Macon wanted to meet her. *For a piece of pie*, the message said.

For the first time in her memory, she didn't want a piece of pie. The very thought of sitting down to a table with Macon Reid made her stomach tie in a knot.

She didn't need this right now. With Dirk's future hanging in the balance, the last thing she wanted was to deal with a man who had broken her heart, over and over and over again. Why hadn't he just left well enough alone? Why hadn't he just left *her* alone? He had been all too happy to do that for so many years. Why break the pattern now?

As she reached for the phone, she thought, *He'd better have cancer or some kind of terminal illness. If not, I might give him one.* Then she quickly banished the thought as unworthy of her. If he really was sick, she'd feel lower than snail slime.

She dialed the motel's number, asked for his room, and waited, pulse racing for him to answer. But when the *Hello* came through, it was decidedly female and distinctly Southern.

"Oh, hello," Savannah said. "I must have the wrong room. I was calling for Macon Reid."

"Sure, darlin', he's in the shower. Hold on." After a couple of seconds, Savannah heard her yell, "Macon, somebody wants to talk to you. I think it's your girl."

His girl? Savannah thought that one over. Funny, she had never thought of herself as Macon's girl. Or any other guy's girl for that matter.

When he answered, his voice sounded older, more feeble than she remembered. A lot older, in fact.

"Hello, Vanna Sue? Is that you sugar?"

Vanna Sue? She hadn't been called that in about twenty years. She'd gladly opt for twenty more "Vanna Sue-free" years.

"This is Savannah, Macon. I received your message and thought I should give you a call."

"I'm so glad you did, honey. How's about I buy you a cup of coffee and a slice of apple pie?"

She wanted to tell him no. She wished now that she had pretended not to have gotten the message in the first place. But it was too late. In for a penny, in for a pound.

"When?" she asked.

"Why right now! I'd just be so proud to see you."

"It's late, Macon. And it's been a long time."

"Too long. That's why we oughta do it now. Say you'll meet me at that little cafe over here in a few minutes."

She sighed, feeling old, tired, empty. Not at all the way a daughter should be feeling before meeting her estranged father.

"Ten minutes," she said. "But I can't stay long."

"That's fine, sugar. I'm mighty proud you're coming."

"Okay."

She hung up the phone and walked woodenly out of her room. As she passed the guest bedroom, she heard Dirk snoring. At least he was getting some sleep, bless his heart. He needed it.

So did she. But, once again, she was putting someone else's interests before her own. Was it because she was a loving, generous woman? Or because she was a fool and a doormat?

She left a note for Dirk on the kitchen table, just in case he got up and found her gone. Then she threw on a sweater and walked out into the brisk, winter, Southern California night.

Halfway to her Camaro, she decided. . . .

Yeah . . . it was the fool/doormat thing. Had to be. She just wasn't all that generous and loving. At least not where Macon Reid was concerned.

The odor of diesel from the eighteen-wheelers in the cafe's parking lot mixed with the aroma of fried food and coffee from the diner itself and made Savannah a bit nauseous as she walked up to the door. Or maybe it was her topsy-turvy emotions bouncing around in there that made her feel like she had just ridden a loop-the-loop roller coaster.

She didn't want to do this. She *so* didn't want to do this.

You don't have to do this, a voice inside told her. *You could just turn around and walk away.*

And run out on him? asked a more humane, kinder, gentler voice. Possibly the voice of a doormat.

Hell, yeah, run out on him. Just like he did you and your

mom and your brother and your sisters, over and over and over. . . .
Show him what it's like to be sitting, waiting for someone you love
to show up. On your birthday, on Easter, on Christmas Eve.

But by then she was already inside the cafe. And he had
spotted her and was rushing to meet her.

Well, not exactly rushing. She noticed that he limped a
bit. Obviously, it wasn't only his voice that had grown more
feeble over the years. His formerly auburn hair had turned
white, and even though he had never been considered a lightweight, he had definitely gained thirty or forty pounds—all
around the middle. Heart-attack city, just waiting to happen.

He met her in the aisle and they shared an awkward
moment as they decided whether or not to embrace. Finally,
they gave each other a halfhearted hug and an air kiss in the
general cheek vicinity.

"We've got a booth right back here," he said, ushering
her to the far corner of the room full of chrome-and-red-
leatherette seats and pearlized gray tabletops. Overhead hung
wagon wheels sporting lanterns with red hurricane globes. But
the lighting did little to illuminate the room, and Savannah
didn't realize until she was nearly sliding into the booth that
they had company.

After making the phone call and hearing the woman's
voice, she had briefly wondered if Francie would be there. She
had quickly dismissed the idea. Not even Francie would be
tacky and tasteless enough to show her face at this meeting.

But, as with everything relating to her father, Savannah
had underestimated the situation.

Francie was older, too, than the last time Savannah had
seen her. Her blond hair had turned as gray as Macon's. The
heavy makeup she had always worn now looked pathetically

garish on her aging face. Her figure had once been voluptuous, but gravity was having its way and her ill-fitting polyester stretch pants and too-tight T-shirt did nothing to camouflage the problem.

"Have a seat, sugar," Macon was saying as he gently shoved her into the booth bench and slid next to Francie on the other side. "I'm just so glad you could make it. Does me a world of good to see your pretty face."

"You *are* looking good!" Francie gushed. "My goodness you've turned into a pretty girl."

Savannah could smell the strong odor of alcohol on her breath. Between dark black lines of heavy eyeliner, her eyes were bloodshot and bleary.

"Thank you, Francie," she murmured, sounding anything but grateful. "I didn't know you were going to be joining us tonight."

Macon reached over and covered Francie's sun-spotted hand with his. "I wanted her to be here, when I tell you the good news."

Savannah was fairly certain she didn't want to hear this "good news," but she heard herself saying, "What's up, Macon?"

"Well . . ." He looked a bit disappointed. "I wanted to sorta work up to the subject, but since you ask me outright like that, I guess I'll just spill the beans now."

Savannah waited, her hands folded demurely in front of her, projecting an image of calm that she didn't feel.

"Well," he began, "I reckon this might not be the best news as far as you're concerned, but I'm really happy about it, and I want you to be, too. If you can be, that is."

"What is it, Macon?" she asked, trying not to jump up

out of her seat and run out the door without hearing what he had to say.

"I've asked Francie here to marry me. And she said she would. In fact, she wants to ask you something special."

"Something special?" Savannah's fists were clenched in her lap under the table. "Special how? What?"

"I want you to stand up with me. To be my maid of honor. I think it's high time that we acted like family. One big, happy family, 'cause I'm gonna be your stepmomma, you know."

Savannah searched Francie's face to see if she was serious. Regretfully, she was.

Amazed, Savannah slowly shook her head. "I don't quite believe this. I . . ."

Macon gouged Francie in the side. "See there, honey bunch. I told you she'd be surprised. Just look at that. She's pleased as punch. She can't even talk straight."

"Then you'll do it?" Francie said. Without waiting for an answer she plunged ahead, chattering on about wedding plans, something about Las Vegas and twenty-four-hour wedding chapels that played Elvis music while you walked down the aisle.

"Wait a minute," Savannah said, when she finally found her voice. "Hang on just a darned minute." She took a deep breath and turned to her father. "You tell me that after all these years, you're finally divorcing my mother? You and Mom *are* still married, right?"

He nodded. "Yeah, but I'm gonna get one of those quickie divorces as soon as we get to Vegas, before the wedding, of course."

"Of course. And as soon as you've divorced my mother, you're going to marry the woman you've been having an affair with for as long as I can possibly remember. The woman you used to drop off at that seedy little motel on the edge of town the few days a year that you actually came home to your family. The one the whole town talked about behind Mom's back and behind us kids' backs, but loud enough that we could all hear and be embarrassed as hell about. The woman that you would swing by and pick up on your way back out of town, leaving Mom pregnant with my next brother or sister. Is that what you're telling me, Macon?"

She turned to Francie, whose badly lipsticked ruby red lips were starting to tremble. "And *you*. You have a more than twenty-five-year affair with a married man. You run all over the country with him in his rig, while his children practically starve at home because of his neglect. And then you have the gall to ask me, the oldest of those nine kids—the one who remembers you best—to be your maid of honor? Did I hear you correctly? Is that what you two just told me?"

Francie shrugged. "Well, if you put it like that, it don't sound like such a good idea. . . ."

Macon bristled and put a protective arm around his bride-to-be's shoulders. "Now look here, Little Miss Savannah Priss, I'm not going to sit here and let you insult the woman I'm gonna marry. That just ain't right."

"And we all know how concerned the two of you are about doing what's right. Right?"

"Don't you give me none of your sass, young lady. I could still—"

"What, Macon? Put me over your knee and give me a whuppin'? Let's get real. The day of you taking your belt to me is long past. So don't even start down that road with me, or I'll slap you stupid, just for old times' sake."

"You're a lot like your mama," Macon said, shoving his cup away and slopping coffee onto the table. "You got a big mouth and a big butt. Always did have."

Savannah stood and silently counted down her temper before replying in a studied, calm voice, "Listen to me, Macon and Francie. In spite of what I just said, I don't wish either of you ill. It would bring me no happiness to hear that misfortune had befallen you. I don't hate you. But I don't love you either. Too much water has gone under the bridge to even pretend that I do."

She saw her father wince, but she decided to continue. "And I can't give you my blessing for this upcoming . . . union of yours. If you want to get married, get married. If you'd had the courage to do it properly years ago, you might have saved us all a lot of grief."

She started to walk away. Then she came back to the table. "And one other thing, Macon. I used to resent the fact that you weren't there to raise the children you brought into the world. I used to resent the childhood that I missed as the oldest, acting like a surrogate parent while you drove your rig and your girlfriend all over the country, while Mom sat in bars and drank enough booze to kill an elephant trying to drown her pain. I used to resent all the diapers I changed, the skinned knees I doctored, and the snotty noses I wiped."

Tears flooded her eyes, and for once, Savannah didn't bother to blink them back or wipe them away. "But then, I realized that you were the one who got the bum end of the deal. You weren't there when Atlanta took her first steps, or when Waycross hit his first homer in Little League, or when Vidalia came waltzing into the living room wearing her prom dress and looking like a fairy princess. You've never held her sweet babies. You missed all that. But I was there, Macon. And those moments were worth the dirty diapers and the hours of homework and the sleepless nights when they all had the chicken pox. I wouldn't have missed it for anything."

She leaned over, offered her father her hand, and, to her surprise, he shook it. "Have a good life, Macon," she said. "And you, too, Francie. Go get married and be happy if you can. Just don't contact me anymore. Okay?"

She didn't wait for an answer. She walked out the door and into the night air that reeked of fried onions and diesel fuel.

But she had said some things that she had needed to say for a long, long time. And the strange combination of onions and diesel had never smelled so sweet.

CHAPTER EIGHTEEN

The next morning, Savannah and Dirk sat in the back of John Gibson's Bentley and stared out the window at the panoramic view below them. John and Ryan sat in front, John in the driver's seat, as always.

"Can you imagine having the bucks to live on a piece of property like this?" Savannah said as she took in the sweeping vista: orange and lemon groves directly below them, the city of San Carmelita a bit farther down, embracing the gently sloping hills, all the way to the beach. And the glorious Pacific Ocean reaching to a hazy pink-and-aqua infinity.

Definitely a nice view, if you could afford it.

"Naw, I wouldn't want to live up here," Dirk said with his usual effervescence. "One good earthquake and the whole thing's gonna fall right into the ocean. In fact, you couldn't pay me to live up here."

"Well, a lot of people have paid a great deal for these lots," Ryan said. "In fact, even the smaller ones are going for seven figures."

"As in a million bucks or more?" Dirk was traumatized at the very thought of such extravagance.

"And that's just for the dirt," Savannah added, shaking her head. "Imagine, a million dollars for dirt."

"The developer is collecting a tidy sum," John said. "Acquiring this property and overcoming numerous obstacles to having it rezoned by the city was one of his finer triumphs."

"This is all well and good," Dirk said, shifting nervously on his seat, the sumptuous leather wasted on him. "But I didn't come up here to sightsee. You said you'd found somethin'."

Savannah cringed at Dirk's lack of diplomacy, but by now, John and Ryan knew Dirk too well even to notice, let alone be offended.

"We have uncovered something indeed," John said, glowing with self-satisfaction. "After we left your home last evening, Savannah, we spent much of the night making telephone calls. I must tell you, more than one of our friends is upset with us, but it was worth incurring their wrath."

"It certainly was," Ryan interjected. "We were so pleased with what we learned that we were waiting at the courthouse this morning when they opened their doors. It took a while, but we confirmed what we were told last night."

"Which was?" Savannah had to fight the juvenile urge to cross her fingers and toes.

"We were searching for a connection to our fine Lieutenant Jeffries and someone named Cooper." John waved a hand at the open, freshly bulldozed lots. "And there it is."

"This land," Ryan said, "was purchased by one Ethan Cooper."

"*The* Ethan Cooper?" Savannah asked. "The guy who built Oaks Dale?"

"And many other exclusive, gated communities here in Southern California," John replied. "Exactly such a complex is intended for this area. Building will begin this summer. Custom, five- and six-bedroom homes."

"Okay," Dirk said. "So, people are nuts enough to pay a fortune for land that's gonna slide downhill as soon as the spring rains begin. What's that got to do with Jeffries?"

Ryan and John grinned at each other, savoring their juicy tidbit as long as possible before spitting it out. In unison they pointed to a prime lot, marked off with yellow surveyors' flags, right in the center of the complex.

"That one," Ryan said, "is his."

"Get outta here," Savannah exclaimed. "He bought that property on what a cop makes? Even a lieutenant on the SCPF isn't paid enough to keep a cat stocked with Kitty Gourmet."

Laughing, Ryan said, "I kid you not. Our poor, underpaid public servant is going to retire like a king."

"He won't be buying it with old family money," John added. "We checked. And he loses more money than he wins in Las Vegas."

"Our man is connected," Savannah offered.

John nodded. "He is connected to Ethan Cooper. We were just beginning to put that together, along with an interesting profile on Mr. Cooper, when we left to rendezvous with you two."

"Let's go back to my house, and I'll fix us some lunch," Savannah suggested. "We'll compare what you have against what Tammy's been working on. She's been glued to that computer screen since dawn-thirty."

"And then," Dirk said, his voice soft, his expression sorrowful, "I have to go ... somewhere ... for a while."

Savannah reached over and took his hand between both of hers. "We're all going to go, buddy," she said. "We've already talked about it."

He brightened slightly, but only for a second. "You don't have to. I mean, you guys hardly even knew her and, Van, I know you didn't even like her."

"What does that have to do with anything?" Savannah laced her fingers through his big, thick ones and squeezed. "We're going for you."

Dirk looked astounded. His voice got husky. "But why?"

"Because you would be there for us if we needed you," she replied. "That's what family is all about."

"Ethan Cooper?" Tammy exclaimed. "I know Ethan Cooper! My old boss used to play golf with him."

"Ah, yes. Your old boss. What a fine fellow he was," Savannah added. "We got him on first-degree homicide for hiring a hit man to kill off his enemies, if I remember correctly ... and I do." She slapped generous dollops of Dijon mustard on the giant hero sandwiches she was building on her kitchen counter.

Ryan stood beside her, layering ham, cheese, lettuce and tomato slices on the bread she had prepared. Dirk sat at the kitchen table ten feet away, scribbling on a legal pad, while Tammy and John consulted their laptop computers opened in front of them.

"What can *you* tell us about Mr. Cooper, love?" John asked Tammy as he clicked away at his keyboard.

"He's as crooked as the Pacific Coast Highway," she said. "He even cheats at golf . . . or so my boss used to say. He has an enormous amount of money, incredible power, and no morals whatsoever. An-n-n-nd . . . he was involved in quite a scandal last summer. You remember . . . that sweet old couple whose house burned down . . . up there on the hill."

Savannah nearly dropped her mustard knife. "On the hill . . . right where those expensive lots are now."

Tammy grinned and reached over to slap Dirk on the arm. "There, you crotchety old fart, how's that . . . coming from an air-headed, flaky, blond bimbo?"

"I never accused you of being a blonde."

She slapped him again, harder.

"That's enough, children," Savannah said. "I'll have to send you to opposite corners for time-out."

Dirk ignored the threat, tapping his fingers thoughtfully on the legal pad. "Didn't Nathan, Lynn's little brother, say that Kevin had bragged about burning some people's house down for enough money to buy a Corvette?"

"He sure did. That's exactly what he said." Savannah licked the knife clean and stuck it into the dishwasher.

Ryan looked up from his mountain of ham and cheese slices. "Who do you suppose the investigating officer was on that case?"

Savannah smiled. "I'll bet you dollars to doughnuts, our lieutenant handled that one all by his lonesome self."

* * *

Savannah supposed that the trip out to sea with Polly's ashes could have been more miserable. But she wasn't sure how.

She stood on the bow of the fifty-foot fishing boat with Tammy and shivered. Dirk, John, and Ryan stood at the stern . . . also shivering.

"How can it be so warm and sunny on land and foggy and friggin' cold out here?" Savannah said, pulling her lightweight cardigan more tightly around her. A sailor's wool pea coat would have been more appropriate. A sailor's wool gloves, wool muffler, wool cap and socks. . . .

"The offshore flow of air from the desert warms the coast," Tammy said, "while the ocean air is—"

"It was a rhetorical question, Tam. I'm far too cold and nauseous to absorb any meteorological words of wisdom you might have now."

When Tammy's lower lip protruded ever so slightly, Savannah reached over and wrapped her arm around the younger woman's waist. "I'm sorry, sweetie. Just a bit grumpy under the circumstances. It's hard, you know. I feel like I should . . . I should feel worse than I do. I mean, this is the woman's funeral—what there's going to be—and she deserves to have people here who mourn her. At least people who knew her, and preferably liked her a little."

"I know what you mean," Tammy said, looking out into the silver-gray fog that deadened the sound of their boat's engine and the horn of the lighthouse in the distance. "I can't tell you how many phone calls I made, trying to get people to come to this . . . for Dirk's sake. Polly just didn't have very many friends. She knew a lot of people, but they were all mad at her over one thing or the other. I lost track of how many told me that she had used them one time too many."

Savannah nodded. "I understand how they felt. She never took advantage of me, but it's because I saw the way she treated Dirk, and I refused to let her get close enough to screw me."

Looking back at Dirk, she saw that he was talking to Ryan and John in a companionable, male way. Their presence seemed to be comforting to him, and she blessed them for caring about a crusty curmudgeon with a thick head and good heart.

Sitting on the starboard side of the boat in a deck chair was a middle-aged woman with hair that was five shades too dark for her sallow complexion. She was wearing a fake leopard coat, black leggings, and black knee-high boots. Savannah envied her the clothing, even if it was a bit garish for a funeral. At least *she* wasn't shivering.

"What's the story with her?" Savannah asked Tammy.

"She's Polly's hairdresser. The only one who would agree to come."

"What's her name?"

"Joleen Palmetto. She has that shop downtown on Harrington Boulevard, near all the new boutiques. Polly went there at least once a week for her hair and nails."

"Let's go chat with her, see if we can get anything out of her."

Tammy gave her a reproving look. "You mean 'see if we can console her in her hour of grief.' "

Savannah shrugged. "Yeah, sure. Whatever."

They walked over to Joleen, Savannah sat down on a chair beside her, and Tammy leaned against the rail on the other side.

"Hello, I'm Savannah Reid, a friend of Dirk's . . . Polly's ex." She extended her hand and Joleen shook it. The beautician's acrylic nails were outrageously long, painted white, with glittery red hearts accented with tiny, glued-on rhinestones.

Joleen must have noticed her looking at them. She smiled crookedly, and said, "Valentine's Day's coming up."

"Yes, of course," Savannah replied. "I understand you were Polly's beautician?"

"That's right. And you're the private detective who's investigating her murder." It wasn't a question. Joleen appeared to have done her homework.

"As a matter of fact, I am," Savannah said. She nodded toward Tammy. "And Ms. Tammy Hart is my assistant."

"You're the one who called me," Joleen said. "I'm glad I came. Doesn't look like a very good turnout."

Tammy shrugged. "People are busy these days."

"Too busy to pay their respects, it seems," Joleen replied. She toyed with the shiny jet button on the front of her leopard coat. "But then, if I were honest, I'd have to admit that I'm not really here to grieve, either."

Savannah tried to look surprised. "Oh?"

"Yeah. I came to talk to you."

"Oh." She had Savannah's full attention. "How did you know about me?"

Joleen chuckled. "You're sort of a local celebrity. I read about you every now and then in the newspapers."

"Mmmm, that's not an altogether good thing," Savannah said. "Flattering, maybe, but part of being a private detective is staying private. And I'm afraid that, usually, when my name makes it into print, it's because I've done something stupid or pissed somebody off."

"There's nothing wrong with pissing off the bad guys," Joleen told her. Savannah decided, then and there, she liked this woman's attitude. A sister-in-arms.

"Yeah, but the bad guys I go after are usually in high places, and that makes things a bit complicated at times."

Joleen's dark eyes glimmered. "Somebody's got to bring the big cats down. Might as well be you, if you can do it."

Savannah had a feeling there was more to Joleen than jungle prints and Dragon-Lady nails. And there was some special purpose for her being on the boat today . . . hopefully something having to do with justice.

"Why did you want to see me?" Savannah asked, lowering her voice. "Tell me what you've got."

Joleen opened her mouth to speak, then glanced over at Tammy and hesitated.

"Whatever you have to say," Savannah told her, "you can say in front of Tammy. If she doesn't hear it firsthand right now, she'll just worm it out of me later."

Joleen's eyes widened. "I'd like to think you're discreet," she said, "that you will keep whatever I tell you in confidence."

"Oh, I'm the soul of discretion," Savannah said. "Except with her. She's really good at squeezing information out of people."

Joleen grinned. "I suspect you're both pretty good at that."

Savannah returned the smile, then got serious. "So, tell me what you came here to say."

Joleen began to twist the button around and around again. Her grin evaporated. "I think I know why Polly was murdered."

Savannah leaned toward her. "I would like very much to know that myself."

"Polly had been dating this guy, a cop. Well, not exactly

dating him. I think they'd only been out a couple of times, and I got the idea that she liked him a lot more than he liked her."

"Do you know the cop's name?" Tammy asked.

"Not for sure. It was Jeff . . . maybe Jeffrey . . . something like that. But she was really proud of herself for nabbing him, because he had a high rank." She glanced over at Dirk and lowered her voice. "I remember Polly saying this guy was going somewhere in the department, not a deadbeat detective like her ex."

"Polly always did have a way with words," Savannah said dryly, "and her priorities in order. Go on."

"Anyway, one night she was over at this guy's house and she overheard him talking to a doctor friend of his, some plastic surgeon, about a good deal they could get on a lot up on the hill. But the cop said he was going to have to do a big favor or two for the developer. Polly got the idea from the tone of his voice that it wasn't something they would tell their grandmothers about."

"No, I don't suppose they would. And . . . ?"

"And then, a few weeks later, she was over there again, hanging out by the pool when this big shot named Ethan Cooper dropped by to see the cop. They went into the study to talk and Polly listened in the next room through a vent. She heard them talking about how the cop had made a bargain with a couple of the criminals he had arrested for armed robbery . . . a bad dude named Snake and another one named Donaldson. They were supposed to burn an elderly couple's house down."

"Any idea why?" Savannah asked.

"Because they refused to sell their old home place there

on the hill to the developer, and without their land, he couldn't go ahead with his plans to build this fancy gated community." She paused to catch a breath "Does any of this make sense?"

Savannah smiled up at Tammy. "Oh, yes. More than you might imagine, Joleen. Just keep it comin'."

"Well, Polly didn't say anything more about it to me, but then, a few weeks later, she told me she was getting a boob job and her teeth capped. That was something she'd been wanting to do for a long time, but hadn't been able to afford. When I asked her if she'd won the Lotto, she just smiled and said her new boyfriend had connections."

"Do you think she was getting these goodies in exchange for her silence?" Savannah asked.

"I don't know for sure, but I think so. I also think things went wrong a little while after that. She acted really nervous when she came in, jumpy. You know, like somebody was after her. She said she was thinking of going back with her old man."

Savannah scowled. "You mean Dirk?"

"Yeah. She said she was having some problems, and he would look out for her."

Savannah felt a sickness in her stomach that had nothing to do with the roll of the boat on the ocean waves. Polly had been kissing up to Dirk so that she could have a free bodyguard. He had been used right up to the very end and didn't know it.

"Does anyone else know these things you've told us?" Savannah asked. "Anyone who works with you there in the parlor, or—"

"No, just me. A girl named Shawna does nails with me,

and she worked on Polly sometimes. But I'm sure Polly didn't tell her anything."

Savannah leaned over and patted Joleen's knee. "You have no idea how helpful you've been. Would you be willing to just keep this in your bonnet for the time being and then go with me to the proper authorities when the time comes?"

Joleen grinned broadly. "Sure. I'll do whatever I can to make sure you get the bad guys. Whatever she might have done, Polly didn't deserve to get killed like that."

"Good girl."

"Do you think I might get my name and picture in the paper?"

Savannah thought of Rosemary Hulse and the exclusive story she had been begging for. "I can almost guarantee it," she said.

The boat's engine was slowing to an idle, signaling that they had reached their destination, the required distance from shore for at-sea burials.

"Guess it's about that time," Savannah said, rising. "We'll take your number and address before we get back to shore," she told Joleen. "And thanks again, a million times."

"Glad to do it."

As Savannah and Tammy walked over to where Dirk and the others had gathered at the railing with Polly's ashes, she whispered, "The part about why Polly came back to Dirk. . . ."

"For protection?" Tammy added, a grim look on her face.

"Yeah. That part. We're gonna keep that to ourselves. Right?"

She nodded. "Sure. I understand."

"I know you do. Thanks, sweetie. I owe you one."

"No, you don't. Dumb ol' Dirk is my friend, too."

Savannah chuckled, thinking of all the times she had stood between them to prevent bloodshed on her living room carpet. "Since when?"

"From this very minute . . . until the next time he calls me a bimbo."

"Well, it won't be the longest-standing friendship in history. Probably fifteen minutes at the most."

Ten minutes later, the ashes had been poured over the railing into the water, the flowers that Tammy had brought were floating in the same spot, and everyone had gone below for a cup of hot coffee, to take off the chill.

Except for Dirk, who stood at the stern, watching as the boat slowly pulled away, leaving the site unmarked as even the flowers began to drift away with the tide. And Savannah, who stood beside him.

To her surprise he slipped his arm around her waist and pulled her closer to him. She put her arm around his, too. Dirk wasn't the demonstrative type. If he needed a hug, even a sideways one, he was feeling pretty bad.

"It's hard to give her up, Van," he said, staring at the flowers. "I feel stupid, like a real putz for even saying it. But I don't want to let her go."

"You shouldn't feel stupid," she replied, hugging him tighter. "You had your reasons for caring about her. You don't have to apologize to anybody for that."

"But she wasn't a very good person. I know that. She used people. She cheated people." He swallowed hard. "Hell, what am I talking about? She used me. She cheated me. She fooled around on me and looked me square in the eyes and told me she hadn't. She took my money. What I didn't give her, she stole. To tell you the truth, Van, I don't even think she ever loved me. I think the only one she ever gave a damn about was herself. So why am I such a dope? Why did I care about her?"

Savannah fought the urge to agree with him. For years she had told him all of these things which he, only now, seemed to understand.

It would feel oh so good to say, "I told you so."

But that was the last thing her friend needed to hear right then.

"Don't be so hard on yourself, Dirk," she said. "There are many, many reasons why we love someone. No, maybe I didn't understand what you saw in Polly, but I didn't have to. She wasn't my wife. Obviously, she was someone different to you. Behind closed doors, lovers share something that the rest of the world doesn't see. In your private moments, she must have made you feel loved."

"*Needed* is more like it. I guess that made me feel like a big man. God, Savannah, did I have to keep a loser like her in my life just to boost my ego? Was I . . . am I that insecure?"

"Everybody's insecure, honey. Everybody needs to feel needed. That's only natural."

They stood for a long, silent moment, holding each other, saying nothing. In a move that was far more intimate than their usual interaction, Savannah leaned into him and rested her head on his broad shoulder. She breathed in the masculine scents of tobacco mixed with a spicy aftershave that was cheap, but dear and familiar. The warmth from his body, from his arm around her made her feel stronger somehow, safe and secure.

"Just for the record," she said, "it isn't only needy people who need you. We all do."

He looked surprised. "We who?"

"Those of us who love you. We all count on you—your courage, your strength, the fact that you would always be there if we were in trouble."

He pulled back slightly so that he could look down into her eyes. He wore a slightly puzzled expression, puzzled and maybe a little pleased.

"Do *you* love me, Van?" he asked, his voice husky with emotion. "Do you ever need me?"

She reached up and brushed his windblown hair out of his eyes. Then she allowed her palm to slide down his cheek and along his rugged jaw line, feeling the bristle of his "stake-out" shave.

"Of course I need you, Dirk. Every day of my life. I always will." She stood on tiptoe and placed a long, soft kiss on his cheek, then a quick one on his lips. "And as far as loving you . . . you shouldn't even have to ask. Do you think I'd be standing out here, freezing my bee-hind off for just anybody?"

She grabbed his arm and pulled him away from the rail. "You get a cup of hot coffee in you and you'll feel a heap better. Especially after I fill you in on the latest. . . ."

CHAPTER NINETEEN

In San Carmelita, small-time crooks who hadn't collected much in the "wages of sin" department spent many of their evening hours at the grubby little bars on Lester Street. Those establishments were decorated with dusty stuffed marlins and swordfish hanging on their walls, dusty fish netting strung from hooks on the ceiling and dotted with dusty shells and the occasional, scantily clad, plaster mermaid . . . also dusty.

Crooks who had raked in the bucks, either because they were smarter or luckier, whiled their evenings away at the Oyster Bay House. The Bay, as locals called it, was perched on a cliff high above the town, with a breathtaking view of the city, the pier, and the ocean. Fountains cascading into ponds stocked with koi, the pink-marble-and-brass entry, an atrium brimming with exotic orchids, gave the Bay a facade of tasteful gentility. But beneath artistic tiled murals of sea gods and their goddesses, swindles were plotted, frauds were perpetrated, and even cold-blooded murders were commissioned.

And Savannah had been told that Ethan Cooper, land developer and self-made quadzillionaire, spent much of his leisure time holding down a barstool at the Bay.

Her sapphire silk dress had been chosen to highlight the cobalt blue of her eyes ... and of course, to show off her magnificent cleavage to its best advantage. A generous amount of makeup, a long blond wig, her best cubic zirconia earrings and tennis bracelet, and four-inch-high heels with ankle straps made sure she caught his eye when she sashayed, Dixie-style past his stool and took a seat at the opposite end of the bar.

Yeah ... she had "Floozy" down pat.

"Floozy" was only a couple of notches above "Professional Working Girl" which was a few steps higher than "Scanky, Drugged-Out Hooker."

She could play them all. But "Floozy" was more fun. Because, like the crooks that hung out there, she could pretend to be classier than she was. The facade of finery afforded them all the illusion.

And one look at Ethan Cooper told her that he was living the delusion of illusion.

He was probably in his mid-sixties, and at one time might have been considered a hunk or maybe a jock. Remnants of his faded good looks and athleticism remained, and his shoulders, which were slightly stooped, were still broad. He could have been a football player in his youth.

His hair might have been black; now it was a dignified

salt-and-pepper . . . heavy on the salt. His dark eyes were aglow with interest as Savannah gave him the benefit of a demure dimpled smile. He quickly sent a second whiskey sour her way.

"Mr. Cooper wants you to join him," the bartender said as he set the napkin and glass in front of her.

She sent her benefactor another coy grin. "Tell Mr. Cooper," she said in her silkiest Georgian accent, "that a gentleman meets a lady halfway."

The bartender looked surprised and more than a little uncomfortable. "Are you sure you want to send Mr. Cooper a message like that?"

"Oh, I'm sending him all sorts of messages," she said with a deep-throated chuckle. "Let's see if he gets them and meets me in the middle of the bar."

Cooper didn't look pleased when the bartender delivered the message. But, along with his displeasure, she saw his interest level rise. Ethan Cooper appeared to be a conceited jerk who enjoyed a challenge.

He waited, just long enough to save face, then casually picked up his tumbler of straight-up scotch and sauntered to another stool closer to the center of the bar. Of course, he took care to project a don't-give-a-damn attitude, but he wasn't fooling anyone in the place. And several people were watching them.

Just as slowly as he had, she picked up both of her drinks and strolled over to sit on the stool next to his. As she sat down she watched his face closely, looking for any signs of recognition. If he had any inkling who she was, this little undercover routine would be down the drain before it began.

But he didn't seem to know her. Didn't seem to notice the fake wig. Funny, men could spot a bad toupee a mile away on another guy, but they never noticed when a woman wore a wig. Especially if it was long and blond. And worn with a low-cut dress.

"Hey, little lady," he said, lifting his glass in a toast. "You like playing hard to get?"

She grinned at him and clicked his glass with hers. "Oh, I don't play at it. I *am* hard to get."

"Well ... we'll just have to see if you're worth it...." He gave her a lecherous grin that made her instantly despise him. She would enjoy netting this mangy bobcat.

"If I'm worth it?" she replied. "Oh, what I have to sell doesn't come cheap."

He looked a bit put out, as though his ego were slightly wounded. "Oh. You're a pro. I should have known. How much do you charge?"

She laughed and took a sip of her drink. She waited until the bartender had walked away before answering. "That's not what I'm selling, Mr. Cooper."

He reinflated. "So, you know who I am."

"I certainly do. I came here tonight specifically to see you."

"And sell me something ... besides yourself, that is."

"That's right."

"So, what are you unloading?" he asked, switching from lecher to entrepreneurial scoundrel mode.

"My silence."

The crooked businessman instantly disappeared and a hard-core street thug took his place. Savannah had seen colder eyes, but she couldn't recall when.

Yes, this man was definitely capable of what they suspected and more. He had hired his arson and killing done out of convenience and self-preservation, not squeamishness; instinct told her that.

"Exactly what am I supposed to pay you to keep quiet about?" he asked out of one side of his mouth, just like a Hollywood gangster.

She glanced around quickly, but no one seemed to be watching. The other patrons had gone back to their own drinking and miscellaneous flirting.

She leaned toward him until their shoulders were touching. She could feel he was very aware of the contact.

"You need to pay me . . ." she said, ". . . for keeping quiet about how you hired somebody to whack my sister Polly."

The guy was good; he didn't even flinch. He stared her straight in the eye, and said with a smile, "Bullshit."

She smiled right back. "No shit, Mr. Cooper. You did it. She told me she was afraid you were going to, what with her leaning on you for the plastic surgery and the new teeth and all that stuff. She even went back to her old man, the cop, for protection. But you had your guy go right into his trailer and kill her."

"And who else have you told about this?"

"Oh, I haven't said a word to a soul . . . except for what I wrote in the letter that's in my safe-deposit box at my bank. The box that my attorney has been told to open if anything were to happen to me."

"And what would you say if I told you, 'I don't know you. I didn't know any Polly. And I don't have the slightest idea what the hell you're talking about.' "

"I'd say you aren't half as smart a man as people tell me you are."

Cooper threw back the rest of what was in his glass and motioned for a refill. Savannah declined another herself and waited for him to receive his fresh one before she gave him further zingers.

"I loved my sister a lot," she said, feeling her nose grow several inches. "Polly was a great gal."

"Oh, yeah? Well, I thought she was a bitch, myself. You should be glad she's not around."

Savannah chuckled. "Okay. That's true. She was. But she owed me a lot of money. And now I'll never get paid back."

"You wouldn't have been paid anyway . . . from what I've heard about the lady. No firsthand knowledge, of course."

"Of course." Savannah turned on her stool to face him directly. "I want fifty thousand. One time. In cash. You won't ever hear from me again, I promise." She donned a haggard, street-weary look. "I want to get out of this stupid town and back to Miami. And I want to fly first-class."

He thought long and hard before answering. "And what about your . . . letter?"

"There's only one copy, and it stays in the safe-deposit box. Just for a bit of life insurance."

"And what if you die before I do. What then?"

"Well, I'm at least twenty-plus years younger than you. If we both kick off through natural causes, you won't have anything to worry about, huh?"

His fingers were wrapped so tightly around his glass that she half expected it to crack in his hand. Obviously, Mr. Ethan Cooper didn't like having a gun—even a figurative one—to his head.

She, on the other hand, was loving every moment of it. Though she had the definite, uneasy feeling that if they were alone and not in a public place, he would have his hands around her throat instead of that glass.

But, upset or not, Cooper was also a man of keen, swift decision-making capabilities.

"One time," he said. "Fifty thousand, once. If you ever come back for more, I swear you'll die. And this time, I wouldn't bother hiring it out. I'd do it myself."

A shot of adrenaline went through her, sweeter than any sugar fix or alcohol buzz. Hot damn! A confession!

"Tomorrow night. Right here," she said. "Don't forget— it's to be in cash."

"Don't *you* forget," he replied. "One time. And your ass goes to Miami to stay."

"Absolutely. Good night, Mr. Cooper."

"Go to hell, lady."

It was all Savannah could do not to run across the restaurant parking lot to get into the large black van parked there. But she restrained herself and walked casually, trying not to skip or whistle, "Zip-a-dee Doo Dah!"

As she approached the van, she whispered, "It's me. Open sesame!"

A side door of the van slid open and a hand reached for her. She took it and was pulled inside, where she was hugged, kissed, and slapped on the back by the entire Moonlight Magnolia team who had squeezed inside the van with all the highly technical surveillance equipment. The vehicle was owned and driven by John Gibson, who also gave her a kiss on the cheek.

"You did it, Van!" Dirk said, pulling her onto his lap and slapping her rear. "I can't believe he actually said it."

"And you got it?" she asked, looking anxiously at the digital readouts and blinking lights on the recording equipment.

"Every word," Ryan assured her. "Loud and clear."

"We were all listening," Tammy said, beaming even in the semidarkness. "You did great!"

"Well, I hope you took notes, kiddo," she told her. " 'Cause tomorrow, it's your turn. I got Cooper; and first thing tomorrow morning, you'll go after the good doctor."

Although Savannah had found it difficult to sleep while still flying high on the wings of Sweet Victory, she had finally dropped off around 1:00 A.M. An hour later, she tossed and turned, dreaming. It was an older sister/surrogate mommy's nightmare.

One of the kids was crying. Sobbing in their sleep.

It was the baby. Atlanta.

" 'Lanta, honey . . . what's wrong?" Savannah whispered, fighting to wake up. Even after all these years, she was on duty. Big sisters could never really desert their posts.

"I'm coming, sweetie," she said, rolling onto her side and throwing back the bedcovers. "Atlanta, you shouldn't have eaten all that ice cream. You know it gives you a bellyache. . . ."

But it wasn't Atlanta. The voice was male.

"Waycross?"

Her only brother. He seldom cried in his sleep. Something bad must be wrong.

It wasn't until Savannah was standing and walking toward her bedroom door that she realized . . . she was fully awake. But the nightmare crying was continuing.

Dirk?

Alarmed, she hurried down the dark hall toward her guest bedroom. In all the years she had known him, she had never seen Dirk cry. Tear up a bit, get husky in the voice, maybe, but never actually cry. And certainly not these horrible, wracking sobs.

She didn't bother to knock but went directly into the bedroom.

The golden light from the streetlamp shone through the gauze curtains and across the bed that was spread with Granny Reid's tulip-patterned quilt. She saw Dirk lying there, under the quilt, his face in shadow, his broad shoulders heaving as he wept.

She rushed to his bedside, leaned over, and tugged on his arm. "Dirk, are you all right, darlin'? No, of course you're not all right. What a stupid thing to ask. I just . . . oh, honey. . . ."

Without thinking of mundane things like propriety, she crawled into the bed beside him and rolled him over onto his back. He continued to cry, his hands over his face.

"Dirk, buddy, come on. Talk to me. What is it?"

"She's dead," he managed between hitching gasps. "She's gone, and she's not coming back. Ever."

"Oh, I know, hon. I know. I'm so sorry."

As she would have done with any of her siblings, Savannah slid her arm under his neck and pulled his head over onto her shoulder. She wiped his tear-wet hair back from his forehead and placed several soft kisses there. He tasted salty with sweat; his body was cold to her touch.

She had to remind herself that, in spite of their earlier triumph with Cooper, Dirk had just buried his murdered former wife's ashes at sea, and he was entitled to grieve. She just hated to see him taking it so hard.

"It's over now," he said. "All over."

"Yes, it is," she said, hoping to comfort him.

But her words seemed to only intensify his sorrow. "You don't get it," he said. "Now I can't make it right with her. Not ever. No chance now."

"Oh, I see." Savannah realized he had not only lost Polly, but the fantasy of ever having a successful relationship with her. Bygones would never be bygones. No kiss and make up was possible now. Even hope was dead.

"I yelled at her," he said, his face pressed against the bodice of her flannel nightgown. "The last time I saw her, I yelled at her."

"It's okay," she said. "You didn't know. You couldn't have known."

"I called her rotten names and told her to get out. I . . ."

She hugged him tighter as he fought to catch his breath and continue, "I . . . told her I never . . . wanted to see her again. And then . . ."

"Sh-h-h-h. It's all right. You didn't mean it like that. She knew you didn't mean it. You threw her out all the time, but you always took her back. She knew you cared for her."

He put his arm around her waist and rolled against her, his body, warm and hard, pressed against the length of hers. For half a moment, Savannah realized they were finally in bed together. After all the years. After all the fantasies. After all the maybe . . . no, maybe nots.

But in her fantasies it had never been like this. Nothing so sad.

He buried his face against her breast, his tears wetting the front of her gown. She stroked his hair and murmured incoherent, soothing sounds as he continued to confess.

"I told her I was sorry," he said. "When she was dying, and I was holding her. But I don't think she heard me. I think she was already . . ."

"She heard you, sweetheart. People hear everything when they're leaving. She heard you, and she knew what was in your heart. Polly died in the arms of someone who loved her. We should all be so fortunate when our time comes."

She bowed her head and kissed some of the tears away from his cheeks. "You helped her, darlin'. Really you did. You made her passing more gentle by being there, by holding her. That's all you could do. It's all anyone could have done."

That seemed to help a little.

Gradually, his sobs subsided and his grip on her lessened. She could feel his body relaxing, the hardness, the tension melting from his muscles.

She rocked him gently, back and forth, like her grandmother had her years ago, when her own world had come tumbling down. His breathing became slow and easy.

Ten minutes later, Dirk was asleep, his arms still around her, his face still buried in her chest. In the dim yellow light of the streetlamp, his street-tough face had softened, and he looked years younger.

Ten minutes more, and he was sound asleep, even snoring a bit. He was back to being Dirk.

But dawn was breaking before Savannah finally slipped her arm from beneath him and returned to her own bed . . . tired, but infinitely glad she had been able to help a friend.

CHAPTER TWENTY

Savannah expected things to be a bit awkward between them the next morning, but Dirk woke with a "Let's Go Git 'Em" attitude, and even refused breakfast before they piled into his Buick and took off for Tammy's apartment.

"Do you think the bimbo can pull this off?" he asked as they headed along Harrington Boulevard toward the seaside area where Tammy lived.

"She isn't a bimbo and, of course, she can. You should give her more credit." Silently, Savannah cursed him for uttering the words of doubt that echoed the ones in her own mind. "Besides, Tammy has to do it," she added. "I can't go see the doctor, saying I'm yet another person. He and Cooper might compare notes and find the two of me too similar."

"I just don't trust her to get it right. This is important."

"Well, you have to trust her. Unless one of you guys want to dress up in drag and pretend to be Joleen the hairstylist."

"Not me. Maybe Ryan or John would want to—"

"Don't even go there," she warned him. "After all they and 'the bimbo' have done for you lately, I'd think you'd be a bit more gracious than usual. It wouldn't take much," she added under her breath.

"You're right. I'm sorry."

Savannah nearly gasped. Such a heartfelt apology from Dirk was a rare commodity, indeed. His emotional state was obviously far more fragile than she had thought. She vowed to handle him a bit more gently.

"No apology necessary," she said.

They drove along in silence for a while. She could feel his mood deteriorating by the moment. A sideways glance at his face told her his thoughts were far away and sad. She wondered if he was embarrassed about crying in her presence last night.

"Are you okay today, buddy?" she asked.

"Yeah, I guess so," he replied.

She thought for a moment, choosing her words carefully. "You don't need to feel weird about . . . you know, anything. I mean, there's no shame in grief. There's nothing wrong with letting it out, even crying a little when—"

"I wish I could," he said brusquely, cutting her off.

"Could what?"

"Cry. You chicks have it good. When you feel rotten, you blubber. Us guys don't get to do that."

She turned and stared at him, not sure she had heard him correctly.

"You wish you could cry?" she said "Do you mean, like, now?"

"Now. Anytime. Sometimes I just wish I could let go and bawl like a baby. Shit, I haven't cried for years. It would probably feel good to just let it all hang out."

She continued to stare at him, her mouth open. Could it be that he didn't remember? Had he been asleep the whole time? Sleep*walking* was one thing. But sleep *crying*?

She shook her head. Men. Such weird creatures. Who could figure them out?

Ten minutes later, they pulled up in front of Tammy's apartment and tooted the horn. She came running out, dressed in her idea of what a hairstylist/cosmetologist would look like. Far too made-up. Hair much too big. A bright, floral-print shirt and hot pink capris that were way too tight.

"The Cosmetologists' Union should hang her from a lamppost by her three-inch-long nails," Savannah said as she watched her assistant bounce merrily down the sidewalk to their car. "Such gross misrepresentation."

Dirk shrugged. "Oh, I don't know. She looks kinda cute."

Savannah shook her head. "Your taste in women leaves something to be desired. The next time you tell me I look great I'm going to go right back into the house and change clothes."

Tammy climbed into the Buick's backseat, amid the fast-food wrappers and old newspapers. "Well, what do you think?" she asked proudly, throwing her hands wide.

"Are the nails glue-ons?" Savannah asked.

"Yep. So is half of the hair. Pinned on, that is."

"What's your name?" Dirk asked gruffly.

"Joleen."

"And what do you do for a living?"

"I'm a hairstylist who doesn't make nearly enough money to keep quiet about everything I know . . . all kinds of sordid details that my customer, Polly, told me just before her untimely death."

Dirk nodded approvingly. "Not bad."

"How much money are you asking for?" Savannah quizzed her.

"Fifty thousand . . . and liposuction on my thighs."

Savannah and Dirk both grinned. She said, "Good girl."

He added, "Maybe we don't have so much to worry about after all . . . with the bimbo on the job."

Tammy beamed, actually pleased with the compliment.

Savannah made a mental note to compliment the poor kid a little more often.

After rendezvousing with Ryan and John, who were driving the "Bat Van" as Savannah called it, they drove to a small coffee shop across the street from San Carmelita's Community General Hospital. Savannah and Dirk left the Buick parked on the street, while John pulled the van into a lot behind the restaurant. They all congregated inside the van.

"Check your wire to make sure it's working," Ryan told Tammy as he switched on blinking red, green, and yellow lights on black-box equipment and adjusted various dials and toggle switches.

"Testing one, two, three. There once was a girl from Nantucket . . ." Tammy stopped and giggled. "Sorry, I've been hanging out with Savannah too long."

Dirk glanced at his watch. "Enough nonsense. It's almost

eight hundred hours, the time the old doc orders his hotcakes and sausage. You'd better get going."

"John will be in there with you, sitting at the bar, if you run into trouble," Savannah said. "And we'll be listening to and recording every word out here. Remember the cue: 'I have to go to the john.' If we hear that, we're comin' in. Got it?"

"Got it."

Savannah gave her a quick peck on the cheek. "Scared?"

"More like excited."

"Good. Then you're ready."

Tammy started to open the van door, but Dirk reached out and held her by the arm. "I just want to say, I really appreciate you doing this," he told her. "You don't have to, and . . ."

"No problem." She patted his hand, then threw the van door open. "And don't thank me . . ." she said, climbing out, ". . . until we get something good on that tape."

"Nothing good yet," Savannah sighed as they sat tensely in the van, listening to Tammy's and the doctor's voices that came from the small speaker in the ceiling over their heads. "This guy's smarter than Cooper. He's not going to give us anything we can take to the bank."

Tammy and Dr. Julian Rafferty had been talking for more than ten long minutes, and he had skillfully avoided anything even remotely resembling a confession.

"So, let me get this straight," he was saying. "You expect me to give you fifty thousand dollars and perform complimentary liposuction on you, so that you won't go to the police with some ridiculous rumor that I had something to do with some woman's murder. A woman I never met."

"Oh, but you did meet her. You gave her a boob job. But maybe she gave you a different name. Here's a picture of her."

Some rustling as Tammy took the photo from her purse.

"Nope. Never saw her before. You're barking up the wrong tree, young lady. For ten cents I'd call the cops and have you arrested for attempted blackmail."

Again, a bit of rustling. Then a click of metal.

"There you go, Doctor," Tammy said. "I'll supply the dime. Go make your call."

Savannah raised one eyebrow. "The kid's got moxie," she said. "But a call's a quarter these days."

"I don't have time to make any calls, and I certainly don't have time to waste with you," Rafferty replied. They could hear him sliding the coin across the table. "Get out of here and leave me alone. My pancakes are getting cold."

"Here's my pager number," she said. "I'll expect you to give me a call before the day is over. If I don't hear from you by midnight, I'll—"

"You'll what? Go crying to the authorities that your pigeon wouldn't pluck? I don't think so. Get lost, lady."

They heard Tammy rise from her chair. Savannah sighed. Dirk sagged. Even Ryan looked discouraged.

"Midnight," Tammy said. "That's how long you have. Otherwise, tomorrow morning the People of the State of California will be buying your pancakes. And I don't think they provide maple flavoring in the syrup."

A minute and a half later, a discouraged Tammy climbed back into the van. "Sorry, guys. He just wouldn't say it."

"The game isn't over yet," Ryan said as he looked out the front window of the van and saw John walking toward

hem. A few paces behind him came a very worried-looking
Dr. Rafferty.

John got into the van and started the engine. "Ladies and
gentlemen, our disgruntled surgeon didn't finish his breakfast.
The moment our Miss Hart had left him, he pulled a cell
phone from his pocket and made a phone call. It was short, but,
judging from the unpleasant look on his face, rather urgent."

They watched as Rafferty hurried to an enormous navy
blue Mercedes and got in.

"Hey, hey!" Ryan said. "He's going to do it! Dirk, old
boy, you were right!"

"What?" Tammy asked, confused. "What's he doing?"

John chuckled, a smug, self-satisfied, very British chuckle.
"Let's just say, dear chaps, we're going to have the opportunity
to use some of our new toys. What bloody great fun!"

CHAPTER TWENTY-ONE

As Dr. Rafferty left the restaurant parking lot and headed west, toward the beach area, Savannah called Jake McMurtry on her own cell phone and gave him a heads up about the latest development.

"Get that buggy of yours rolling in this direction," she told him. "With any luck we'll need somebody with a badge on the scene."

"What scene?" Jake asked.

"The scene remains to be seen. Call you back in a few."

It didn't take long for them to figure out where the doctor was going. Following a discreet distance behind the Mercedes, they watched as he pulled into the public parking lot for the city pier.

They found a spot nearby, getting out.

Savannah gave Jake another ring. "We're at the pier, in

the southern lot, in a black van. Get here as soon as you can, but don't let him see you. Park on the right side of us and we'll let you in."

For the next seven or eight minutes, the doctor continued to sit in his Mercedes, and they continued to watch him. A few passersby strolled along the walkway leading to the pier: a pair of lovers walking arm in arm, fishermen with poles over their shoulders and tackle boxes in hand. Since it was a school day, the swing sets on the beach were empty, and the only "kid" romping on the beach was a golden retriever chasing a Frisbee.

They could sense the doctor growing impatient as he fidgeted inside his car.

"Don't you love it?" Savannah said with a broad grin as she watched his anxiety mount. "It's great . . . rattling their cage and seeing them squirm like the snakes they are."

"Do you think he's as nervous as we are?" Tammy asked, then gulped from a bottle of mineral water.

"More so," Ryan said as he continued to adjust his various equipment instruments.

"Go easy on that water, kiddo," Savannah told her. "The number one rule on a stakeout . . . if you're a female, limit your fluids."

"Why if you're female?" Tammy asked innocently.

"Because we guys can use an old coffee cup, or anything else with a lid," Dirk replied dryly.

She made a face. "Way more information than I needed. Sorry I asked."

"Ah, ladies and gentlemen," John said, "our pigeon is on the wing."

Rafferty had gotten out of his car and was walking along the beach toward the wooden stairs leading up the pier.

"Shouldn't at least one of us go up there?" Tammy asked. "You know, trail him?"

"No," Savannah answered. "Now that he's seen us all at one time or another, we can't risk him recognizing anyone. If he realizes we're here, it'll ruin everything."

"Besides," Ryan added, "that's what this new gadget is for." He flipped a switch and they heard scratchy static coming from the speaker overhead . . . along with amplified sounds of the surf and the occasional seagull squawk. "It isn't the best fidelity," he said, "but it should do the trick if I get it pointed in just the right direction."

"Is the tape recorder going?" Dirk asked anxiously.

"It certainly is," Ryan replied. "And, yes, I triple-checked it. Everything's a go."

"Oh! Oh! Look!" Tammy nearly jumped off her seat. "It's him! It's Cooper! Walking over from the jetty!"

Savannah chuckled. "Ain't it great?"

"What?" Tammy said.

"When a plan begins to unfold. When the bad guys are stupid, and you're smarter. When they do exactly what you want them to do."

Dirk grumbled, less optimistic. "Yeah, well, the fat lady ain't singing yet. Let's hear what they've got to say. And where's Jake? He should have—"

"Speak of the devil, and he'll appear," Savannah said, as Jake's Mitsubishi pulled into the parking space beside them.

They slid the van's door open and yanked him inside. It made the quarters more than a little snug, but they were glad to have his company.

"So what's going on here?" he said. "What are we . . . ?"

"Sh-h-h-h," Ryan told him. "Just listen."

"To what? Sounds like a bunch of seagulls to me. I—"

"Hush up," Savannah said, gouging him in the ribs. "Ryan's got a high-powered, directional mic. As soon as Cooper joins up with Rafferty and they start talking, he'll be able to tune in on what they're saying."

"Really?"

"Well, in theory," Ryan replied, scowling as he continued to adjust. "The beach makes it a bit challenging. There's not usually this much background noise."

The first human sounds began to filter through the speaker. A female's voice saying, "Of course I'm sure. I'm never this late. It's been two weeks since I was supposed to start."

And a male's reply, "Well, I think we should wait until we know for sure. I mean, marriage is a big deal and—"

"I'm sure. I peed on the strip and it was pink. That means positive."

"Maybe blue means positive."

"No, pink means pregnant . . . and it's a girl. I read it on the instructions."

"Well, if you're sure . . ."

Dirk snorted. "Sucker."

Ryan laughed. "Sorry, folks, wrong conversation."

A moment later they heard a fisherman mumbling about his lousy luck in colorful sailor's terminology.

Then, just as Cooper and Rafferty met on the pier, the exchange they were looking for came through—not exactly loud and clear—but audible.

"I told you this wouldn't work, using street scum to do

important work," one of them said. They realized it was Rafferty by his gesticulating.

Cooper responded, "There wasn't a lot of choice at the time. You can't exactly find a professional in the Yellow Pages to take care of this sort of thing for you. Besides, we don't know for sure there's a problem."

"Come on," Rafferty said. "We both get approached within twenty-four hours by women blackmailing us. They've got to be cops or something. I'm telling you, Donaldson confessed. He ratted us out."

"No way. Jeffries told him that if he even so much as mentioned our names, he'd be hanging from a sheet noose in his jail cell."

It was all the Moonlight Magnolia gang in the van could do to contain their excitement. "That's it," Savannah whispered. "Say it all. Tell us all-l-l-l-l about it."

The two men continued to walk out toward the end of the pier, and Ryan had to adjust for the distance, to keep their voices clear.

"Jeffries." Rafferty gave a disdainful snort. "What a loser. We shouldn't have let him in on the deal either. I don't even know if I want him for a neighbor up there."

"We needed him, too," Cooper reminded him. "In case you've forgotten, he's the one with the list of thugs willing to do what we need done. He's a bargain. Besides, he won't be such a bad neighbor. By the time the houses are built, the guy's gonna be chief of police. And Hillquist will be mayor. We'll be nicely situated for a lot of land deals in the future."

"Hillquist is another problem," Rafferty said. "Jeffries told me he's figured out what we're doing. We may have to cut him in, too. Where's this going to end?"

Savannah nearly danced a jig, right there in her van seat. Hillquist, too? That would be much too sweet. Far too good to be possible.

"Hillquist won't say anything," Cooper said. "He's already endorsed Jeffries, said publicly that he's been grooming him for his spot."

The twosome had reached the end of the pier and were turning around to walk back. With a pair of binoculars, Savannah could see their faces. They looked oh so worried . . . just the way they wanted them. It was somebody else's turn to have sleepless nights, sweating the fact that they might spend the rest of their lives in jail. She and Dirk had had enough. It was the bad guys' turn.

"I wish I'd never let you get me involved in this mess," Rafferty was complaining. "All I wanted was a good deal on some view property. I'm not making the big bucks on this like you and Jeffries are."

"Look, all you did was a free boob job to keep some stupid woman happy and quiet. Jeffries is the one supplying the muscle to take care of problems and—"

"And look what happened! He gave the job to an idiot who hit her in a *cop's* house! He went in there with a stupid sword to do it. How ignorant is that? It took McMurtry and that detective agency ten minutes to find him. And then, when *he's* got to be taken care of, Jeffries sends another moron with a bow and arrow to do it! Don't tell me what a great organizer Jeffries is. He's screwed the whole thing up, and now we're in trouble.

Cooper stopped abruptly on the pier and turned to face Rafferty. Savannah could see his face, and, if she had been the surgeon, her blood temperature would have plunged about sixty degrees. "Look, Doc, if you don't like the way we do business, if you're going to freak on us, get out. We'll let you out. No-o-o-o problem."

Rafferty was silent for a long, heavy moment. "I know how you 'let people out.' No, thanks. I'm in."

"Good. Just keep your cool and everything will be fine. I'll get in touch with Jeffries, tell him everything that's going on, and he'll have somebody take care of those two women, whoever the hell they are."

Rafferty shook his head. "This is getting too big, man. In the beginning it was just going to be one house burned down. That was all. And now three people are dead, and it's still growing. Is it worth it?"

Cooper laughed, a mirthless, cold, empty sound. "It sure is. This fall, Jeffries will be police chief, Hillquist will be sitting in the mayor's chair, and we'll have that whole hill to ourselves, and maybe those marshlands down by the beach that I've been after for the past twenty years. We're gonna fuckin' own this county. Oh, yeah . . . it's worth it. You just keep your mouth shut and let us work out these final details."

Savannah reached over and gave Tammy a high five. Ryan turned to Dirk and Jake, and said, "What do you say, boys? Got what you need?"

Jake still look a bit dazed.

Dirk, on the other hand, was beaming.

"Oh, yes! Yes, yes, yes. Way more than I could have hoped for." He turned to Jake. "Are you going to call for backup before you make this bust, buddy, or would you like this gang to accompany you up onto the pier?"

Jake took a few more seconds to assimilate the information in his stunned brain. Then the realization hit him: A bust like this was a major coup for any detective, let alone a rookie. Considering the players, it would be a major news event. His career had just been made.

He grinned from his left ear to his right. "Let's go get 'em."

The Moonlight Magnolia gang piled out of the van and strolled casually toward the pier. What was the hurry? Like . . . where were Cooper and Rafferty going to go?

CHAPTER TWENTY-TWO

"You know we *had* to be here for this," Dirk told Jake as they and Savannah headed down the hall of police headquarters toward Jeffries's office. "I mean, we just couldn't miss this for anything."

"No sweat," Jake said, a new look of confidence and determination on his face that hadn't been there two hours before. Funny, how a little thing like arresting a successful surgeon and one of the county's most powerful developers could do for a guy's ego. "You guys wrapped it up," he said. "You deserve to be along for the kill."

Savannah smiled, half-suspecting that Jake—even with his new infusion of bravado—was thankful not to have to arrest his superior alone.

And she had to admit that walking down these halls . . . the halls she had been unjustly banished from several years ago . . . on this sort of a mission was delicious. With every step, she could feel the old wounds healing. There was nothing quite like the feeling of taking back some of the power you had lost. Most satisfying, indeed.

When they entered the reception area where Dirk had so recently been arrested, Savannah glanced over at him and knew he was recalling that humiliating moment, too. She wasn't the only one taking back the power. This was deeply satisfying all the way around.

She shot him a bright smile, which he returned. Then and there, she decided that the evening would end in an orgy of pizza, beer, and Ben & Jerry's ice cream sundaes. If she and Dirk knew anything, it was how to celebrate!

"You can't . . . you can't see the lieutenant right now," the receptionist sputtered as they sailed past her desk. "He's got the chief in there and—"

Savannah laughed out loud. "All the better," she said. "Two pigeons with one great big rock! Yeah!"

They barged into the office and found Jeffries and Hillquist sitting by the desk, deep in some sort of conversation. Neither man was stupid, and it took only a couple of seconds for their faces to reflect their realization of what was up.

Jake seemed to freeze momentarily. Dirk stepped forward and leaned over Jeffries. "Tell me something," he said. "Did you get the feeling when you woke up this morning that this was going to be a ba-a-ad day?"

Jeffries didn't say a word, just glared up at him.

"Yeah," Savannah added. "You know . . . one of those mornings when you're on your knees, scooping the cat poop out of the litter box, you throw it into the toilet, and the water splashes up and gets you right in the eye. One of those kinds of mornings?"

Hillquist stood and turned to Jake. "McMurtry, what the hell is going on here?"

"I'm here to arrest the lieutenant," Jake said. Savannah could hear the waver in his voice, and so could Hillquist.

"Don't blow it, Jake," Hillquist said quietly, with deadly deliberation. "This is your career, right here, right now. Don't throw it away on a really bad mistake."

"There's no mistake, sir. I arrested Ethan Cooper and Dr. Julian Rafferty a couple of hours ago. I have the evidence I need."

"And is that evidence solid, Detective?"

"Yes, sir."

Jeffries suddenly snapped out of his state of shock and jumped up from his chair. "What have you got? What?"

Savannah looked over at Dirk. "Do you notice how nobody has asked what he's being arrested for?" she said, smiling. "You bust a street punk, and the first five things out of his mouth are, 'What did I do? What did I do?'"

Dirk nodded solemnly. "I did notice that, Van. I suspect they know exactly what he's done. All they're worried about now is the evidence. Why don't you show 'em the evidence, Van? Go ahead."

"Sure. Good idea."

Savannah pulled a small tape recorder from her purse and switched it on. A second later, Rafferty's and Cooper's voices filled the room.

"This is getting too big, man. In the beginning it was just going to be one house burned down. That was all. And now three people are dead, and it's still growing. Is it worth it?"

"It sure is. This fall, Jeffries will be police chief, Hillquist will be sitting in the mayor's chair, and we'll have that whole hill to ourselves, and maybe those marshlands down by the beach that I've been after for the past twenty years. We're gonna fuckin' own this county."

Savannah switched it off. "It's a nice, long tape," she said, "with lots of nice, juicy details. But that gives you some idea of the content."

"Let me see that thing." Norman Hillquist reached over and grabbed the recorder out of her hand.

Savannah snatched it back and held it tightly against her chest. "No way, Chief. You took a major piece of evidence from me several years ago, and I couldn't do a thing about it because you were my boss. But I'm a civilian now. And I own this tape. My detective agency recorded it, and my guys are delivering the original to the DA right now. Oh, yes . . . and my assistant is giving a copy to a friend of mine, a reporter at the *Star*. She asked for an exclusive, and she's got it."

"You don't have anything on *me*," Hillquist said. "I'm not involved in any way."

"Maybe you weren't directly involved in the murders, but you knew what was going on."

"I did not. I have no idea what you're talking about."

"Cooper says you know . . . right here on the tape," Savannah said, holding it, tantalizingly under his chin.

"Big deal. A crook says something about me. That's not evidence."

"No, but it's gonna play well on the evening news. It may not put you in jail, but it'll sure as hell keep you out of the mayor's office."

She took a step toward him and shoved her face close to

his until they were almost nose to nose. "And because I know how very, very desperately you want to be mayor of our fair town . . . that, dear Chief, is enough for me. I'm not a cop anymore because of you. And you're never going to be mayor because of me and my agency. I gotcha back, you dirty rotten bastard, and it feels nice, like sugar and spite."

Sticking her tape recorder back into her purse, she headed for the office door. "I'm off to buy a bottle of Dom Pérignon. Have fun arresting the lieutenant, Jake."

She paused, her hand on the doorway. "Oh, yeah . . . He looks like a pretty desperate criminal. Be sure to frisk him good before you cuff him."

"Here's to freedom," Ryan said as he lifted his champagne flute to Dirk. "And to your continued career in law enforcement."

John joined the toast. "May criminals everywhere quake in their boots. Once again, Detective Coulter patrols the streets."

"The world's a safer place," Savannah added.

Tammy just giggled.

Dirk blushed. "Bunch of friggin' smart alecks," he said, but he grinned broadly in spite of himself. The Dom Pérignon bubbles had hit his bloodstream and lifted his spirits considerably. Savannah knew he would have choked on the champagne if he'd had any idea how much she had paid for it.

Oh well, this was a special occasion, and who needed to buy groceries or pay the electric bill?

They sat around the table, a much cozier, far less tense group than the last time they had assembled there. Half an hour before, they had all watched the evening news. And it had been spectacular! Quince Jeffries's face, along with Norman Hillquist's, had been on every station at eleven o'clock, and the headlines included a lot of tongue clucking that such promising careers were cut short in their prime. Along with the sordid and sensational details of the murders, it made great copy. Political intrigue with the Medieval Faire as a backdrop ... Savannah had heard that several of the TV magazine shows were picking it up.

Norman Hillquist's career was dog poop! And she couldn't be more overjoyed!

"Seriously," Dirk said after they had clicked glasses all the way around the table. "If it hadn't been for you guys, I'd be sitting in jail right now, feeling miserably sorry for myself. You saved my life, and I won't forget it. I'd much rather be sitting here, feeling miserable with you guys for the rest of my days."

"And making us miserable with all your complaining and pessimism," Savannah added.

He shrugged. "Hey, it's my gift. I have to use it. But I just wanted you to know that, when all this was happening, I didn't feel alone. I felt like ... you know ... like I had family. And it really helped. You all really helped."

"Better watch it, Coulter," Ryan said. "You're starting to sound like a sensitive sorta guy. We can't have that. Next thing we know, you'll be asking to wear my blue tights."

"Not on your life. The next time I'm going to one of those faire things, I'm wearing a corset. Why should Savannah get all the looks?"

Savannah refilled everyone's glass and thought, as she passed from loved one to loved one, how very blessed she was. How many people in the world had this many friends they could truly count on? Wasn't this what family was all about? Not only those who were related to you by birth, but those your heart chose to love and trust.

"Drink up," she said, lifting her replenished glass. "Enjoy! Celebrate! Good friends, good drink! Life just doesn't get any better than this!"

An hour later, everyone had left, except Dirk, who was fidgeting nervously, as though he had something on his mind. "Be back in a minute," he said as he jumped up from the table and headed out her front door.

She heard his Buick door slam, and a moment later he returned, holding something behind his back and wearing a goofy sort of smile on his face.

"Come into the living room and sit down on the couch," he said.

"Oka-a-a-ay. You wanna tell me why?" she asked, doing as he suggested.

"Nope. You'll see in a minute. Close your eyes."

"If I close my eyes, how am I going to see in a minute?"

She wanted to continue to tease him, just to watch the color mount in his face. He was genuinely embarrassed . . . a rare state of mind for this street-worn, cynical thug. But she shut her eyes tightly and extended her hands, palms up.

"Don't you dare put something gross, wet, or slimy in my hand," she said.

"Would I do that?"

"In a heartbeat."

She felt the weight as he laid his object across her palms. About two pounds, she'd say from the heft . . . and from the mouthwatering, chocolate smell she'd conclude. . . .

"Godiva! No way! I don't believe it." Her eyes snapped open. Yes! It was true! A gorgeous gold foil box with a dark red satin ribbon tied around it. Wonders never ceased.

"If you make one crack about me being cheap, I'm taking them back," he said. "And I'm going to eat them, one by one, right in front of you."

"No way. You're not sinking your chompers into these beauties." She untied the ribbon, opened the box and beheld culinary hedonism at its best. "These are mine . . . all mine."

He laughed and plopped down beside her on the sofa. "You deserve 'em, kiddo. You really bailed me out this time . . . literally and figuratively."

She fished out a truffle, bit into it and groaned with orgasmic delight. "Consider the score even. Mmmm, these are exquisite."

"Ah, speaking of scores"—he reached for the TV remote control that was lying on the coffee table—"there's a heavy-weight fight on tonight . . . on HBO. Would you mind if . . . ?"

Lost in the oblivion of taste bud heaven, she easily agreed. "Whatever you want—just let me savor this experience in peace."

He flipped on the fight and settled back to enjoy, the picture of contentment. Kicking off his sneakers, he propped his feet on the coffee table.

She opened her eyes incrementally. "Get your clod-hoppers off my furniture. I'm not *that* far gone." She nudged the box a little closer to him. "Have one."

"Really? Naw, they're yours. I bought them for—"

"I'm not going to offer again."

He nabbed three and munched along with her for several minutes, watching the prefight commentary.

She had just bitten into a mocha cream-filled when she felt his huge hand engulf hers and squeeze gently as he laced his fingers between hers. "Does this mean you're my Valentine?" he said, as shyly as a first grader giving a handmade, lace doily heart. "I mean, you're eating my chocolate and we're sitting here on your couch, watching the fight together."

"If that don't make me your Valentine, boy, nothing will," she said, returning his affectionate squeeze.

He looked pleased as strawberry punch, then seemed to reconsider. "Don't tell anybody," he said. "You know . . . it ain't none of their business that I bought you candy . . . expensive candy. It'll ruin my reputation as a cheapskate and then everybody will expect me to start paying for stuff."

"Well, we certainly can't have that. It'll just be our little secret . . . along with the fact that we're going to eat this entire box of sinfully rich chocolate before the tenth round."

He snagged another truffle. "Mum's the word."

Please turn the page for
an exciting sneak peek of
G.A. McKevett's
newest Savannah Reid mystery
SOUR GRAPES

coming in hardcover in February, 2001

SOUR GRAPES

Savannah Reid, transplanted Georgian belle, was never happier than when those she loved were seated around her kitchen table, and she was stuffing their faces with good, Southern home cooking. And at that moment, four of her favorite people were finishing off a platter of fried chicken, a bowl of mashed potatoes, and a boat of cream gravy.

Well ... three of them were eating the calorie-laden goodies. Savannah's health-conscious assistant, Tammy Hart, was enjoying her usual salad. At least, she said she was enjoying it, though Savannah couldn't grasp the concept of "savoring" lettuce.

"Tammy, you need to eat something," she told her, passing a golden drumstick under her nose. "You're so skinny now, you'd have to run around in a rainstorm just to get wet."

The petite blonde reached down and patted her nonexistent fanny. "Actually, I've got to watch it. I've put on a couple of pounds lately."

Savannah tossed the chicken leg onto Dirk's plate and tried not to urp. A couple of pounds . . . on that size zero butt. Please.

She had decided long ago to feel no envy, only deep sympathy, for this emaciated waif. Okay, so Tammy might look great in a bikini, but she would never know the deep, soulish thrill of eating a huge slice of cheesecake, double-dipped in chocolate and topped with raspberry liqueur.

The poor child wasn't svelte; she was tragically deprived.

Savannah turned her attention to the opposite end of the table, where the object of most of her sexual fantasies sat . . . Ryan Stone, tall, dark, gorgeous, suave, debonair, her dear friend and sometimes fellow private detector.

And next to Ryan sat the reason why those delicious fantasies would never become reality—John Gibson, Ryan's life partner, an older, silver-haired, completely sophisticated and charming British fellow. She very simply adored them both. Sadly, so did Tammy and every other female who crossed their paths.

On the other hand, Dirk—being a red-blooded, all-American, highly heterosexual and not particularly tolerant male—had only recently learned to appreciate their unique skills. As retired FBI agents, they had used their expertise to help both Dirk and Savannah solve some difficult cases. Savannah had noticed that, after they had pulled Dirk's butt out of the proverbial wringer a few times, he had dropped the "fairy" and "twinkle-toes" comments.

At the moment, he was making no comments at all, because he was quickly dispensing the chicken leg off to "drumstick heaven." Dirk was never particularly conversational in the presence of food. Especially free food.

"This meal was absolutely delightful, my dear," John said, dabbing at his silver mustache with his napkin. "I can't believe I've lived my entire life thus far without the pleasure of Dixieland cooking."

She walked over to the kitchen counter where she began to slice a fresh-from-the-oven apple pie. "Then you should come over more often and make up for lost time," she said. "We can't have you walking around with a cholesterol level less than three hundred."

She slid a piece, dripping with French vanilla ice cream and caramel sauce, under Ryan's nose and was rewarded with a breathtaking smile. "Savannah, you spoil us rotten. Please don't ever stop."

"Never. Besides, we've gotta celebrate Dirk's big bust here."

She saw him glance down at his chest, and she was thankful his mouth was too full for him to make the predictable, corny joke.

"Yes, congratulations, Sergeant Coulter," John said, lifting his teacup, which was brimming with his own special blend of Earl Grey. "A most impressive showing on your part . . . and Savannah's as well."

"Five wanted felons and nine guns'" Ryan added. "Good haul."

Dirk grunted, and his face flushed slightly. He wasn't particularly adept at accepting praise . . . receiving so little of it.

"Mmm, yeah, thanks," he muttered. "Those damned gangbangers . . . bunch o' punks. I'm tellin' you, when I see the kids today, I just wanna get myself neutered, if you know what I mean."

Savannah reached into a drawer and pulled out a can opener. "If you're serious, I can take care of that right now for you."

"Gimme some pie instead."

"Say, 'please.' "

"Oh, yeah . . . please."

She gave him a double-sized piece. Might as well, she figured, and save herself a trip; he was sure to ask for seconds.

As she joined them at the table, her own generous serving in hand, Ryan asked her, "How is your schedule now, Savannah? Do you have time for a little extra work?"

She perked up instantly. As a private detective, she often found herself on the "famine" side of the "feast or famine" wheel of fortune.

"Work? *Real* work . . . like for *real* money." She gave Dirk a loaded, sideways glance, which he conveniently ignored.

"Well, I don't know how much work will be involved," Ryan said between sips of coffee. "It's more like presenting a presence. I've been hired by a beauty-pageant promoter to 'guard' some lovelies who are competing for the 'Miss Gold Coast' crown."

"Miss Gold Coast?" Tammy asked, nearly choking on her salad. "What a disgrace . . . evaluating women on the basis of physical attributes like a herd of cattle."

"Yeah," Dirk agreed. "Disgusting. Do they need an off-duty cop as a chaperone for those chickie-poos?"

"I heard they have one more position to fill, and they specifically asked for a female," Ryan said.

"Reverse sexual discrimination. That's what it is. A

middle-aged, white guy can't get a break in this country anymore."

"Hush and eat your pie, Dirk," Savannah said, nudging him under the table with her foot. "Guarding a batch of beauties would be bad for your blood pressure."

She turned back to Ryan. "Is the pay good?"

"Listen to her," Tammy said, snickering. "Like she's picky these days. I balance her books . . . or try to. Believe me, if it pays minimum wage, she'll jump on it like a hound on a T-bone."

"A hound on a T-bone?" Savannah laughed. "You've been hanging out with me too long, New York girl. I'll have you eating grits and gravy before you can shake a lamb's tail."

Tammy gagged. "No way. No grits, no gravy, and certainly nothing to do with a sheep's back end."

Savannah scooped up a big forkful of pie, dripping with the caramel and pecan sauce. "I'll take it," she told Ryan. "Looking out for some girlie-girl beauty queens, making sure they don't stub their pretty toes and ruin their pedicures, maybe breaking up a few catfights over false eyelashes and hair mousse. How hard could it be? I mean . . . what could happen at a beauty pageant?"

The beauty queen sat at her dressing table, wearing a pink chenille bathrobe and hair curlers, staring at her reflection in the brightly lit, Hollywood mirror. The dozen bulbs around the mirror's edge illuminated every tiny blemish on her nearly perfect complexion, and she studied each one, frowning, as though it were a critical issue that demanded an immediate solution.

The walls and shelves of her bedroom were laden with

the spoils of her victories in the pageant world. Trophies, some over three feet tall, cluttered every horizontal surface. Vertical surfaces were covered with photographs—beautiful pictures, professionally taken over the years—showing a little girl who had been groomed to look like a woman at the age of six.

The closet door stood open, and inside glimmered an array of sequined and rhinestone-studded evening gowns of every hue, jostling for space with feathered boas, a hundred pairs of glittering shoes, and miscellaneous faux fur accessories.

Having decided on a course of action, the girl at the dressing table chose a particular cream from the dozens of bottles before her and began to dab the lotion on her "trouble spots." From time to time, she glanced to her right, at the lighted glass case that sat on its own special table and held her pride and joy ... the Miss California Sunshine crown ... in all of its cubic zirconia glory.

She was good at what she did.

Very good. And she knew it.

She looked across the room at the younger, far less attractive version of herself stretched out on the twin bed against the opposite wall.

"Go downstairs and get me a soda," she told her sister. "And make sure it's a cold one from the back of the fridge."

"Get it yourself."

"I said ... get me a soda, now!"

The well-trained younger sibling stirred from her bed, grumbling under her breath, but obeying nevertheless, trudging across the bedroom in penguin-spangled, flannel pajamas.

In their little sorority, hierarchy had been established long ago, and it was too late to challenge authority now.

"Diet! Make sure it's diet!"

"Eh, screw you." The objection was mumbled low enough that it didn't constitute outright mutiny.

As soon as sister number two had left the room, the beauty queen picked up the telephone and punched in some numbers.

Her party answered almost immediately. Keeping her voice low, she said, "It's me. Yeah. Did you think it over . . . you know . . . what we talked about?"

She frowned, not liking what she heard.

"That won't do. That's not what I want. I *told* you what I want."

She listened again, but not for long. "No! I don't care what you say; it's gotta be the way I told you before."

More objections on the other end.

She shook her head, sending curlers tumbling, and stomped her bare foot. "No, no, no, no! You better listen, or you'll be sorry. A lot of people are gonna be sorry if you don't listen to me."

As the party on the other end continued to fill her ear with unpleasantries, the bedroom door opened and her sister appeared, diet cola in hand.

Time to end the conversation.

"You heard me," she said in her most ominous tone—a voice she would never allow a panel of pageant judges to hear. "I made it very clear to you what I expect, and this isn't negotiable. I want action . . . very soon. Understand?"

She slammed the phone down and snatched the soda out of her sister's hand. "What are you grinning at?" she snapped. "What's so damned funny?"

"You." The younger girl walked back to her bed, flopped across it, and began to chew her thumbnail. "*You* trying to get your way with people."

"I don't *try*." She took a long swig of soda and smiled. "I *do* it."

"Yeah, well, you're gonna squeeze the wrong person one of these days, and you're gonna get it . . . something you *don't* want, that is."

Beauty set her soda aside, took another look at her Miss California Sunshine crown, and went back to dabbing pimples with lotion.

"No way," she said. "I'm a woman who knows what she wants . . . and how to get it. Every time. You just watch me, Squirt, and take a lesson from an expert."

The younger sister groaned and rolled over to face the wall, mumbling minor obscenities . . . just loud enough to express her disgust . . . but low enough not to incur Her Highness's royal wrath.

Yes, in this tiny kingdom . . . everyone knew her place.

An hour later, on the sidewalk across the street from the beauty queen's modest suburban home, a figure stood in the shadow of some oleander bushes, watching.

The upstairs bedroom light had been out for twenty minutes. Twenty-three, to be exact. But the watcher still waited. Thinking. Planning.

Having observed the house before, the person knew that four people lived there: mom, pop, the beauty contestant, and her younger sister, and knew which bedroom was hers . . . the little bitch on the phone . . . the one making demands.

The watcher knew what had to be done. The only questions remained, "When?" and "How?" Some things had to be done properly. Carefully. And murder was certainly one of those.

The first time the thought *murder* had crossed the watcher's brain, it had been like an electric shock, terrifying, repulsive, foreign. But with each subsequent thought, the concept seemed less revolting, more possible, even necessary. The would-be victim had chosen her own fate. The rest was a foregone conclusion.

But when?

Now wasn't the time. Not on a quiet, residential street in a house full of people. Not without a plan . . . a good, well-thought-out plan.

The pageant.

The Miss Gold Coast Pageant began in two days. An event full of emotion, confusion, hundreds of people running around in semiordered chaos.

Yes . . . what better backdrop could there be than a beauty pageant . . . ? The perfect stage for murder.

Please turn the page
for an exciting sneak peek
of the rest of the
Savannah Reid mysteries!

JUST DESSERTS

The first Savannah Reid mystery

Memphis-born Detective Savannah Reid is in her element cruising for crime in one of southern California's most exclusive enclaves . . . until a shocking murder rouses San Carmelita from its star-studded stupor—and places Savannah in the center of a sensational case that soon erupts into a media feeding frenzy.

With suspects abounding—and a cast of characters that includes an ex-CIA agent and a computer genius with the technology to take the case into the twenty-first century—Savannah finds herself sifting through a nasty mess of sex, adultery, and down-and-dirty politics that could prove the *crème de le crème* of her detective career, *if* she can use her own appetite for justice to unmask a cunning killer.

In Savannah Reid, G.A. McKevett has created a vibrant new sleuth in a spicy, suspenseful mystery that's sure to keep readers devouring every page.

BITTER SWEETS

The second Savannah Reid mystery

Savannah Reid, that big, sexy, Southern-born sleuth with a black belt in karate, has finally established herself as a P.I. in posh San Carmelita, California. All her Moonlight Magonlia *from* SOUR GRAPES

Detective Agency needs now is enough business to pay the rent and put some serious sweets on the table.

No sooner does Savannah complete her first case—finding the long-lost sister of a local real estate broker—than murder enters the picture. Framed in a diabolically clever double-cross, she sets out to find the real culprit . . . only to discover that she's the prime suspect among the lovers, losers, and liars lurking in the shadows of the victim's past. Each of them has a motive. Not one of them has an alibi. Now Savannah must call upon all her resources to sort out the baffling clues, clear her own name, and corner a killer whose appetite for murder is growing every day. . . .

KILLER CALORIES

The third Savannah Reid mystery

Sexy private detective Savannah Reid may be built for comfort and not for speed, but she likes herself just fine as she is. So the only way she's likely to set foot in a health spa is over a dead body—somebody else's—along with a hefty fee to sweeten the deal.

The irresistible combination of murder and money brings Savannah to Royal Palms to investigate the death of spa owner and former cult-flick actress Kat Valentina. The medical examiner called it a fatal—but accidental—mixture of booze and hot tub, but Savannah's anonymous client thinks otherwise. Savannah quickly learns there's no shortage of likely suspects from ex-lovers and would-be lovers, to employees and prior co-stars with unsavory pasts. As for Savannah and her sweet tooth, this may prove to be a costly case. For if the strict regimen of exercise and nasty spa cuisine doesn't kill her, there's a murderer close by who's prepared to finish the job. . . .

COOKED GOOSE

The fourth Savannah Reid mystery

It's hard to get into the Christmas spirit when the Santa Ana winds are blowing at a balmy ninety degrees. It's also hard to live in a "Baywatch" world when you're an overly voluptuous size fourteen. But Savannah Reid has never been one to believe that good things only come in small packages. Right now, the only present Savanah wants wrapped up is the one of a serial rapist who dresses as Santa. Thanks to his twisted brand of holiday visits, Savannah has a full-time job teaching self-defense to San Carmelita's terrified women.

But the feisty detective is less than thrilled when Captain Bloss, her ex-boss from the San Carmelita PD, asks Savannah to be his daughter's personal bodyguard. It seems the rapist has turned vicious cop killer, making the captain and his daughter prime targets. With enough chaos swirling around to make Tiny Tim grouchy, Savannah looks over her list of suspects to figure out just who's been naughty. From the ex-con cop killer just released on parole to the bookie with more than a few debts to collect, Savannah considers them all, plus a few others, while she tries to keep danger from dropping down her chimney and bringing a killer home for the holidays. . . .